Holly McCulloch lives in Oxfordshire and bakes beautiful (and delicious) cakes for a living. *Just Friends* is her debut novel.

www.penguin.co.uk

Just Friends

HOLLY McCULLOCH

CORGI BOOKS

TRANSWORLD PUBLISHERS
Penguin Random House, One Embassy Gardens,
8 Viaduct Gardens, London SW11 7BW
www.penguin.co.uk

Transworld is part of the Penguin Random House group of companies
whose addresses can be found at global.penguinrandomhouse.com

First published in Great Britain in 2021 by Corgi Books
an imprint of Transworld Publishers

A CIP catalogue record for this book
is available from the British Library.

ISBN
9780552177252

Typeset in 12/14 pt Dante MT Std by Jouve (UK), Milton Keynes
Printed and bound in Great Britain by Clays Ltd, Elcograf S.p.A.

The authorized representative in the EEA is Penguin Random House Ireland,
Morrison Chambers, 32 Nassau Street, Dublin D02 YH68

Penguin Random House is committed to a sustainable
future for our business, our readers and our planet. This book
is made from Forest Stewardship Council® certified paper.

To Friends

And one friend in particular – Mr Rick Barbaria

Chapter 1

I am not happy.

I am angry. On this, my Best Friend's Wedding Day, I am angry.

And not (just) because I haven't eaten.

I am angry because some dickhead has just made me angry on a day when I want to be genuinely full of happy. I have spent the last eighteen months helping my best friend, Mia, gear up for this day, agreeing to wear a dress that doesn't suit me and shoes that hurt, running increasingly random errands, glue-gunning (is that even a verb?) diamantés on to orders of service, and kindly offering to sit next to her crazy Uncle Geoff at dinner the night before. Who even spells Jeff that way? He spoke to me for hours about his coffee preferences, and I listened kindly, my jaw muscles aching from all the over-enthusiastic fake smiling. And why? Why am I doing this?

I'm doing this because, no matter where I am or what friend group I'm in, I am always known for being the happy one, and happy people don't flip their lid at having to listen to Uncle Geoff drone on about the proper way to make an Americano.

But the truth is, inside, I am not happy – I'm a mess. I

don't know what I want to do with my life. I'm stagnating at work. I avoid all awkward conversations, and instead live with a growing well of frustration inside me and an increasingly loud internal narrator, who I try to keep quiet because not many of my thoughts are that happy these days.

But I pretend to be happy because I want to be happy. And because all of my friends like this happy version of me, and because I like my friends and I want them to stay my friends, I keep up the ruse. It's really fucking tiring.

Most days I manage it quite well.

But today is not most days.

Today I am on the verge of losing it. Today I have worked hard to be the best maid of honour a person can be. I helped calm people down in the morning, I helped find ribbon, I stood where I needed to in church, I left my wedgie where it was throughout the whole ceremony, and I even delivered a thoughtful yet amusing maid of honour speech. I haven't eaten a proper meal in two days because of the nerves. But I was happy to do it.

And now this fool has had the audacity to tell me that I need to work on the way I answer the question 'Do you have a boyfriend?' Apparently my reply ('Ha, no') totally put him off. He kindly informed me that he *could* have been my next boyfriend, if only I'd answered that question differently.

There's too much rage in me to reply like an adult – a happy adult. And so instead, I've been standing here, silent and open-mouthed, for an uncomfortable amount of time, unable to make any words reach my mouth.

Eventually I decide to say nothing and hobble away as fast as my pinched feet will take me. But as soon as I leave, I worry that I have disappointed all the feminists. I've definitely disappointed myself.

Already too late to turn back with a quip (and still too stunned to think of one), I continue on my path. As I head past the obligatory awkward dancing and over to the bar, I hear someone yell my name.

'Bea! Bea! Let me buy you a drink!'

I turn and see Peter – Peter Bodley, Oddly Bodley to his closest friends. I do feel kinda bad that the name stuck. I probably should have kept it to myself.

But the thing is, Peter is just a bit odd.

He can speak Latin but he can't bake a potato, he knows every European capital but he can't paint a room without getting more paint on himself than the walls, and he wears some of the most subtly strange outfits. At university it became quite a well-known fact that his mum would try to organize his clothes for him in a way that made it impossible for him to pick out offensively clashing colours and patterns. He frequently found ways to go rogue.

Looking at him now, not much has changed. He's wearing a very nice suit, but he's also wearing a really old-fashioned shirt and the grubbiest trainers I have ever seen.

'It's an open bar, you idiot. And I can get my own drink.'

But still, we wander over together and order a couple of whisky sours.

'Ugh. I know Tomorrow Me will regret this. The older I get, the more I like whisky, but the less it likes me.'

'I've always liked whisky. Although I do prefer a sherry.'

Of course he does.

I take a sip and let out a noise that's somewhere between a sigh and a groan.

'God, it's nice to get away from people. I love Mia, but being her maid of honour has been like having a second full-time job, with no benefits, no lunch breaks and a restrictive uniform.' I'm slouching more than I should in public, and more than I should in this dress, but the idea of pulling my shoulders back makes me want to cry. As it's only Peter, I continue to slouch.

He looks at me and appears to be taking in the tulle and the corset for the first time. Not that he knows what tulle is. He nods in appreciation and feigned understanding, and I take it as a sign that it's OK to keep the tirade going.

'The thing I find most odd is that Mia has really good taste in clothes – she always looks amazing. But I think I've finally found her one weakness: she has shit taste in bridesmaids' dresses. Unless she's done this on purpose, but I don't think she would have.' I drop my head into my hands.

'It does look rather restrictive. But it's nice to see you in something other than black or grey.'

'Hey. Wearing monochrome is easier both from a washing perspective and a fashion perspective.'

I am about to launch into part two (possibly three?) of the tirade against the dress, but have to quickly steel my face when Mia appears seemingly out of nowhere, which is no small feat considering her skirt is the width of four people.

'Mia! You OK? Do you need anything? Can I do some-thing?' I really hope she didn't hear anything I just said, because in truth I would be her maid of honour any time she asked. I'd do it all over again in a heartbeat, and be genuinely happy to do so.

She smiles and turns to Peter, leaving me clueless and increasingly sweaty from the anxiety. I try to hide my awkwardness by paying more attention to my drink than it really deserves.

'Peter! Thank you so much for coming. I hope you're having a good time? I put you on the table with my fun cousins.'

'Ah yes, they were very welcoming, thank you.'

'Good – I thought you would all get on.' She does then turn to me. 'Could you fix my hair? I keep getting poked by a pin.'

To me, she looks perfect – she always does – but I nod, un-slouch, put down my now-empty glass and get ready to clock back in. Game-face on.

'Right, well, I think that's my cue to go get a restora-tive bacon sandwich.' Peter kisses her on the cheek, smiles at both of us and heads back towards our wider group of university friends who have gathered around the snack table. Not quite an introvert or an extrovert, I only have the energy to maintain strong friendships with a limited number of people. Mia and Peter are the chosen two from my university days.

'Is it just me or has Peter scrubbed up really well this evening?' Mia sounds unsure.

'It's just you.'

'No, really. Once you get past the eclectic wardrobe, he really is quite good-looking.'

'Peter?'

'Yes, Peter.'

I look over and catch him just as his larger-than-life laugh booms out of him. It's so innocent and genuine. He's speaking to someone who's not known for their humour. I can't imagine the joke warranted the laugh, but Peter is a generous soul.

'I've never thought about it.' This is a slight lie. Whenever we used to play 'Kiss, Marry, Dismiss' at university, Peter would always be in my 'Marry' column. He's the type of handsome that you would want to grow old with. But these games were just games. Hypotheticals. Unlike my current issue: Mia's hair.

I stare at her hair for a while and try to remain calm. There are so many pins. Which one is sticking into her? They all look like they're sticking into her. I take out a pin and hold it between my lips for safekeeping, then mumble on. 'The idea of dating a friend is not one that appeals.' And I should know. There's too much risk, too much potential for heartbreak. Besides, 'Stop looking at men that aren't your *husband*.'

She grimaces at this. 'That word's going to take some getting used to.'

Right before I poke her with a pin, Mia chirps, 'Bea, if I haven't said it before, thank you for being my maid of honour. There is nobody else I would have chosen.'

I stop the poke, add the pin to the collection in my

mouth, half hug her shoulder with one hand, and try to tell her through a mouthful of hair accessories that it's me who's grateful. Being her best friend is a title I proudly bear. It's the only reason I'm also happy to bear the title maid of honour.

She turns to face me more quickly than I'm prepared for and I narrowly miss stabbing her in the eye. 'Huh?'

I motion at the pins in my mouth and gesture for her to turn around, feeling a tad weepy. And I would do it all again; Mia is my best friend and my strongest advocate. She even supported me through a painfully honest pink lipstick phase.

I stab her (accidentally) for a final time. 'All done.' Thank goodness she can't see the back of her head. It definitely did not look like this at the start of the day, but in lieu of having a professional hairdresser on tap, my efforts will have to do.

'I have one more favour to ask. In about five minutes can you start handing out the sparklers? That way everyone will have them at midnight, so they can ring in the new year in style.'

'Of course.' The line between friend and minion is a fine one this evening.

Still, I hunt down the sparklers and start handing them out. They're the biggest sparklers I've ever seen, and I decide to 'accidentally' miss out the more inebriated guests, becoming increasingly nervous about the fire and safety regulations.

The countdown begins – although I have no idea who was aware enough to keep track of the time – and I take a quick scan of the area. Everyone, or at least all the worthy guests, has a sparkler.

Good.

Shit.

I look around again. I am not with anyone I know. This is precisely why I never go out on New Year's Eve, I would far rather be in a room by myself than in a room full of people who all love each other, but where nobody loves me.

I decide to run away and hide until midnight has passed.

'Bea! Bea! Where are you going?'

For the second time in the night Peter has caught me trying to escape.

'Come here.'

He pulls me under one arm, meaning there really is no running away.

Shouts of 'Three! Two! One!' fill the air, and I don't know what to do. Everyone else has found someone to kiss, but I feel awkward and tense. My shoulders are up to my ears. I don't want Bodley to kiss me, even if Mia is right, he does look good this evening. But it wouldn't be *just* a kiss between us, it would be . . . something else. I hope he doesn't think he has to kiss me merely because we're standing together. I smile at him awkwardly. He starts to come towards me, and my body reacts. I step a little closer.

He kisses me. On the cheek.

I'm sure I feel relieved. My shoulders sink back down, and I smile up to him. I should have realized that he wouldn't want to *kiss*kiss me either.

'Happy New Year, Peter.'

'Happy New Year, Bea.'

After a while, once all of the bizarre, overly enthusiastic and totally undeserved congratulations are over, Peter turns to me once more. The music has kicked back in. 'Now that's finished with, can I treat you to a dance?' Peter has many skills, but dancing isn't one of them. His limbs are too long for his body, and he's incapable of moving them in a consistent, predictable manner. My feet are killing me and I know he'll step on them, but I don't want his smile to fade so I nod.

The night continues as expected. There is some mild scandal, excessive eating of fairly bland wedding cake, more terrible dancing, and some questionable confessions of love. We score full wedding bingo when one of the bridesmaids starts crying.

I say one of the bridesmaids – it's me.

I have a weep on poor Peter's shoulder.

I blame it on the fact I drank too much, an activity I typically avoid as neither my finances nor my hangxieties can handle it. Unluckily, the open bar made the former issue irrelevant and the latter was quite forgotten.

'See, the thing is, I want to be *genuinely* happy. I have all the reasons in the world to be *genuinely* happy, but I'm not.' Good lord, have I ever sounded so pathetic? 'Everyone here is happy. I want to be happy too.'

Peter puts an arm around me as I really scrutinize the room. Everyone looks happy. Everyone looks content.

Everyone looks paired off.

I squint a little, trying to see the root of my problem.

'Huh.' I look again to make sure. Every single person who is attached to another person is smiling. 'Look!' At this moment I hit Peter on the knee, a touch harder than intended, and point to the couples glued together, drunkenly swaying on the dance floor, propping each other up. 'Look at them all. They all look so happy. Like nothing is missing, not even rhythm. Maybe it's because they're loved by someone who's not genetically predisposed to love them.' I breathe again, finding it hard to keep my thoughts on track. 'Maybe I need that too?'

I haven't been interested in having a boyfriend for a while, so my own dating history is exactly that – history.

Nevertheless, I take a breather so my thoughts can make their way through the whisky haze. 'Is it silly to wish to be happy?' I shift slightly so I am almost facing Peter.

'Not at all. I think happiness is a great aim.'

I slouch a little less and use his body to anchor myself. 'OK! I've decided! I'm going to start dating again!' I wipe the last of the tears from my eyes and decide to stop feeling sorry for myself. 'I think I need to see if I would be happier if someone out there who isn't genetically predisposed to love me, loves me. Know what I mean?' I turn to face Peter and smile. He smiles back.

'I love you.'

'Yes, but, Peter, you don't count.'

Chapter 2

I wake up the next morning and feel absolutely horren-dous. I swear I can feel my brain physically banging against my skull. I can't even do a full body assessment of how I feel because it hurts too much to think that hard.

I look at my phone, which I magically remembered to plug in to charge when I rolled into my hotel room early this morning.

I have one update – a text from Mum.

> Bea, Happy New Year my darling! Let me know you're
> alive when you have a moment. I hope the wedding went
> well. Please send my love to Mia. xoxo

Typing out my reply takes longer than it should, but Mum will worry if I don't message her back.

> Happy New Year, Mum. The wedding was great, but I've
> felt better. I hope you had fun last night? Sorry I wasn't
> there. I love you loads. xx

I check the time before I put my phone down.

I only have half an hour before I'm required to be down-stairs for breakfast and, working back, I need another four hours to get ready. An extra four hours would give me just enough time to have a salty snack, rehydrate, shower, nap, and then wake up with renewed vigour before getting dressed and applying some make-up to hide my face.

But, alas, I do not have an extra four hours, so with an overly dramatic groan I push the covers back and get ready to crawl out of bed, hoping that I won't feel as bad as I fear I will when I eventually stand up.

My hopes are quickly dashed. I stand up and feel worse.

When I manage to reach the bathroom, I am met with an unfortunate sight. I look dreadful. At least the part of my face I can see looks dreadful; half of it is obstructed by the message I left myself on the mirror last night when I still felt like a superhuman, as opposed to the squashed, bruised banana of a human that I currently resemble.

DATE.

I have no idea how I'm going to get that off the mirror. It would be a simple task if my limbs and brain were still able to understand each other. Maybe I should leave it up there for the next occupants? I've written it quite well – the 'D' is particularly pretty, and I am impressed with how neat the handwriting is overall, especially as I wrote it in lipstick. A lipstick that I can see I totally destroyed in the process. I can't fathom the energy to be overly upset about this. Besides, I always have issues wearing red lipstick. It looks quite good on me, but only until I eat or drink or talk or breathe, and then I get that extra lip below my actual lip that adults should be able to avoid.

I sit on the loo, hoping the stability of the seat will help stop the slight spin.

DATE.

This is precisely the kind of silly, drunken declaration I should be avoiding at my old age.

As I sit, I move my head from side to side, simultaneously trying to relieve my headache and remember the last date I went on.

The sad fact is that I have only ever had one boyfriend worthy of the title, and it didn't exactly work out very well. Sam, my first and only love and one-time best friend, utterly broke my heart.

I can't help the sigh that escapes.

There are many issues with being hungover, but one of the worst is that it makes everything so much more sad, and my memories of Sam are interwoven with a whole load of other memories and feelings. Memories and feelings I try not to feel when I have to be sociable any time soon.

A knock on the door is a welcome interruption.

I look at the time and realize I've been sitting on the loo for fifteen minutes with only my sad thoughts and pale thighs for company.

I make myself as decent as possible in my delicate state and open the door. Why are there so many locks?

'Rise and shine, it's breakfast time!'

Christ alive. Too much. Too soon. Too early.

Adjusting my eyes to the outside world, or at least the world beyond my bedroom and into the hotel hallway, I see Peter standing with a grin across his face and—

'Are those hash browns?'

'Yes, and some orange juice. I thought you might need them if you were going to make it to breakfast.'

'Thank you so much.' I grab the plate of hash browns and, knowing Peter's presence is part of the package, open the door wide enough to let him in. I bury the vague memory I have of stepping towards him for a kiss. I wish alcohol didn't make me so stupid. Or so hungover.

'It was no problem. The kitchen ladies are extremely kind.' He enters the room, shuts the door and plonks himself on the bed. The kitchen ladies are not extremely kind, but Peter has a way with people.

I feel better already and I've only smelt the salty starches.

'Now hurry up. I should have some fresh pancakes ready for me in fifteen minutes.' Peter winks and I shuffle to the bathroom, clutching at the last of the hash browns and the remainder of my soul.

Thirteen minutes later, Peter barges in and leans against the door-frame.

'That's a bit intense.'

'Huh?' My face? My outfit? His entrance?

'The message in aggressive red caps.' He points to the mirror, cup of tea in hand. I assume he made it using the weird hotel kettle, the type I never really trust.

DATE.

I can't help but grimace.

'Ah yes. I remember now. Your New Year's resolution.'

'It's not a resolution. People always break resolutions. I am not a resolution person.'

He raises his eyebrows and eyes me with scepticism. 'Well, you came up with an *intention* for the new year. I would say that is a resolution.'

I shrug, trying to act casual about it. 'Call it what you want. I guess I didn't want to forget.'

In truth, all I want to do is forget about it. I'm happy as I am.

OK, I'm not happy as I am, but in the cold, sober light of day I don't see how exposing myself to other people is going to make me any happier. I wish I'd drunk less last night. If I'd drunk less, I wouldn't have made any pathetic and pointless *intentions*.

'What is that noise?'

'I put an alarm on to let me know when my pancakes would be ready.' He nods at me as if he assumes I will be proud of this plan.

I roll my eyes in response. 'Of course you did.'

We get down to the breakfast room and Peter makes a beeline for one of the kitchen ladies, who scuttles away as soon as she sees him and returns with a stack of pancakes and a huge smile on her face. He has a way of bringing out the best in people. It's infuriating.

'Oddly Bodley up to his old tricks, eh?'

I turn to see David and his heavily pregnant wife next to me. David was Peter's housemate at university. He's nice enough, but is currently standing closer to me than I would like. He's always been one of those people who doesn't understand the concept of personal space.

Still, I smile politely before sitting down. 'Some things never change, I guess.'

With a full plate and no shame, Peter takes his place next to me and gives me one of his pancakes. Sure, there were some initial teething problems in our friendship, namely his extraordinary intelligence, as well as a very posh accent that proved a little tricky to understand, but his character quirks made him instantly approachable. Unlike me, he sits solidly in the extrovert camp, and sometimes I worry I rely on his shield too much. If this were a rom-com, he'd be some weird kind of knight in shining armour.

'So, how are you going to go about dating?'

All eyes turn to me and my kind thoughts about Peter flip. I have never hated him so much in my life. I don't want my pathetic resolution announced to the world. If it's announced to the world, I'll be less likely to be able to forget about it, like all New Year's resolutions should be. And I especially don't want it announced in this world that is full of perfect people in perfect relationships.

'Oh, I . . . I don't know. I mean, I haven't really thought about it.' This is not a lie. I don't think my head will be capable of thinking for a while.

But as soon as these words are uttered, a myriad of unsolicited advice comes my way. Advice from people I've never known be single.

'Only hang out with single people!'

'No, only hang out with married people.'

'Only wear heels – I heard they give people more confidence.'

And then, 'You should try online dating. Swiping? What harm can it do?'

This is the only suggestion that is met with general agreement, and all I can see is a round table of nodding car dogs.

'Yes, yes. A friend of a friend found their fiancé that way. I think it's how it works these days.'

The nodding continues, and I even spot a thumbs-up.

'How what works these days?'

Mia and Mark appear behind me. She looks so refreshed. I must ask her what moisturizer she uses.

The question forgotten, someone else chirps in for me. 'Dating apps. Online dating. Bea is going to try them out.'

As soon as the words have been spoken, Mia's eyes light up. She's been trying to get me to date for a long time, telling me to put myself 'out there' more. I go out. I just don't like what I see.

I open my mouth to protest. It was only a stupid, drunken . . . resolution. One that I don't mean in real life.

But her face is so happy.

So instead I say nothing, and at some point I must have smiled and nodded back, because before I know it Mia has taken my phone and set me up with a profile that vastly exaggerates how spontaneous I am, and I have a date next Tuesday with someone who's validated his character by providing his Uber rating and a 'quote' from his mum.

Chapter 3

It turns out that swiping can cause a lot of harm. Modern dating is causing me a lot of harm. Mainly to my already precarious confidence, but also to my bank balance, my tolerance for terrible chat-up lines, and the early onset of RSI in my right thumb. *Left. Left. Left. Oh! Maybe! Let's dig deeper. Oh no, is that real? Is that even the same guy? Left. Guy with a dog! RIGHT. Left. Left. Left.*

Who knew that trying to date should come with a health warning?

Despite the fact I eventually set myself up with a new, slightly more accurate (but still optimistic) profile on a more feminist-friendly version of the Flame of Shame, the results still haven't been great. In either quality or quantity.

Quality-wise, most of the men I've been on dates with baffle me. How have they not been arrested? How do they have jobs? Were they even raised by humans? One man hit on our waitress whilst we were still on the date. Another kept throwing things, almost like a kind of macho test, a test that he failed many times. And too many potentials sent unsolicited dick pics; one even sent a slow-motion video.

My mum bought me this phone. I can't be watching that on a phone my mum bought me.

Quantity-wise, I've not exactly been struggling to find a date, but I've quickly learnt that finding a date and actually going on the date are two different things. The number of times a date (the person, not the event) would mysteriously disappear on the day is shocking. Turns out a lot of men get ill/run out of battery/find better plans at short notice. Mia says it's a consequence of the casual nature of online dating. But I've always thought of myself as being witty when I make an effort, and I can't help wondering if my messaging skills aren't up for the challenge.

I've also come to the conclusion that we need a new term for these 'dates'. To me, the word 'date' still has quite a romantic connotation to it, drumming up ideas of flowing conversation, a proactive plan, a nice outfit, on-point personal hygiene, maybe some flowers – this last one is a bit of a reach, but a girl can dream. These social meetings that I've been subjecting myself to are in no way romantic. They do not deserve the term 'date'. 'Investigation' might be a better word.

And I never get a second 'date'. I also never really want to go on a second date, but the fact that no one wants to go on a second date with me is damaging my self-confidence. What is wrong with me? What kind of signals am I giving out? What am I doing wrong? Maybe it's my face. I try really hard to appear interested. I'm sure my actions say I'm interested, but I'm also pretty sure my face says I would rather be somewhere else.

I've given myself one more try at a 'date' before I give up, and I'm hoping it will be a quick one this evening. I've already prepped my date, Tom, with the news that I will have to leave early because I'm travelling with work tomorrow. This is not exactly a lie as I do have an errand to run that will take me out of the office, but it is a stretch of the truth.

The saving grace tonight is that Tom has opted for a pub. Most of the men I've met have been doing Dry January, which means a lot of people have been suggesting increasingly involved date activities but have then been a touch too self-conscious to really enjoy them. The worst so far was an indoor axe-throwing session. As someone who does limited physical exercise, mainly because I lack coordination and have precisely zero sporting ability, I knew this would be a bad idea. But it turns out I'm actually a pretty good axe-thrower, much to the annoyance of my date, who found my decreasingly modest character increasingly irritating.

Nearing the pub I can see a man who looks vaguely like the pictures I've seen of Tom, although he's got much less hair than his profile would suggest.

In a momentary panic I almost forget his name.

'T-om?'

'Bea?'

'Hi.'

We go in for an awkward almost-touch of the cheek.

I plaster over our bumbling with a chirpy question.

'Shall we go in?'

*

Despite it being really grey and dark outside, the pub is uncomfortably light, which wouldn't be so bad if it wasn't also extremely empty. I feel very, very on show.

'Can I get you a drink?' I always like to get in the first round because then I feel no guilt if I leave after one.

'OK, great. I'm not actually drinking, so I'll take a Diet Coke.'

What. The. Actual. Fuck.

I've been hoodwinked. Lured into a false sense of security, and now I don't know what to do. At least on openly dry dates I know I shouldn't drink, even if I still choose to. But this is new. This is a sneakily dry date. It's making me yearn for the axe-throwing days.

I have been standing still for too long.

'Sorry, didn't I tell you I was doing Dry Jan?'

'Oh no, it's fine.' It isn't fine. None of this is fine. Why am I here? 'I'm just surprised you wanted to come to a pub if you aren't drinking.' That came out a touch more harshly than it should have. 'I'll go get you your Diet Coke and you choose where to sit.'

There is absolutely no queue at the bar, so my thinking time is shorter than I would ideally like it to be. The girl behind the bar gives me a knowing glance. She can tell it's a first date of the swipe variety.

'You OK?'

I contemplate asking her if there is a back exit.

'I'll get two Diet Cokes, please.'

Turning around with two whole pints of Diet Coke in my hands, I see that Tom has added insult to injury by choosing the worst seating option possible. He had the pick of the place but he's gone for a dirty table right in the middle of the room. I already know that I don't want a second date.

'So, why choose a pub when you aren't drinking?' I worry that I sound like an alcoholic, but I want to understand.

'Oh, I love the smell.'

'The smell?'

'Yeah. I love the smell of a pub.'

Now I worry that he sounds like an alcoholic, but still I nod and say, 'Oh my goodness, me too!' I hate myself. Why do I do this?

'Let's cheers to that!'

He lifts his glass up and I think he's being serious. He wants to 'cheers', but to what I am not entirely sure. Still, I raise my glass and toast him in pretend solidarity.

'So, your accent, where is it from?'

'Liverpool. I moved to London a couple of months ago.'

This is the other thing about dating apps. They're frequently used by people who are new to the area, and I'm not interested in being a travel guide. I want someone who already knows the best way out of the tube without having to follow the signs.

Still, I say, 'Oh, cool. Are you liking it?' I know he'll say yes – everyone loves London when they first move here, and even if they don't, they say that they do.

'I love it. I'm living with a really nice girl. It's actually

her who made me sign up for this online dating thing.'
I'm sure she did. There is nothing worse than having a
housemate who's in all the time. 'So I should thank her,
I guess.'

'Ha, I guess.'

'Cheers to that!'

Seriously?

His glass is already up there, and I'm not quite rude
enough to leave him hanging.

Our glasses clink again and I'm even more embarrassed
when I see that the girl behind the bar is watching us. I
can't blame her, I'd watch us too.

After an incomprehensible amount of cheersing, our
glasses are finally empty.

'Gosh, I hadn't seen the time.' I look down at my wrist,
though I haven't worn a watch for many, many years.

Looking at the clock on the wall, I can see that it's only
seven thirty. How we have only been on this date for
forty-five minutes I don't know. It's earlier than even I
think is an acceptable time to leave, but my cheers quota
for the year has been used up and I can't take it any more.
I have to leave before I hit him. Or cry.

'Sorry, but I really should go.'

I can see in his face that he doesn't quite believe me.

'Well –' he's going to be polite, and I instantly feel so
guilty that he's clearly a genuinely nice person, whereas
I am disillusioned and tired – 'this has been great. I
would cheers, but it seems odd to cheers with an empty
glass!'

'I guess it does!' I manage one last smile, possibly the

only genuine one of the evening as I can sense freedom is near. I reach for my bag and start to stand.

'But we could do it anyway!' He smiles up at me, face full of innocence. 'Cheers!'

And fuck me, but I sit back down and lift my glass one last time.

Chapter 4

I frequently wonder how long it would take my co-workers to notice if I stopped showing up to work. I find it so odd that five days a week I go into an office, wear (increasingly less) office-friendly clothes and exhaust myself trying to seem busy.

I wasn't always this way. I used to care a lot about my job – it was quite exciting to work for a start-up company doomed for greatness and spearheaded by a fearless, hard-working female leader, my inspirational boss, Mansi. But now I despair when I look at our plans for getting more and more time-poor and money-rich people inter-ested in personalized vitamin regimes that attempt to improve your wellbeing. Especially when I've found that being less and less interested in them myself has actually improved my wellbeing.

Today's task, which, true to my word, did briefly take me out of the office to pick up some bookends, has been to rearrange my boss's books according to the year of publication. Of course, as soon as she saw the result, she decided colour was a better way to organ-ize them.

So I've chosen to take myself off to the disabled loo for

a pitiful cry at the stupidity I feel at being upset by this unsurprising, but still quite humiliating, event.

Luckily this isn't my first rodeo, and, as any practised weeper knows, you should always take your phone with you, so when you're done crying you can flip through your required reading and carry out your personal admin, giving your eyes and face some time to calm down.

Today the majority of my personal admin is related to my alternative career as owner and creator of CARDi-ology. I set it up a couple of years ago on a bit of a whim, but it has since become an outlet for my terrible sense of humour. I really had no idea people could be so inter-ested in high-quality, screen-printed cards with puns on them. Calling it a business is slightly optimistic, but who knows, maybe one day.

The only time my two careers (if I can call either a career) have ever clashed was when I accidentally handed my boss my latest list of political puns instead of the lat-est health-related news round-up. She finally caught on when she realized 'There will be hell toupee' wasn't a real headline.

'Career' all seen to, I turn my attention to my social calendar.

I unmatch the cheery Tom from last night. I book my place at yoga for next week, I organize address labels for the numerous clothes I need to return (only getting momentarily distracted by some shoes that I send to Mia – they're far too expensive for me), and order food for the upcoming Games Night.

Games Night, which rather confusingly can take place at any time of day, is a tradition that started at university. It's actually how Peter and I met – at the first meeting of the Board Games Society, whose tagline was 'Don't Get Board, Be A Player'. I still remember the first time I met him; he made such a big impression, even outside of the weird clothes. He was charming and funny and just the right side of competitive. He was one of the only people I could be myself around from the start. He still is. Unfortunately the society lost its funding after the first year, but a group of us kept it going on a casual basis. Our meet-ups have dwindled from weekly to monthly to quarterly, and attendees are always in flux, especially since some members have been procreating (hence the move from night-time to any time that coincides with nap time), but everyone is keen to keep it going. Every time we meet up we always have fun, even if we also only need to see each other a couple of times per year.

And every time we meet up, we always have a theme.

The next Games Night, which is to be held during the day on a Saturday, is in February, and so obviously I'm theming it around National Tortilla Chip Day. It's my turn to host, but because I live in a one-bedroom apartment too far away for the majority of people to visit, I hope to use Peter's flat instead. It's the obvious choice, and we've hosted together before.

When I asked Peter if I could use his place, his reply – 'Of course. My only request is the layered dip' – came in far more quickly than I expected.

I jump at the soft knock on the bathroom door.

'Bea, it's me.' Recognizing the voice of Penny, my work wife, I get up and slowly unlock the door.

She peeks in.

Penny quickly became my work wife out of necessity; I had snuck out of the office to buy some more animal-print clothing, only to come back and realize I'd missed the beginning of the monthly staff meeting – a staff meeting I was meant to be taking minutes in. Without batting an eyelid, she covered for me and ended up taking the minutes. Her cover story was far better than anything I would have made up, and since that time we have been like two pendulums, swinging back and forth between who owes who the next coffee, who owes who the next cover story, and who owes who the next weird and overly friendly insight into their life.

'I've got to run and jump on a call, but I thought you'd like a cup of tea.' She fumbles behind the door, using her foot to keep it open enough so she can pass me the mug, but closed enough to keep me safe from unfriendly eyes. From the sound of things, Joan, the office dragon, is stomping around nearby. If there is one person you want to avoid crying in front of, it's Joan. She's the kind of person who passes off bullying as camaraderie. As Penny hands me the tea, I can see that it's exactly the colour I like. 'Oh! And I brought you these.' She magics a packet of cookies from her pocket and gives them to me. Double chocolate chip.

'I don't deserve you. Thank you.'

She blows me a kiss and lets the door close. I lock it after her, not quite ready to resume the day.

Chapter 5

With Valentine's Day right around the corner all I see is red. And not because of all the stupid red Valentine's hearts, but because I'm so angry at all the red hearts. Not only is the glitter unable to be recycled but the hearts seem to be encouraging people to do things like hold hands and kiss in public, so I am surrounded by the sight, and what's worse the *sound*, of affection.

I purposefully bump into at least three couples on my way to yoga.

Truthfully, I have a constant struggle between wanting to be a yogi and wanting to give in and embrace my lack of flexibility and tummy rolls. The latter outcome is much more likely, because no matter how hard I try, or how many yoga classes I go to, I constantly surprise myself with my lack of progress. And for such a small amount of movement, I sweat a lot. The only saving grace is that I have so far managed not to fart in class.

As I reach the studio I spot Tilly, who does actually like yoga.

'Tilly!'

She turns towards me and my overly high-pitched voice,

flashes me her Insta-worthy smile and envelops me in a hug. She is quite lithe, but her hugs are deceptively strong. I often have to brace myself against them.

We break apart and I take in a restorative breath.

'I'm so excited that we're finally doing yoga together.' She squeezes my arms, probably to exaggerate her excitement.

I don't normally let anyone see me exercise, but I had to make an exception for this evening.

'Are you kidding?' Meeting up with Tilly is a bit like a celestial event – you gotta enjoy it whenever it comes around, and when she asked if I could do something tonight, I was loath to cancel the class and lose my money. 'I worry it's going to be slow for you.'

'Oh, Bea, I don't care.'

She's impressively flexible.

After a quick bag drop, we rush into the studio just in time, feeling flustered and un-yogic and not in the least bit zen. We find a spot that is almost big enough for two, and squeeze in. The people around us give us insincere smiles and move *very slightly* to give us more space.

I lie down and fight the constant urge to fidget. I hope I don't sweat too much.

Tilly lies down and immediately seems at peace.

Tilly is by far my most trendy friend. We found each other one year when we happened to both be working at a very random, very local food fair where I was trying to make some extra money selling overpriced (and, quite frankly, fairly mediocre) brownies. I made no money, but I did make some fantastic memories. In particular, learning that Tilly made out with not one but both members of the duo who ran 'R&Brie Bingo', an entertainment stall hosted by two men who combined cheese puns, fake French accents, homosexual stereotyping, R&B and bingo all in one go. I've never seen them anywhere else, but I hope they've found success.

I am smiling to myself at the memory as Sal, my favourite yoga teacher, walks in.

Nothing if not a creature of habit, I always try to go to this specific class. Unlike the majority of yoga teachers, who have a perma-tan, a gravity-defying arse and a positive outlook on life, Sal keeps it real. He's bitter, he has a bit of a belly, he wears old-man shorts that pose a serious sexual harassment risk, and he doesn't waffle on about 'practising with the body you have today'. And no matter how shit I am at yoga, I imagine that he's even shitter. I've never actually seen him in a yoga pose (thank goodness, because the shorts really are inappropriate), and I'm not entirely convinced that he practises yoga at all.

We go through all the yoga poses without too much drama. I sweat an acceptable amount, and only get my lefts and rights confused a couple of times. But something is off. Sal is uncharacteristically happy.

We are all lying on our mats, the (acceptable amount of) sweat now drying, when Sal chirps in with a final piece of optimism.

'I hope you found time in this practice to relax and refocus, allowing yourselves the space and freedom to really connect with and appreciate who you are. And remember this –' insert dramatic pause for effect – 'you are enough.'

Seriously, what has got into Sal? He must have got laid last night.

'See you all here again next week. *Namaste*.' There are echoing whispers of *'Namaste'* throughout the room, and, so help me, despite my continuing bitterness, all of a sudden I feel emotional. Bloody Sal and his 'you are enough' has made me feel all kinds of things, and for some unknown reason I start crying. This might be worse than an accidental fart.

There is a lot of shuffling and movement in the room as everyone goes to hang up their mats and file out of the studio. I can hear Tilly getting up beside me but suddenly I'm not quite ready to leave, so I hide my eyes with a faux casual placement of my hand, and motion that I'm going to stay for a little longer but she should go get showered. I'll meet her soon, once my eyes have stopped betraying me.

For a while I concentrate on my breath and try to get my tears under control.

But even with my eyes closed, I sense someone coming closer until they're standing over me. I take a peek and see Sal looming, regarding me with a mixture of pity and kindness.

'Yoga can sometimes be an emotional release. Don't be embarrassed about crying. Realize that it's doing you good to let go, to feel the emotions.' He pauses and rests a warm, tea-tree-infused towel over my eyes. I feel like I'm in a spa, but also kinda gross, because *where did the towel come from*? 'Breathe, have a sip of water, and only leave when you feel ready. There is no class in here for an hour, so you have plenty of time to collect your thoughts.' With that he leaves me alone.

Post-shower and make-up removal I'm still a bit puffy and numbed, like when you have a cold. I can't quite walk properly, but eventually I zombie out of the changing room and spot Tilly ogling the overpriced yoga clothes.

'Bea! I loved the class. And I love these leggings.'

They are far too patterned for me, but I can see that Tilly would look great in them, so I nod.

'Shall we get some food?' I'm starving. Crying makes me hungry.

'Oh, I'm doing this alternative day fasting thing, so I can't really eat, but I could have tea? We have so much to catch up on!'

And we do. Somehow we haven't seen each other for at least four months. How does this happen?

My hunger can wait, but hanging out with Tilly can't. I'll pick up food on the way home.

'You grab the seats, I'll grab the tea.' She heads towards the seating area in the entryway whilst I potter over to the massive urn, fill a couple of glasses with an unknown herbal tea and narrowly miss knocking over a tray with my bag on the way back.

I sit down and try to shake off my feeling of numbness and concentrate instead on the friend sitting in front of me.

'Tills, how was the yoga retreat?'

Part of the reason I haven't seen Tilly for a while is

because she's been travelling. I don't know where she gets the money from. I don't think she really has a job, but I know that her parents aren't bankrolling her either.

'It was amazing! I didn't realize until I got there, but it was a silent retreat, absolutely no talking allowed.' The one thing Tilly loves more than yoga is talking. 'I loved it so much that I ended up staying for a whole month!' A nod is all the encouragement she needs to keep going. 'It was so enlightening. When I first emerged into the non-silent world, I felt so rejuvenated. The effect was transformative. It's such a shame because, as with all these things, I can no longer feel the full effects, but when I feel low, or over-whelmed, I try to remember what I felt like during that month and I immediately start to feel more in control again.' A mini pause as she gazes up to the ceiling, prob-ably trying to remember what it was like to be silent. 'I kept a diary. Wanna see it?'

She looks so excited I can't say no.

'Is it long?'

'It's a visual diary of sorts.'

Tilly then gets out her phone and proceeds to show me one of the most depressing photos I've ever seen. Zoom-ing in, you can see that she used twigs that she found on her walk around the compound (the only exercise in addition to yoga that she was allowed to take) to mark the date, with each day represented by a random object. The backdrop is a cracked concrete wall and floor with a couple of dead bugs strewn about.

'What is that?' I ask, pointing to something that looks like an old, chewed piece of gum.

'That's dried banana, to remind me of, well, the dried banana. It was the only thing we were allowed to eat at dinner time, and even then we were restricted to five pieces.'

No wonder she's looking so thin.

'Day fifteen was a good day!' She zooms in to the washing-up liquid. 'I finally managed to signal to someone that my water wasn't working. The kindest man with the most sparkly eyes came to fix it, so I could take a bath and flush my loo.'

On day fifteen?! She had spent more than two weeks not showering even though it was blisteringly hot, and not flushing the loo, even though day three was ominously represented by loo roll? I had purposefully zoned out when she recalled that day. I haven't eaten yet.

My eyes scan the rest of the photos to try and find something positive so my face doesn't have to work as hard to keep a neutral expression. 'Day twenty-five looks interesting.'

Day twenty-five is represented by a condom.

'Oh yes! This was really the apex of my stay. Helped by the fact it was Buddha's birthday, I managed to achieve a Buddha-enlightened meditative orgasm.'

Huh.

'And –' she takes a breath and leans in – 'I met someone. He's great. As soon as we met, we totally clicked even though we couldn't talk for the first month of knowing each other. In fact, he's the reason I came back early. I actually cut my trip short so I could help him find an apartment here in London. His name is Jeroen.

He's Dutch, tall and gorgeous, and I am madly in love with him.'

'Oh, Tills, that's so great. What's he like?'

From this point on I hate myself a little, because instead of being totally and completely happy for Tills – poor Tills who really has been on a bit of a rollercoaster with relationships – only a small part of me feels genuine happiness, whilst the bigger, louder part of me feels jealous and sad and even more lonely and confused. She went travelling with no interest in finding a man. In fact, before she left, she had started referring to men as sperm donors. But not this time. This time Jeroen is a partner, her partner. And despite actively looking, I am still alone.

If I were wearing plimsolls and badly fitting shorts under a totally bizarre but mandated skirt, this would be just like school sports all over again. Always awkwardly last to get picked. Less and less hopeful that my luck will change. And wearing clothes that aren't cool.

Chapter 6

Games 'Night' has arrived and I've been at Peter's flat since 10 a.m. prepping all the dips. It shouldn't be taking as long as it is, but Peter has a unique way of helping.

'Leave it alone.'

'But it's fun.'

'No, it's not fun, it's going to spill all over the counter. Stop stirring it.'

'It's like a mini whirlpool.'

I know he's doing it on purpose – he's smiling the same smile he uses when he knows he's doing something he shouldn't. Like that time I caught him secretly swapping dust jackets in a random bookshop. I try not to find it charming.

I ignore him in the hope he'll stop if I don't pay him any attention, and go back to wiping the board so I can start chopping the coriander.

'Oops.' I look over and see that the counter is now splattered with blobs of refried bean.

I probably should get mad at him, but he smiles and instead I decide to simply clean it up, cloth already in hand.

Peter leans across the breakfast bar to watch me chop the coriander. 'So what are we playing today then?'

After squishing his massive sofa to the side, we managed to squeeze in four playing stations. Any game is allowed, except Twister, which we had to stop playing because too many of us were getting injured in our old age. Personally, I normally steer away from games like Monopoly and Risk, and steer towards games like Scrabble and Pairs, or if I'm feeling particularly unadversarial, a calming puzzle. Some people are good at dealing with confrontation or taking risks, endangering their prawns or queens. But not me.

'Well, I thought we'd go with Scrabble, Snakes and Ladders for Jess –' who has recently had a baby, and requested a mindless game that is still fun, but will allow her some peace so she can breastfeed – 'Shithead and Cranium.' I have also bought extra play-dough as that's everyone's favourite part of the game.

'A well-rounded selection. I like it.'

The doorbell rings. I'm still chopping, so Peter goes to open it. I can hear Mia and Mark before I see them, looking fresh-faced from their mini-moon, followed by the usual gang of regulars. At the back of the group I can see a timid-looking Isla peeking through. She doesn't often come, which is sad as she's also an advocate of the quieter games.

I take a fortifying breath, stop chopping, wash my hands and start hugging everyone. I'm smiling on the outside, but on the inside I worry I didn't order enough food.

'You can't do that! That's cheating!' Someone slams their hand on a table and I jump, just a smidge, from the safety of the kitchen. Shithead has proved to be quite popular today, so after Jess left with the baby in tow, we converted a second table to the enemy-making card game.

Mia is uncomfortably competitive, a trait I'm quite glad I don't possess, so when she comes charging over having lost, my main focus is on trying to calm her down and make her realize that it's only a game. She might have lost tonight, but she's still very much winning at life.

She takes an unusually large sip of wine and cuts right to the chase.

'Distract me. Tell me something funny.'

I look up and right, searching for a funny anecdote to distract her with. I could talk to her about my dating life, but that's more sad-funny than funny-funny, so I opt for something else instead.

'We're bringing out a range of edible vitamins, mainly aimed at kids, but they taste a little too good, and some kids are eating far more than they should and are actually changing colour.' I shrug. 'Apparently orange is the most vivid.'

Mia looks genuinely aghast. 'Really? I thought there would be controls on that sort of thing.'

'Well, there are, and they should only be having one a day, but a lot of the kids in the test group are having to eat the vitamins because their diets aren't great anyway, so they're used to eating quite a few sweets and can't tell the difference.' I rephrase. 'Well, they couldn't tell the difference until they started changing colour.'

'This is like a real-life chocolate factory situation.'

'I know, I'm trying to stay out of it.'

'And dating? How is dating going?'

This will make her feel better about herself. 'Terribly. The last guy kept making me cheers after every sentence.'

'That doesn't sound too bad.' She's happily married, so I forgive her lack of understanding. 'What else did he do? Was he nice?'

'He was really nice.' And that was part of the problem.

'So are you going to see him again?'

I go back to the washing-up so I can avoid looking at her, knowing that my answer is going to disappoint.

'Oh no. I've actually blocked him. He was *too* nice. And I know I should have messaged him instead of wimping out and going silent, but I couldn't face turning him down.' I risk a peek at Mia.

She just sighs.

'You're looking for the perfect person, but I don't think that person exists.'

I have to disagree.

'I don't think that's it. I'm not seduced by the idea of the potentially perfect person who exists just around the corner if only I could be the one to find them, but I'm not interested in dating someone I can't bear to be around. I want to *want* to be with them.' Like Tilly wants to be with Jeroen. Like Mia wants to be with Mark.

Peter's laugh cuts through the general din, and I look through to the games. He's playing Scrabble with Isla, who in turn is smiling, no doubt amused by his word choice.

'Well, sometimes you have to give these things time.'

She starts to help with the washing-up by grabbing a tea towel and drying. 'When I first started going out with Mark I was so apathetic. It took me about four dates to realize that he was actually OK and then another year to realize he's actually great.'

I do remember the first days of Mia and Mark. She kept complaining about his backpack.

I've never really reached that stage in a relationship where you can exist in peace alongside each other. Apart from my relationship with Sam, my whole dating history has been an amusing collection of short stories. Although I didn't date at university, what with my lack of desire during the first two years post-heartbreak and then the lack of single men in the third, I did have quite an active dating life when I first moved to London. Active, but still fruitless. Fruitless, but still funny.

'Maybe I'm being too optimistic, but I had hoped that I would have more luck on the dating scene this time around.'

'What, as opposed to that OAP and the gym guy?' Mia's memory has always been impeccable. She's referring to the only two men, since Sam, to have made it past a second date.

'They weren't *that* bad.'

'They were.'

I met Philip (an OAP in all ways bar his actual age) at a time when Sunday became more than the day of rest and turned into the day to announce your engagement on social media, a depressing (and pressurizing) state of affairs that meant I gave him more time than I otherwise would have. A whole six months totally wasted. At first I thought he was shy, but actually he was really boring. Making marmalade was genuinely one of the more exciting things that he did.

And then there was Jimmy Gym, whom I started dating when personal training became quite the fashionable career choice. Rather depressingly, he was probably one of my longest relationships, at least according to my recollection. In my eyes we were dating for ten months. In his eyes, we weren't dating at all. In his eyes, we were 'casually seeing each other', which meant he and his teeny tiny pencil penis were having a great time hanging out in many other pencil cases.

'OK, maybe they were.'

Washing-up all done, I distract myself with a chilli chip. 'Anyway, it's fine. I think I might cave in and give up.'

She shakes her head. 'You can't do that. Give it some more time.'

As if time will make these men more appealing.

Chapter 7

But I do. Despite my reluctance, I take Mia's advice and give dating some more time. I never really thought of myself as a (deluded) optimist until now.

I text her to keep her updated, and also to try and make her evening go more quickly. I know she's working on a big boring case, and the one thing I can provide is some entertainment to distract her.

> On my way to a date! I'm cautiously optimistic about this one! I'll let you know how it goes! Don't forget to eat dinner! xx

And I am cautiously optimistic. Toby, my date, seems just the right level of keen. In a turnaround of events, he was the one who asked me to go for a drink, and he even chose the bar and booked a table. From the outside the bar looks cute, and from the inside, which is where I now am, I'm delighted to see that they also offer a charcuterie board.

Sitting at the table, practising my casual look, I get a text from Toby.

> Sorry I'm running late, saw a lost dog on the road and had to find the owner.

It's as if he's reading my mind, and I immediately accept this as a satisfactory excuse.

Don't worry at all! Take your time! Poor little puppy.

Turns out he's twenty-five minutes late. My casual pose doesn't last for twenty-five minutes. Its cut-off point is eighteen, and my maximum wait-time is thirty. He's cutting it pretty fine.

A man casually points at me.

'Bea? Are you Bea?'

I nod.

The man then points to himself. 'Toby. I'm so sorry I'm late, so rude of me.'

At first glance he's quite attractive, but obviously shorter than his photos would lead you to believe.

He takes off his jacket and settles into the seat opposite me.

'Did you find the owner?'

'Huh?' He looks at me as if I have two heads, and then his eyes widen in understanding. 'I mean, that might have been a lie, sorry. I was running late and thought the dog story would be an acceptable excuse. You seemed pretty dog-obsessed.'

I can see how he came to this conclusion. I sent him a lot of dog memes to illustrate my varying moods. It seemed a safer option than using words. And it's true, I do love dogs, but I don't particularly like that he lied or that I was gullible enough to fall for the story.

It all rests on his answer to my next question.

'How do you feel about cats?'

'Not good. I don't understand why their skin is so stretchy.'

If he'd been pro-feline, I would have stood up and walked away.

A bottle of wine and a surprisingly pleasing plate of meat, cheese, crackers and some odd pickled items later, I am delighted to report that what happens is a pleasant surprise. I like him just enough to potentially date him. We have a nice evening; he tells me about his family (his mum sounds nuts), his job ('I'm kinda like Santa' – by which he means he runs a website that sells cheap gifts, a comparison I find quite amusing, unless he genuinely thinks he's like Santa Claus, in which case we have a problem), and his friends. I even think there is some flirting going on. Part-way through, I note that I keep copying his physical movements, so I try to stop, but then I become even more stilted, so decide to let my body pose in whatever way it likes.

Unbelievably there are no lengthy silences, and like a modern-day romance, we have a cheeky goodnight kiss outside the bar. He's a good kisser, despite being short. (Maybe he's a good kisser because he's short? Have I been missing a trick here?) Mainly I'm proud of myself that I actually remembered how to kiss someone. I had plenty of time to prepare when I noticed he came back from the loo chewing gum. All in all, a good date. There is hope! I feel the giddiness of hope!

On my way to the bus stop I reach for my phone. Mia

will be twitching with anticipation; she'll start calling soon if I don't send her an update.

> It went well! He seemed really nice and most
> importantly – normal! We even had a cheeky kiss!

I add in the teenage gossip because I know Mia will be proud. Her reply is instant.

> Oh yay! This is great! Was the kiss good?

I'm about to type out my answer as my phone rings. It's Mum. It's quite late for her to be calling.

'Hey, Mum! Are you OK?'

'Bea! Yes, I'm fine. Are you OK? You sound happy. What have you been up to?' How can mums always tell when there is something juicy going on?

'I'm OK too.' I haven't told her about any of my dates as she would get her hopes up, so I remain purposefully vague. 'I've had a good day. And I had a charcuterie board for dinner.'

'Oh, that is good.'

'How are you doing? How's Hugo?' Hugo is my mum's dog and best friend.

'Oh, he's fine. He's currently napping.' I can imagine the two of them now. Both snuggled with a blanket. One of them lightly snoring.

'I was wondering if you were thinking of coming home soon. I saw your favourite face wash on offer and I thought I would pick some up.'

I do need to go see her. I haven't been home since before Mia's wedding. My dad isn't around any more, so my brother Fred and I like to visit her at least once a month. Sadly my dating escapades have made it harder to find the free time.

I lie slightly. 'I was actually hoping to come home in the next couple of weeks. Would that be OK?'

'That would be lovely. You lead such busy lives, you and your brother. But only come home if you can. Just let me know beforehand so I can pick up something for dinner.'

Mum fills me in on all the town gossip, including a shocking case of petty arson at the local park. I listen happily, glad to be distracted from my more anxious thoughts. I had a good time tonight, but what if I read the situation wrong? What if I was a little too 'me'? What if he thought my bum was a little too big, my wonky walk a little too wonky, my conversation too meandering?

I look up in time to see my bus pulling in ahead of me. I half run towards it, hoping nobody I know is around to see.

I reach the doors in time and make a big faff trying to get my card out to pay. It's hard to do with a phone in one hand. 'Mum, I've got to go, my bus is here.' The idea of a bus full of people overhearing my mum's fairly middle-class problems makes me cringe, so I keep the goodbye short and meander my thoughts back to Toby as I find my seat.

He did kiss me. He wouldn't have kissed me if he had a bad time. I let myself feel hope again.

Chapter 8

I get to work thirty minutes before my contracted start time, which is late according to everyone else in the office, sit down at my desk and ease myself into the day.

Keen not to put too much pressure on the date with Toby, but rejuvenated by the thought that not all dating is bad, I decide to reassign some of my online shopping time to the online man hunt. I choose to think of it as self-care and decide to be proud of myself for recognizing when I need some me-time, instead of being depressed that once again my contribution to the workplace is so minimal that spending two hours doing absolutely no work goes totally unnoticed.

So I swipe whilst pretending to catch up on emails, but despite my refreshed attitude it's still a bleak world out there, and at the peak of my despair I sign up for speed dating next Tuesday evening, a decision I immediately regret.

Of course, I don't forget Toby. I texted him this morning and eventually he replied, but, like an avocado, with dating there is a very short period of time when it's just right, and I fear letting too much time lapse between date one and date two. Still, the one thing I have learnt from mistiming the ripeness of my avocados is that if you shove enough lime, salt and chilli in there you can make an excellent guacamole.

So this is essentially what I do with Toby, except I swap lime, salt and chilli for GIFs and puns. This time we have promoted our choice of date day to a Thursday, which works well as speed dating is on Tuesday, giving me a whole day and a half to ready myself to socialize again.

By the time I've finished swiping, a generous hour has passed and there is no point doing any work today. I'm leaving at lunch(ish) for a smear test and if I start anything now, I'll have to redo it tomorrow morning.

Besides, I am distracted, and I can't work when I'm distracted. I'm worried about all the potential mishaps that might happen during my smear test. What if I fart? I didn't last time, but a fart during a smear test would be bad, probably worse than a fart in yoga.

I could just not show up, but I've left it for longer than I should have and I've intentionally worn a wrap dress instead of jeans to make getting undressed slightly more dignified than my last experience.

I'm busy getting up to speed with the 'news', also known as the sidebar of shame, when I hear a louder-than-office-acceptable greeting. 'Bea! Good morning!' I look up and see Penny striding towards my desk, smiling her room-lightening smile, leaving a trail of ogling eyes in her wake. Annoyingly, although her beauty is undeniable and I often feel like a lowly peasant in her company, she's also one of the kindest people in the office and I can't help but love her.

'I just remembered that you're out of the office this afternoon. Do you need me to do anything? And what are you up to? I hope it's something scandalous.' She winks at me. 'If it is, can I come with you?'

'Nothing scandalous, I'm afraid. I have my smear test.'

'Ah, nice. Good outfit for it.'

This is why she's my work wife. Great minds think alike, and fools seldom differ. With us, the latter part of the saying is definitely more suitable.

'I remember the last time I got my smear test. God, it wasn't great.'

I worry her anecdote isn't going to make me feel better about my upcoming appointment.

'The nurse had to keep getting bigger implements. Eventually she actually said to me, "I've never seen such a big vagina on such a small girl." I swear that's exactly what she said. Since then I've been doing Kegel exercises for at least fifteen minutes every day.'

I look at her suspiciously. 'Were you doing them in the comms meeting yesterday morning? When everyone was talking about how to handle the kids-changing-colour issue?'

'Oh my God – yes! How did you know?'

'I remember glancing over at you and thinking it looked like you were concentrating really hard, but I knew you weren't. Good idea doing them in meetings.'

'I know, right? Really keeps me looking present.'

I look at the clock.

I'm definitely not going to start any new work now. 'Wanna get lunch?' I can go to the doctor's straight from there.

Penny's smile widens. 'Sounds great. Let me go get my money.'

'Who you texting?' She nudges me.

Penny knows all about my dating life, so no doubt she thinks my smile is for Toby. She's wrong.

'It's my mum. I've asked if I can go home this weekend. She's now panicking that she won't have time to clean the house and is already apologizing.'

'Ah, a classic mum problem.'

We head out of the building and turn left towards the tube.

'Sushi place round the corner?' Penny is always a bad influence when it comes to spending money on food.

'Sure. Let's treat ourselves.' I'll get some batch-cooked soup out of the freezer for dinner.

She strides next to me, her long legs making me walk a touch quicker than normal. 'Thanks for suggesting we go to lunch. I don't know what it is, but the office has had a really bad vibe recently. Is it just me?'

I hadn't really thought about it. To me, work always has a bad vibe. 'I guess we have had a lot of new people start recently, which I think makes people like Joan a bit on edge. All the extra competition.'

'I don't like it. Every time I go into a meeting, the first five minutes are taken up by people boasting about why they're so great and all the impressive things they've done. I've done impressive things too, but forgive me if I'm not a shouter.' She's getting louder and louder as she talks. 'I worry that if I don't shout about how great I am, people will forget me.'

We reach the sushi place as she finishes talking. I take the volume down to an inside voice. 'Penny, people could never forget you. You are not a forgettable person.'

We take a quick break in our conversation to pick our sushi, pay and perch on the bar stools in the window.

As I distribute the pickled ginger, I keep going. 'I do see what you mean though. I just don't know how to help. I've never been someone who shouts about their strengths and achievements.' I also feel my own particular strengths and achievements can be slightly harder to find.

'It's fine. I think I'm just in a slump.' She does actually slump when she says this. It's not a look I normally see. She's usually very poised. 'I need to not care so much.'

I shrug. 'This has been my solution.' I dip a piece of sushi into the soy sauce and shove it into my mouth so I can't finish the second half of my thought. The half that admits this solution is a great way to get forgotten about.

The waiting room at the doctor's surgery is too warm and I'm already sweating thinking about taking my clothes off behind that useless curtain they use. Oh God. I hope I'm not sweaty *down there*. I should have thought about this earlier, but I can't do anything about it now – my name has been called.

Eventually I knock on what I hope is the right door and peek in before I enter.

'Sorry – it took me a while to find the right room.' The totally illogical numbering system didn't help.

A happy-faced, friendly nurse looks up at me from behind a computer screen.

'Bea?'

'Yes.'

'Wonderful. Take a seat. My name is Mary and I will be carrying out your exam today.'

She then makes sure I am who I say I am and confirms who she thinks I am, weighs me (why don't they do this after you have undressed?) and takes my blood pressure.

'Your blood pressure is quite high. Is your blood pressure normally high?'

'Erm, no, I don't think so.'

'Probably white coat syndrome.'

That sounds bad.

'Oh God – what is that?'

She looks at me with a weighted gaze. It takes me a moment to catch up.

'Ohhhhh. White coat syndrome. I get it. Patient panic.'

'Exactly. I see you've had a smear test before, so you know what to do. I'll pop behind the curtain so you can get undressed. Let me know when you're up on the bed. There's a sheet there for you to cover up with, and a blanket. It's quite chilly today.'

Here goes. Bag off. Coat off. Sit down. Shoes off. Stand up. Tights off. Nope, underwear came with them. Every time. Assess height of bed. Can't hop up bum-first, way too high. Knee-first it is. Done. Apart from ripping the paper sheet a bit during the twist to lie down, I handled the partial undress pretty well.

At this juncture I panic. What is an appropriate thing to say to let her know I'm in position? *Welcome to the bat cave. Enter if you dare. Trespassers will be prosecuted.*

'Are you ready?'

Thank God she's made it easy for me. 'Yes!'

I sound way too chirpy.

'Is there any chance you could be pregnant?'

With a confidence that I rarely feel when asked a question, I reply, 'Nope.'

She moves my legs into position. 'Right, try to relax. You will feel a small amount of pressure.'

I look up to check out what is going on, but she's dived under the sheet. I do as she says and I try to relax, but forcing yourself to relax is very hard.

'OK, all done.'

I can feel my right eyebrow rising an unnatural amount. Whaaaat? I didn't feel a thing. Maybe I have a numb vagina. Maybe it has actually died from lack of use.

Amidst thoughts of my dying vagina, I get up only to realize that I did so much thinking about getting undressed that I didn't think about getting re-dressed.

The nurse is mumbling something, but all I can see is the tumbleweed of tights and pants currently getting twisted further by my sweaty hands. Mocking me. I can practically hear them saying, 'Ha, this is for all those times you left us on the bathroom floor, cold and alone, a mere ten centimetres away from the safety of the laundry bin.'

I look down and somehow I've already put on my coat, which will make it even harder to put my underwear and tights back on. The extra bulk. The extra layer. The lack of flexibility at my elbows and shoulders. I will definitely tuck my dress into my tights. I can feel the sweat on my upper lip forming.

In a split-second decision I decide to leave as I am, wearing no pants and no tights. Instead, I shove them into my coat pocket and make a run for it, an errant tight foot with fluff on it poking out of the pocket. My shoes are not shoes that should be worn without a barrier between them and my feet. My feet are going to rub.

I reach the freedom of outside and immediately regret my decision to forgo the tights, for many reasons.

Firstly, Mary was right, it is quite chilly, certainly a lot chillier than I remember it being – probably because I had tights and pants on before. Secondly, it's also windier outside than I remember it being, making it highly probable that I will flash someone, particularly because my previously perfect outfit choice has a big flap at the front due to its 'wrap-around' nature. And thirdly, I haven't shaved my legs for a while, so I will have to walk home to avoid the close human contact and the harsh, hair-emphasizing lights that both come with public transport. Next time I go for a smear test I will wear trousers. Wearing trousers means I have no choice but to put them back on, and the potential embarrassment of letting the nurse watch me struggle to dress myself far outweighs the more than likely embarrassment of flashing too many unsuspecting strangers with my cold, dead vagina.

Chapter 9

My weekend at home was gloriously restful. Apart from walking the dog with my mum on Sunday morning, I did impressively little moving. Mum made me chicken pie and mashed potato for dinner. She brought me cups of tea and dunking cookies. She even let me sit in her usual spot on the sofa. The best seat in the house.

But the issue with going home at the weekend is how blue it makes me feel on Sunday afternoon, a deep navy blue that bleeds into the start of the week, meaning Tuesday and speed dating has rolled around a lot more quickly than anticipated and I'm not emotionally sharp enough to be my most charming self.

The situation is made even worse by the fact I'm the last of my friends to still be single, meaning I couldn't find anyone to take the second ticket I'd purchased in the hope of not being alone at an event for people who are alone. What possessed me to even buy one ticket?

What have I done?

I breathe and try to quiet the anxious part of my brain.

As soon as I enter the room, I am immediately glad I decided to come late, as late as possible to avoid the awkward pre-speed dating chat/lack of chat. And there is wine. Horrible, horrible wine I imagine, but wine nonetheless.

I look around the room as I head to collect my drink. It's busy but everyone I can see seems quite normal. I check out the girls first; I want to gauge the competition. I would say we are all within the median range, a solid four to seven rating. It's a good thing I didn't bring Penny; she's more like a nine and nobody here wants a nine. Probably not the boys, and definitely not the girls.

The boys also appear to be fairly average, which is a good thing. There is one ginger and a couple of people who definitely have issues with keeping eye contact. On the whole, an encouraging bunch of singles.

With a loud clang, we are called to order, and all the awkward conversations come to a sputtering stop. Personally, as soon as I had my glass of wine in hand, I busied myself by searching for nothing in my bag, and therefore also managed to avoid the awkward stop to the awkward conversations.

Someone with a very enthusiastic face starts talking.

'Hello! Welcome! Welcome! For anyone who's new to Speedy Dating, the rules are simple!' She shimmies like a belly dancer as she says 'Speedy Dating', which makes me feel even less comfortable with my choice of evening entertainment. 'You were each given a number when you arrived; this is the number of the table you'll start at. At each table you'll find paper and pencils so you can write down notes on each person. Once the dating is done, you'll have twenty-four hours to go back online and mark down anyone you liked, and matches will then be able to message each other. When I stop talking, go to the table with your number on it. Girls, please sit down in the outer circle, and boys, please sit opposite. I will then ring the bell – this will signal the start of your first five-minute date! I will ring the bell again when the five minutes are up. Boys, you'll be the ones moving, so I'll give you a bit of time between rounds to move on to the next table and begin again! And boys – move to the right! OK. I'll stop talking now. So, ready, set, date!'

Cringe.

Still unable to believe that I'm here, I find the piece of paper I crumpled up and see a hastily scrawled number thirteen. Of course I get number thirteen. The unluckiest of all the numbers. That figures.

The harder I try to squeeze into the seat next to the wall, the more fuss I appear to make until someone (my first speed dater) sees me struggling. In an effort to avoid any more awkwardness, he tries to help me by pulling out the table, which only helps me thump into the seat with a force neither of us was prepared for. I laugh a touch too loud for it to be genuine.

Now, I hate to say it, but after a few five-minute sessions I can see the benefits of speed dating. I've heard more mature people than me say that when house-hunting you can tell within the first seven seconds if you're going to like a property or not. And I think the same can be said of people.

The first two are instant noes; my notepaper remains

blank. The third is a maybe, as is the fifth, until the conversation quietens (briefly), causing him to bring out a list of questions he commonly asks when dating. The questions include: 'What do you look for in a mate?', 'How strong is your moral compass?', 'Do you want children?' and 'If yes, would you be comfortable with your mother-in-law playing an active role in disciplining your child?'

Luckily the bell rings before I have time to actually answer any of the questions, allowing me a breather in which to take a fortifying gulp of wine before my next appointment.

I look up and over to assess my next Speedy Dater.

Crap.

It's Oddly Bodley.

Part of me is relieved to see Peter, a friendly face who will give me some reprieve from the stilted conversations with strangers, but the larger part of me is dying of shame that someone I know has found me speed dating.

And there is no way out. Damn these stupid pub benches with their velvet bum pillows and unhelpfully heavy tables.

He looks at me and smiles. I can't help but smile back.

'Is it just me, or is it mildly depressing being here? I feel like I should give up now and invest in one of those companies that specializes in meals for one.' He takes a seat and leans forward conspiratorially. 'It's nice to see you though. I didn't know you came to these things.'

'Oh no, no, I don't come to these things. I mean, obviously I *do* come to these things because I'm here, but this is my first time.' Why am I blabbering? In my lifetime

I've spoken to Peter for many, many hours. Why am I all of a sudden flustered at having to speak to him for five minutes? My hands are flapping now, which can't be a good thing. I sit on them. 'You don't need to be here, you've never had a problem finding a date. I feel like you've taken a ticket away from someone whose dating need is greater than yours.'

And it's true, Peter has never had a problem finding a date, especially after it got out at university that he came from old, plentiful money. Schools of girls started circling him, angling for a shot at the title. They even earned their own label, the Bodley Babes. His groupies tended to be very tall and very pretty, but also very dim and more attracted to Peter's money than to Peter himself. Proudly, I was never a member.

He has the sense to look a little sheepish. 'Well, yes, I am OK at finding dates, or at least they're good at finding me. But I rarely find an actual girlfriend, and my mother is getting increasingly anxious about my happiness – well, probably *her* happiness, which is currently tied directly to the prospect of me having children.' He puts on a high-pitched, comical voice. ' "Time is ticking, Peter. And I want grandbabies." So I thought it was worth trying something different. Of course, it would be easier if she actually liked any of the girls I bring home. The only female of the species that I have introduced her to and that she's liked is you.' This is a nice surprise to me as I always thought I had a face that people forgot. 'Truth be told, I'm also here supporting a friend. The chap you just spoke to, Al. He says he comes to these things a lot but rarely gets a date out of it, so thought I'd tag along and offer any insights I might have. Not that I've ever actually been very good with women, but I might be able to give him some pointers. You know. How did you think he did?'

'Can I be honest?'

'I would never expect anything else.'

'Terribly. He started off OK, but then he got out a list of unnecessarily intense questions.'

'Ah, I wondered what he was scribbling on his way here. He's even more lost than I had feared.' There is a brief pause, and Peter looks at me for a little longer than I'm comfortable with. 'So if you're not doing anything after, can I take you out for some chicken? I know a fancy Nando's around the corner.'

The odd look gone from his face, I have no qualms in saying, 'Sure. But I would be happy with regular Nando's too. Just so you know.'

The end of speed dating, and the promise of chicken, can't come soon enough. Spotting Peter after the final round is easy; I can't actually see him, but his laugh can be heard even above the noise of the post-speed dating din. Physically reaching him at the bar is harder than it should be though. At five foot one (on a good day), I'm often too short to register for the average-sized human, which can either make navigating crowds really easy (if the crowd size is exactly right), or really hard (if the crowd size gets too big for the allotted space, as it is this evening).

As I near the bar, I can see Peter more clearly . . . and the girl he's talking to. From the look of things, she would have fitted in perfectly well with the Bodley Babes. She reminds me of a magpie: attracted to anything that sparkles.

'Hey, Pete. Ready for some chicken?' I think I can see hesitation in his eyes, so I add, 'Or do you want to hang out here for a while longer?'

'Well, I have just ordered another drink. Can I get you one and then we can go for dinner?'

The idea of being Peter's wingwoman on what has been an already taxing evening is too much for me to handle. I can feel my mask slipping. I must retreat.

'Of course, finish your drink. I'm going to head out though. I didn't have lunch today,' (lie) 'and I have an early exercise class tomorrow morning,' (a bigger lie) 'so I'm gonna go pick up something to eat and head home.'

I think he might be a bit sad, but not sad enough to cancel the order. 'Sure thing.' He pauses. 'Hey, it was great to see you though. Sorry about Al and his list of intense questions.'

'No worries.' I try to hide the disappointment in my face. 'Night, Peter.'

I give him a quick hug and make my way through the crowd. My backpack, which I have put on as added armour, keeps snagging against the shoulders of people who appear to be having a much better time than I am, making me feel even more out of place.

Back at home I curl up on the couch, slightly bruised, with a microwaveable veg pot that is too hot to eat balanced precariously on the arm of the sofa. What I don't understand is that everyone else there seemed to be having a good time. Even Peter, who only went as back-up for his friend. I found it tiring and depressing. I turn the TV on even though I know I'm not in the headspace to watch anything, but the background noise makes me feel slightly less alone.

My phone pings; it's Mia.

How was speed dating? x

I don't know how to respond, so I decide not to.

Instead I put my phone down and look at the sad crumpled-up piece of paper that has my hastily scribbled notes on it. Nobody stood out for a good reason. I crumple it back up and throw it across the room.

Chapter 10

By the time Thursday, aka second-date-with-Toby day, rolls around, I'm ready for a nap. Tensions in the office are at an all-time high as we've had to scrap the kids' vitamins altogether and there are no tea-bags left in the kitchen. I've had to resort to drinking hot water. You can't dunk biscuits into hot water. It's an absolute nightmare.

Even texting Toby has become a chore. My general malaise has bled into my messages, and I know I am bordering on boring, but I have no armour against it.

Dressed in my usual monochrome, this time with a pop of lip colour (but not enough to risk the under-lip), I find I'm actually quite nervous; I'm entering territory I haven't entered in a while – I'm going to a boy's house for a date. I didn't think this would be suggested until the third date at the earliest. But surely just because I said yes to him cooking me dinner at his apartment doesn't mean I'm saying yes to everything. Or does it? I hope it doesn't. Me and my dead vagina aren't ready for that.

But how much do I really know about dating these days? Despite my recent flurry it would appear I am still very naive. Just this morning I overheard a shocking conversation at work about the necessity of getting your anal tone checked out ahead of a date. And whoever this woman was talking to didn't seem shocked at all. Instead, all she said, very casually, was, 'I think that is wise. And a doctor would be able to tell you. You don't want to rely on anyone less than a professional for these things.'

Sitting close to the kitchen comes with both advantages and disadvantages.

And yet, despite this, I'm still on my way to the date. I pop his address into Google Maps and get a seat on the tube. I'm sure it's a sign that this evening will go well – until I'm met with another passenger's crotch in my face. It's the most crotch I'll be getting tonight but it's hard to really enjoy it.

I only go the wrong way once on the walk from the station to Toby's place, so I'm feeling pretty smug as I arrive. I ring the doorbell with a hint of a smile on my face.

After some scuffling noises at the door, I see Toby. In truth I see more of Toby than I was bargaining for. He's wearing an open dressing gown (a little weird, but maybe fine) with his manhood dunked into . . . a can of coconut milk? This is not fine.

The hint of smile drops from my face.

'Bea! Welcome! Come in, come in.' He opens the door a fraction wider to make room for me to squeeze by. 'So, I realize this looks unusual, but I've had a bit of a nightmare and didn't want to leave you out in the cold.' I am glued to the doorstep. 'Please come in. I won't be a second.' He scampers away with his dressing gown flowing out rather majestically behind him. He shouts back at me, 'If you could shut the door behind you.'

I step inside and shut the door, too stunned to do anything but follow simple instructions. I can already feel Captain Hindsight preparing his 'I told you so' speech. But alas, I ignore him and follow Toby further into his lair.

I walk through to an empty kitchen. I can only assume Toby has retreated to the safety of a bedroom. There's a box of food on the counter, partly unpacked, and some of the ingredients are simmering away on the stove.

Should I chop? Should I set the table? Pour myself a glass of wine? Call the police?

'Should we reschedule?' I shout, in no particular direction, around the room.

'No no, I'm fine.' I have to assume his bedroom is somewhere off the hallway, based on the direction of his voice.

With hesitation I tiptoe towards the voice and ask, 'So, what happened? Can I do anything to help?' *Please say no.*

'Erm, maybe.' And then all I hear is some mumbling, and then a request for some . . . paper Jews?

'Sorry, did you ask for some paper Jews?'

With that a door swings open and he steps into the hallway. At least he's body confident.

'Pineapple juice. I don't suppose you have any on you? From my research it might be more effective than the coconut milk.'

Why would I be carrying pineapple juice?

'I can go get some?' I decide that if he asks me to do

this I will go get it, but I won't step back in the apartment. 'If you don't mind me asking, what happened?'

If you don't mind me asking. He has his penis in a can of coconut milk and *I* feel awkward?

'It's been a series of unfortunate events really. The stupid box is meant to contain all the ingredients for dinner, that's part of the appeal. But *apparently* coconut milk and flour are "staples" that you should already have in your cupboard. Well, not this cupboard. So I had to go get those – two separate trips to the corner shop.

'So anyway, I was part-way through chopping the chillies when I realized I was running late. So I went to change and take a quick loo stop. But see, erm, turns out that I hadn't washed my hands since chopping the chillies, and, well, I think they must be very strong because I have an awful burning sensation on my guy. And I didn't know what to do, you know, never having rubbed my dick with chilli before.' Did he say he was rubbing? I wonder what he was doing in the loo? 'But my mum used to make me drink regular milk after eating something too spicy, so I hoped dunking him in coconut milk might reduce the burning.

'And then you rang the doorbell and, well, here we are.' He opens out his available hand in a welcoming motion, whilst the other, I am happy to report, remains otherwise occupied holding the can. I hope he doesn't cut himself.

Right. 'I guess maybe the silver lining is that you had some coconut milk after all?' He doesn't say anything – perhaps it's a bit soon to joke. I try a different tack. 'Is it helping?'

'Not as much as I would have hoped, but the desire to chop it off has stopped, so I think progress is being made.'

I can't help but wonder what would happen if the situation was reversed. If I was the one in the dressing gown, hopping up and down trying to get the burning to stop in my vagina? Apart from the fact this would never happen, I don't see Toby being as patient.

'If it would help, you could stay . . . dunking, and I could finish dinner?' Apparently I'm determined to continue the date with this unsupportive fuckwit. Heaven help me.

He relaxes slightly and leans against the door-frame, looking like a great weight has been lifted off him. 'Gosh. If you don't mind, that would be great.'

The appendage has been dunking for a solid half hour while I prepped and cooked. I wonder if it will look all wrinkly like your fingers do when you've been in the bath too long? I'm not quite curious enough to ask the question out loud. Our conversation has been awkwardly stilted so far, and I don't think it's all because of the appendage issues. I keep asking questions, questions that are getting more and more mundane, but all he's giving me back is one-word answers.

I've been exaggerating my interest in the food prep to camouflage the silence.

Finally I have a momentary reprieve from thinking of things to say when Toby retreats to put some clothes on.

'I think it will be a while before I go near chilli again.'

He enters the kitchen with the swagger of a man who has recently escaped death.

I nod. 'I think that would be wise.' I take a taster bite from the pan and, yes, dinner is more than edible. Hopefully I won't poison either Toby or myself. 'Good timing too, I think dinner is ready.'

Toby holds out the bowls, and I dish us up before we head to the table. It's quite a small table, and I have to sit with my legs squished to one side to stop myself from continually bumping into his outstretched legs.

But fully dressed Toby is no easier to talk to than half-naked Toby. Our first date was full of laughter and joking. Maybe we've already used up all of our funny?

I look around the room for some inspiration. I've already asked him about his work, his weekend, his crazy mum. 'So, have you lived here long? I really like it. I really like all the . . . lamps and chairs and stuff. It's very stylish.'

'Thanks, but none of it's mine.'

'Oh, so it came furnished?' Even as I ask the question I don't care.

'Yep.' He seems more intent on the food than anything else.

I decide to keep talking anyway. 'Well, I really like decorating. Painting walls. Buying soft furnishings. Picking out *objets d'art*.' I am mildly impressed with my French accent. 'I was always the kind of person in those computer games who wouldn't really play, but would build houses over and over again. Obviously I don't own the house I'm living in now. I rent it, but I've tried to make it my own.' I keep going, oblivious, and now also indifferent, as to whether he is finding this interesting. 'And I guess it isn't really worth it. Say I put all this money into making it nice, and then—'

He holds up a hand right in front of my face. 'I'm gonna have to stop you there.'

His face is red and the squirming is back.

'Are you OK?'

'Hold on a sec,' he says and abruptly leaves the table. I finish my meal in silence.

After an uncomfortable amount of time, Toby emerges, once again with his appendage in the can, clothes back on the floor. This time he's even forgone the dressing gown.

'I'm really sorry about this, but the burning came back and I had to touch him again to get him back in the can, but I must still have some remnants of chilli left on my hands so it's got even worse.'

I have no words.

'I don't know what else to do and to be honest, mate, I am worried about my guy.' His face is full of concern, and I do actually feel quite sorry for the guy. Both guys. 'Can you help me down to the hospital?'

You have got to be shitting me, *mate*.

And yet, I find myself helping to conceal his penis and following Google step by painfully embarrassing step to the nearest hospital, because no taxi would take us.

Chapter 11

Sunday can't come soon enough. And when it does eventually reach us, I indulge in what the internet tells me I should be doing: I go to yoga and then meet up with Tilly at our favourite brunch spot. I'm feeling a tad emotionally delicate, so I kept my yoga session to myself. I can't quite handle feeling like a very ill, very old sloth, next to the very flexible Tilly.

We lucked out and got shown to my favourite booth. I imagine Tilly's smile had something to do with it.

She squeals at me. 'I'm so happy that this is our second in-person meet-up in a month!'

I shuffle along the bench. 'Well, if you stopped being so busy and travelling all the time, we could see each other more.'

'Actually, I have a plan that will mean exactly that.' She arranges her napkin on her lap. 'But before we get on to me, talk to me about you. I felt so bad – after yoga, I realized I did all the talking and didn't ask one question about what you were up to.' She reaches towards me from across the table. 'What's happening? Job? Romance? Life? How's your mum?'

I half reach back, but it isn't an action that comes

naturally to me, so I avoid actually holding her hand. If that is indeed what she wants? 'There's not much to report.' I pull back an inch. 'Mum is really good, job is frustrating but that's normal, the cards are bumbling along.' I make a face and nod slightly. 'I have actually been on a couple of dates recently –' Tilly sits straighter as soon as I say this – 'and I did have some hope for one of the guys, but the second date did not go well.'

'You didn't like him? Is it worth trying again? Giving it a bit more time?'

What is it with Mia and Tilly? They both think time will make these men more appealing. I think spending more time with them will have precisely the opposite effect.

'Um, no. We're just very different people.' Tilly looks crestfallen. 'Part of me wonders if it's the online thing. Maybe I would have a better success rate if I date people that I meet in real life. Like at the supermarket. If we both reach for rotisserie chicken, at least we know we have that one thing in common.'

'What about your friends?'

I scoff. 'Oh God no, I don't date friends.'

Tilly slants her head. 'I meant more, do your friends know anyone they could hook you up with, but that's quite a strong reaction.' She raises an eyebrow. 'Spill it. Do you fancy one of your friends?'

My head shakes even faster now. 'No no no, it's not that.'

'Well, what is it then?'

I don't like talking about Sam.

'It's such a pathetic story.'

'Let me be the judge of that.'

I avoid eye contact, and am glad for the moment's reprieve when someone comes over to take our order, but they leave more quickly than I would have liked.

'You don't have to tell me if you don't want to.'

Now I feel like I'm making it into a really big deal. I sigh and reposition myself slightly.

'It's not that big of a deal –' I haven't even told Mia this – 'but when I was younger, we're talking when I was in my last years of school, my best friend Sam and I started dating. And I know I was young and I had nothing to compare it to, but I thought we were going to get married. I did all the stupid things. I practised my married signature, I had photos of us all over the inside of my closet. My parents loved him. And I loved him. I loved dating my best friend. It felt so right.'

'So what went wrong?'

'He stopped feeling the same.' I shrug.

This isn't quite the whole truth. What actually happened was that my dad died, and life became really shit. And eventually Sam stopped coming round so much. He said I'd changed. He said I wasn't happy any more and he didn't want to be around someone who was so sad all the time. He wanted to go back to being just friends. Of course we didn't, so I lost my boyfriend, my best friend and my dad all at the same time.

I can't entirely blame Sam for the lack of emotional support he offered, we were young. But it stung quite badly when two weeks later he started going out with Meghan Smalls, a girl with (ironically) massive boobs and an even bigger smile.

So, since then, unable to change the size of my boobs, I instead decided to pretend to be happier, and to never, ever date a friend in the hopes that when the relationship inevitably ended, I wouldn't be so totally devastated. I can handle losing a boyfriend. I don't know if I can handle losing another best friend.

'Anyway, let's change the subject. It was so long ago.' I really should be over it. Our drinks arrive and I add half a cup of sugar to my coffee. 'So what's this plan that you have?'

'I've decided to change my career. I want to become an interior designer.'

'I think that's a great idea!' And I genuinely do, even though I have no idea what she's changing careers from.

'Thanks, I am excited. So, I'm planning to go back to school and take a course. It's quite expensive, but I think it will be worth it.'

'How expensive are we talking?'

'About forty thousand pounds.'

I choke on my coffee.

'And then there'll be living expenses on top of that.'

'Forty thousand pounds?' I am incredulous, outraged, baffled. 'Could you not learn the same things in a different, less expensive way?'

She looks at me, and a teensy amount of the light in her eyes has died.

'Take my cards. I would love to do them full-time, but the reality of the situation is a bit different.'

'I know, but I want to do something that I enjoy, exactly like you enjoy working on your cards. It was actually you who inspired me to think about what I enjoy doing and to go for it. And if I live with Jeroen then my living expenses won't be *that* much.'

I can't, I can't let her make a plan based on a man she's only just met. She doesn't know anything about him. I don't know anything about him.

'And I want you to do something that you enjoy too, but what if you guys break up?' I am projecting my own worries on to her, and I know it, but I can't help myself.

'Well, then I guess I'll have to figure it out.'

I open and close my mouth like a guppy.

Luckily our food arrives.

I have a vague notion of moving out of the way.

Tilly makes polite conversation with our server, but I'm too busy processing to do anything other than nod. Her answer is so simple, and I have no retort. No matter how hard I process.

Chapter 12

Brunch with Tilly left me feeling oddly energized for a Sunday afternoon, so I went home, put on Classic FM and printed a whole bunch of new cards. They're now drying on every surface in my tiny flat.

There is a lot of stuff to hate about my apartment: the weird yellow bathroom that always makes you look ill, the cantankerous old lady next door, the dodgy stain on the carpet in the bedroom, the really thin walls, the fact my post always goes missing, and the cheap linoleum flooring that isn't glued down properly. But there is also a lot to love: the cat that sits outside and guards my weird yellow bathroom, my view of the city skyline (which is so far away that you can only just about make it out as long as there are no clouds), and most importantly the fact I can make as much mess as I want.

I look at the newly printed cards.

Tilly's revelation – that if things go wrong she'll figure it out – is so refreshing. I've always been more of a planner. But I think somewhere along the way the planning morphed into worrying.

Maybe I could be more like Tilly.

But she was wrong about one thing. I haven't 'gone for

it' with my cards, and if I gave her the impression that I have, then I'm a bigger pretender than I even realize. They're stocked in a total of two local shops, the same two shops that have always stocked them, and I haven't put any real money or time into them since I started; even my screen printer now looks tired.

But I could go for it.

I've been so absorbed in my cards that I have no idea what time it is. I look at the clock in the kitchen. I say 'kitchen', but in reality the kitchen is also the lounge, the dining room, the craft area, the storage space and the laundry room. It's an efficient way to live.

It is almost time for me to think about dinner, which is fine as I have no more space for any more cards. I know I have paint over my hands, and probably most of my face. I'll need a quick bath-time before food-time.

With the steam lending an air of mystery to the bathroom, I test out the water before dropping in.

I stay in the bath until my fingers are acceptably wrinkly, but as soon as I get out, I hear a knock on my door. For a split second I think I'm about to be murdered. A knock on the door this late on a Sunday, or indeed at any time of day unless I'm getting something delivered, is unprecedented. But rationally, being murdered is probably even less likely. Besides, I don't know if murderers knock.

I dry as quickly as I can, put my underwear on so I don't feel completely unprotected, and throw my dressing gown over the top.

I can't help but note the irony of opening my own front door in (almost) nothing but my dressing gown, and I'm relieved to see Mia on the other side. If I had to soak an appendage in front of anyone, it would be her.

'Mia! Gosh, sorry, I forgot that you were coming round.' I assume I have forgotten plans, and panic that I was meant to have prepped some food. I only have left-over cheese.

'We hadn't planned anything, but I thought I would chance it, see if you were in. I was right around the corner, picking up some shoes.'

'It's Sunday evening, of course I'm in.' I say this much more welcomingly than I feel. I hope she can't tell that I don't particularly want her here.

Not that I don't like seeing her – I do, but I'm not prepared, mentally or physically. My house is a mess. I've just had a bath. I'm in Sunday evening wind-down mode. Not Sunday evening talk-to-people mode. Even if that person is my best friend.

'I'll make tea,' I say. I always keep some herbal tea for her. For myself I plan to make a hot chocolate. 'You can show me your shoes. Let's go into the kitchen.'

We rotate ninety degrees to reach our destination.

'I'm warning you now, they aren't exciting shoes. They're amphibious shoes for our trek in the rainforest.' It takes me a moment to realize that by 'our' she means her and Mark, not her and me. She says it as if it's obvious. But it wasn't always that way. 'Our' used to refer to us. Our movie nights. Our favourite dance moves. Our preferred ice cream flavour. 'Apparently they're very quick-drying.' Mia has been known to pack months in advance, so this prep doesn't come as a surprise, but nevertheless this is not what I thought she was going to say. She's the only person I know who wears heels out of choice on the weekend.

'Amphibious shoes?' I ask, in a way that hopefully conceals my sadness at no longer being part of her 'our'.

'Yes! Here, look, they have holes in the sole to enable the quick-drying action.'

I take a look and she's totally right. I didn't even know they made such a thing.

'I didn't even know they made such a thing.' Turns out I have nothing else to say.

'Neither did I. They are truly disgusting.'

I look at the shoes some more. It's almost as though someone has used a hole-punch all over them. 'I bet you get some funny suntan lines.'

She lets out a conciliatory laugh. 'Oh God, I hadn't even thought about that.'

The kettle boils and we sit down on the sofa. I make some space in and amongst the card supplies that are scattered over the table.

'Are you OK? You seem a little off?'

'No, I'm fine.' And I am, but no matter how you answer a question like this, you never sound fine.

'OK. So, how was your weekend?'

'I haven't done a huge amount, but I saw Tilly for brunch this morning, and that was nice. It was good to have a chill weekend after my disastrous second date with Toby.'

'Oh no! What happened? Why was it so disastrous?'

I can't quite bring myself to share the chilli episode. It's a funny story but it requires more energy than I currently have. I shouldn't have brought it up.

'Ugh. It was just bad. I felt like we got on really well on the first date, but it wasn't there on the second.' Probably because his burning penis was in the way.

'I've told you before, you need to give these things more time. I think it would be worth going on a third date, so you can see what happens.'

'I'm not going to give him more time.' I don't know why she always assumes I'm being impatient.

'OK, but I think you're giving up.'

'I'm not giving up.'

'Really? Because, Bea, all you've been doing recently is giving up.'

Ouch.

'No, I haven't.'

'Yes, you have.' We haven't actively moved away from each other, but we're both sitting a little straighter, and there is more distance between us. 'When was the last time you were happy?'

Before you got here. Obviously I don't tell her that.

She asked the question kindly enough, but I almost feel ambushed. 'I am happy.'

She shuts her eyes and shakes her head. 'No, you're not. You're flailing.' She's on a roll now. 'Take your job. You keep saying that you're about to move departments, or you're about to get promoted, but I haven't seen it.' I know that Mia doesn't understand my lack of ambition, but this seems harsh. I never really thought she was paying that much attention to my work updates. Her job has always been more important and impressive and stressful than mine, so I rarely bore her with the trifling issues that come with being someone's assistant.

'You are not this person you're becoming. I was so happy when you said you were going to start dating because I thought it meant that you would actually be doing more than just existing. But no! You're flailing. You're giving up. And you aren't happy. You've been stuck in the same job for almost ten years.' Her tone is condescending, totally unlike her. It stings.

'I think that's kind of unfair. Just because I'm not as career-driven as you doesn't mean I'm flailing. Besides, I have my cards.'

'Your cards?'

I rear up. 'Yes, my cards. What's wrong with my cards?'

'There's nothing wrong with them, Bea, but you don't do anything with them!'

'But I'm going to.'

'Really? Are you? Because your track record would suggest otherwise.'

'Well, what does my track record suggest?' I immediately regret asking this question.

'Your track record suggests you're not going to do anything with them. You stay inside your comfort zone. You hide in your apartment. You never ask for anything. You never fight for anything.'

'I do.' Although I say this with absolutely no fight in my voice.

'You do not.' Mia goes from sounding angry to exasperated. I don't know which is worse.

Some seriously heavy silence surrounds us. I know I must look like a deer in the headlights, but I am a deer in the headlights. I didn't know this was how she saw me. I thought Mia was my friend. I would never say such harsh things to a friend. I don't know how to react, but my body reacts for me.

I can't help the tears that are forming, but I can stop her from seeing them.

'I think you should go.'

'You want me to leave?'

'Yes.' I'm hurt and angry and embarrassed. But I don't want to say something to Mia that I might later regret, even if at this moment I don't really like her very much at all.

'Fine. I'll go.' She gathers up her bag and turns to me before she leaves. 'I love you.'

I think I nod a couple of times, but I don't say it back. She leaves her tea sitting on the table, untouched.

Chapter 13

The few weeks after my 'exchange' with Mia were not the best of weeks in Bea Land. I ended up escaping home so much that my mum now knows something is up, and texts me first thing every morning with a chirpy 'hello' to make sure I'm OK. Things have been going badly at work, where I was so distracted that I included the wrong selection of customers in an email about pregnancy vitamins. Things have been going badly with my cards, because the stores they're in have decided to add more card stockists, meaning my orders are going to decrease. My personal life is going badly, because I've halted all dating activities since the chilli drama, and things are still really weird between me and Mia. And then on Tuesday morning the boiler broke. On hair-wash day! Just as the temperature was due to be unseasonably cold for April. Just when I had fucked up at work, making it super awkward to ask to work from home. Why does this always happen?

But nevertheless, here I am on Wednesday morning, working from home (thanks to Penny and her cover stories), waiting for Colin the boiler man, as my actual work goes up in flames and my card business peters out.

Turns out Colin is very prompt, but even so I jump when he knocks and slightly spill my coffee on the couch.

I open the door.

Holy shit, Colin is kinda hot.

'Bea?'

'Uh huh.'

'Hi, I'm Colin, come to fix your boiler.'

'Uh huh.'

'Can I come in?'

Finally my brain kicks back into gear.

'Yes, thank you so much for coming. Please do come in.' Who talks like that? 'Can I get you something to drink? I have some cookies.' What? What am I saying? Why am I offering him cookies? I only have some old, crumb-covered custard creams and my favourite chocolate ones that I keep in the freezer.

'No cookies, thank you, but coffee would be great. Milk, two sugars.'

I am visibly relieved. 'No problem.' I walk through to the kitchen-cum-lounge-cum-dining room-cum-laundry area-cum-storage space-cum-office, and point to a door. 'The boiler is in there.'

He puts down a useful-looking bag and gets closer.

'Let's have a look at what's going on.'

What's going on is perfect bone structure.

When the kettle finishes boiling I snap, painfully, back to reality. I cannot hit on the boiler man. Even if I knew how to flirt, I cannot hit on the boiler man. But what if this is the person who will show me that life really is better shared with someone else? What if it was fate that made my boiler break and bring me Colin? I shouldn't ignore fate.

I am totally going to try to hit on the boiler man.

'So, how's it looking?' My game needs work.

'Fine, but it does need a service and a clean. Looks like there might be some build-up.'

I resist the urge to make a lazy sexual innuendo.

'Great. Cool. Super. I've, uh, left your coffee on the side.'

'Thanks.'

'No problem.' I roll my eyes internally. Maybe a little externally too. I try to walk away, which is hard to do considering my flat is only made up of one room, and decide to give up with both the flirting and the walking away.

'So how long have you lived here then?'

He is talking to *me*! This could be easier than I initially thought. Ugh, I hope he doesn't talk too much, like some taxi drivers and hairdressers. Maybe I should be more careful. He does know where I live. Who knows what else he's got in that bag.

'Not too long. About a year. It's nice though. I like living by myself.' That's not being careful, that is being reckless. He could be a serial killer. You shouldn't tell serial killers that you live alone.

'Yeah, I have a couple of friends who live right round the corner. There are some nice pubs nearby. The Angel down the road does a lovely Sunday roast. But I have to watch my head on the beams, they're quite low and I'm quite tall, nearly knocked myself out once.'

I have never seen or heard of the Angel. 'Oh yeah, I

know where you mean. And lucky for me, I don't think I
would have a problem with the beams.' I gesture weirdly
at my head, which I somehow feel will communicate
that I'm talking about my height.

'Ha, you're probably right. You should go. Although
last time I was in there, my friend Rich, who bloody
loves to get naked, got naked too early. I think he's
banned from there now, which is a sadness for us all.'

'Probably not that sad for everyone – like unsuspecting members of the public. Is there an acceptable time to
get naked in public?'

'Ha, no, you're probably right. But he loves it. Can't get
him to stop.'

The naked conversation makes me feel as though we
are flirting with danger. I feel very exposed, metaphor-
ically naked if not literally, so I remain silent and stay
standing close, but hopefully not too close, leaning up
awkwardly against the kitchen counter.

From what I can tell he fiddles about a bit more, blows
on something, and then declares that the boiler should
be fixed but I will need to bleed the radiators.

It's at times like this that I feel like a pathetic, ignorant
girl. I know that bleeding radiators is something that
people do, but I do not possess the knowledge of how to
do this.

And I think he can tell by the look on my face that I'm
panicking.

'Do you want me to show you how to bleed your
radiators?'

My relief is obvious. 'Yes please, that would be great. I

know it's something that I should know how to do, but, well, I don't.'

'No problem. I'll show you a couple of times, and then you can do the rest, but don't worry, I'll supervise.' His smile is dazzling. 'We're going to need some paper towels or an old tea towel.' It's the sexiest thing anyone has said to me in months.

Turns out bleeding radiators is really easy. And I think Colin, the boiler guy with lovely bone structure, might be flirting with me, but I can't be sure.

We have now bled all the radiators and I've lost all confidence.

'Thanks so much, I really appreciate it. And double thanks for showing me how to bleed my radiators. I feel like I'm finally becoming an adult.' Once again I do a weird hand gesture, like a half-punch. Did I just fist-bump the air?

He smiles, and I am dazzled again.

I have no idea how to do this. Me, who found a really long chin hair whilst inspecting my face this morning. Resigned, I head towards the door.

'Let me show you out.'

Chapter 14

It's Thursday and Mia's birthday drinks have arrived. I go because I know I need to. If I don't go, I would be further along the path of waving buh-bye to my friendship with her, and I'm not ready to let that ship sail, but my shitty week has made me feel far from sociable.

As soon as I pull open the heavy door I already regret being here. I've totally misjudged the vibe and I'm wearing all the wrong things. Plus it's so dark and so busy that I don't know how I'll find my friends.

Thankfully, from the slightly raised step I can make out the top of Peter's head.

As usual, he's holding court. Talking to people has always been one of Peter's skills; the fact he's a little different makes him approachable to people from every walk of life. A bunch of Mark's trendy friends surround him, along with a handful of Games Night frequenters, and somehow he doesn't look out of place in his suit.

As I'm nearing, a girl's hand appears on Peter's upper arm. He immediately opens out to let her in, taking her under his wing, the same way he normally does with me. But then, in a change of events, she kisses him – briefly, but it still happens.

It's the girl from the speed dating bar.

I decide too late to change direction. Oddly's seen me and waves me over.

'I was wondering when you would show up.' He takes me under his other arm. I feel extremely weird.

'Bea, this is Alice. Alice, this is Bea.'

I give her an awkward wave as both of my arms are being held down by Peter, and she makes the cheers motion at me with her drink. It puts me even closer to the edge.

'We were discussing the finer points of Mark's stag do. Controversially, I hear the boys weren't the ones to order strippers but it was in fact the girls who saw some action. Do you deny these vicious rumours?'

He's talking to me. 'Sorry, guys, but what happens on the hen do stays on the hen do.' I say this with far more energy and amusement in my eyes than I feel.

'Mia has a canvas with an imprint of the guy's butt plastered on it!'

'Again, no comment.' That was one of my better ideas.

Luckily the conversation leads away from our escapades and returns to a competition over who has been witness to the worst treatment of a stag. I'm glad I'm a girl. The worst you get at a hen do is stifling amounts of organization.

Despite not talking or contributing in any meaningful way, I need a break.

At the bar, I am totally overwhelmed by the choice of cocktails. The list is too long, and it's too dark to read it comfortably. I don't want to spend fifteen pounds on a cocktail I might not like. White wine it is.

Just as soon as a barman sees me waiting and deigns to take my order . . .

I'm on tiptoes leaning as far as I dare over the bar, and still nothing. The person next to me has started speaking loudly. I turn to him, my face a picture of dislike.

'I said, it's busy tonight, huh?'

A man is talking to me. I make my face look friendlier.

'It is.'

'Who are you here with then?'

Is he flirting with me?

I hope not, because I am not in the mood. 'Oh, those guys over there.' I point in what I think is vaguely the right direction. 'It's a friend's birthday. It seems like a cool place for drinks, if I ever actually get to try one.' I roll my eyes and point towards the barman. I don't want to be rude, but I also don't want to be overly friendly. It's too loud to talk and I don't want to miss my opportunity to order a drink. Plus, he's standing on my bad side.

Luckily he takes the hint and moves on to someone else.

I'm about thirty seconds away from leaving and going back to my warm apartment when Peter sidles up beside me.

'Looks like you could use a taller escort to help.'

He makes a signal with his hand and, as if by magic, the barman comes over to take our order. Peter orders for a bunch of people before asking, 'What are you having? It's my round.'

I swallow and my eyes widen. I hope I'm not expected to pay for a whole round of drinks. From the look of things, a whole round of drinks would destroy a month's expendable income. Maybe more.

'Don't worry – I offered to get these, but nobody else has signed up to doing rounds. You're safe with me.'

'I was going to get a white wine.'

'Hogwash. You're having an Elderflower Fizz. You'll love it, and you can give me a sip so I can taste how delicious and refreshing it is before going back to my terribly manly craft beer.'

'Who says "hogwash"? Is that word still included in the dictionary?'

He ignores me. 'So, tell me, what's up between you and Mia?'

Trust Peter to notice something isn't right. And to have no subtlety when asking about it.

'Nothing, it's fine.' He looks at me. 'OK, it's not exactly fine. We had a weird thing and we just need some space.'

He nods. 'I'll accept this as an answer because I can see that you don't want to share specifics, but the next Games Night is only a month away, so if it's not sorted by then, let me know and I can interfere if it looks like you guys might get pitched against each other.'

'We'll be fine by then.' It would be awful if we had to share custody of Games Night.

'Anyway, I haven't asked for a while – how is the card business going? I loved the food series you did.'

I'm touched he liked the food series – it was a particular favourite of mine because of all the egg jokes – but I'm also kinda surprised that he would know any details about my cards. 'You saw the food series?'

He looks at me. 'Of course. I'm your biggest fan. I always check to see what you're doing, mainly so I can use the jokes as my own.'

When I first started the business a couple of years ago, I considered keeping the whole venture secret so I could save face when I stopped doing it, either by choice or because of a lack of funds, and it still isn't natural for me to talk about it, especially in public. Especially now when I know how Mia feels. So I keep quite vague about many of the details. I don't want to outright lie to Peter as that does feel wrong, but I also don't want him to see me as flailing.

'I think it's going OK. It's actually probably going better than it deserves. I haven't put as much effort into it as I could, but I want to come up with a plan to make it bigger. The stores I'm stocked in always sell out and they always want more, but I'm not quite in the position to give them more. It's a bit of a catch-22. To give them more I need to make more money, but to make more money I need to give them more.' I realize I'm waffling now, and I shift from foot to foot, uncomfortably aware that what I'm saying isn't clearly thought through.

I can also feel the increasingly angry stares burning into us as other people wait for our order to be completed, waiting less and less patiently for their turn. The sighs and tongue clicks have gained momentum over the last two minutes.

'Well, I think what you're doing is great.' Of course he does, he's always optimistic. 'I don't know if you know this, but should you ever want help, or even a sounding board, there are people who would love to help you. It can't be easy working away on your own. I would definitely go nuts if I only had myself to run ideas by.'

I squirm. 'I'm fine. It's all fine. After all, they're just silly cards.' Silly cards that I'm not going to do anything with.

' "Just silly cards." Bea, you're building a business. No matter what the product is, that is impressive – don't sell yourself short. I couldn't do it. Some day you might actually have to admit that you're braver than you give yourself credit for. And also, to make sure it's on the record, I would like to offer my services.' He bows dramatically, or at least as dramatically as he can in the tight space. 'Two heads are always better than one, and I love this stuff. Besides, "silly cards" are so much more exciting than the kind of companies I normally have to look at.' And he's not lying. He does love this stuff, so much that he's made a career out of telling people how to run their businesses. 'We've actually started a community outreach side project, helping small companies get going, sharing knowledge across a whole bunch of areas. I can take a look to see if there's anything that I think might be helpful for you?'

This sounds like a lot of very important information that I really should want, but would probably have no idea what to do with.

'Thanks. I'll think about it.' And I do mean it. Even if I have no intention of actually taking him up on it.

Peter pays the bill with a credit card that he pulls out of a Velcro wallet. He doesn't even blink at the amount, simply picks up the tray of drinks and heads back to the group.

The Elderflower Fizz is delicious. I offer it to him and he surreptitiously takes a sip before we reach the circle.

He gives me an almost imperceptible wink in return, but from then on I resume the role of the quiet friend.

Once the fizz has fizzled out, I decide to take the plunge and head over to Mia. I should have said hello when I first got here, but she was busy and I was unsure. I don't want to make things worse between us, and I do genuinely want to wish her a happy birthday, so I take a deep breath in and walk towards her.

'Mia! Happy birthday!' I give her a hug, but it's unusually stiff, not at all like the ones we usually share. 'I'm sorry it's taken me a while to get over here. It's so busy!'

'I know, right! I saw you talking to Peter and Alice. She is so beautiful!'

She *is* beautiful. I wonder if anyone has ever used that adjective as a principal description of me. I would guess not.

'Yeah, they wanted details on the hen do, but don't worry, our stories are safe.' I'm trying to be jokey and kind, but it feels forced. I feel so stupid talking about a hen do when we have much more important things to talk about. Like whether or not we're ever going to be best friends again.

I think Mia might be about to say something more, but as she starts to say my name, her attention is grabbed by one of her more forceful, more trendy friends, who claims to be an environmental activist but refuses to take public transport, always opting for a taxi instead. It's too loud to hear their conversation from where I'm standing, so I remain on the sidelines. When it's clear I'm not going to be subbed in, I decide to leave at the next opportunity.

Mia is having a good time, and even if I knew what to say, now is not the right moment. So I make a swift French exit and leave her birthday card on a nearby table.

Now outside, the fresh air is a relief on my face, but it's not enough to distract me from thinking about Mia. I don't know what to do. She was the one who said some not very nice things, but part of me still wants to apologize. For what, I don't know, but I miss her.

Chapter 15

The next day I find it really hard to get out of bed, and not because I'm hungover. My mind is going round and round asking too many questions that I don't have the answers to. It is extremely irritating. I am extremely irritated.

My mum's now usual good morning message pings in. For the first time, I don't reply. I'm swimming in a sea of questions and anxiety.

Do I actually like anything about my job? Do I like living alone? Would it be healthier to live with other people? Should I quit my job and travel the world with my (very limited/non-existent) savings? Could I be the kind of person who goes travelling without a day-by-day itinerary? Should I go back to school and learn how to build websites or write code? Should I get a new haircut? Or a tragus piercing? Should I go on a diet? Should I take up trampolining? Should I stop working on the cards, and spend that time trying to get promoted in my actual job? Do I care enough about vitamins to work there at all? Should I get a house rabbit in place of getting a dog? Can I be bothered to wash my hair this morning, or could I tie a fashionable scarf around it to hide the grease?

I decide not to wash my hair.

And I'm in luck, because despite being a full hour late to work, nobody says a thing, nobody bugs me as I catch up on the 'news', and my boss is absent. It's glorious.

All in all, an OK day to decide to come in. And a great day to come in late with a latte.

As usual, despite a long list of tedious tasks that require my attention, I end up prioritizing personal admin. Today's task? Looking for something to hang above my bed.

I've narrowed it down to five different options across three different sites when an office newbie, probably called Emily, comes over.

'Hiiiii.' I hope she can't tell that I'm unsure about her name. 'How can I help?'

'Hi, Bea.'

She's a chirpy one.

'This is a silly question, but I'm still quite new here and Penny said that you would be the perfect person to ask, 'cause you know all the history and have dealt with her before.' Oh God. I know who she's going to ask about. 'I need to send some feedback to Cathy Armstrong on her latest ad, and I heard that she can be kinda, well, prickly. Joan isn't in today, so can you read over what I've written before I send it?'

'Joan is your manager?'

She nods.

'And she left you to do this by yourself?'

She nods again.

To say Cathy 'can be kinda, well, prickly' is the understatement of the century; she once set someone's tie on fire after he suggested changing the tone of red used in the background. She is a Creative, and sees herself as an Artist.

This poor girl is in for a world of pain. 'Of course I'll look at it for you.' I sigh and minimize my wall art. I wouldn't have actually bought anything anyway.

I'm partly touched that I have seemingly become something of an email-wording mentor for the young Emilys of the world, but also partly saddened that my pathetic contribution to the workplace can now include proofreading.

Emily visibly relaxes.

'Thanks so much. I sent it over before I came, so it should be in your inbox.'

And lo and behold, there it is.

Over the years I have learnt that there is an art to a good email, and this is not a good email. However, having finally reached the end, I can confirm that her name is indeed Emily.

I wonder how best to play this out. I could rewrite it for her, which would basically entail using far fewer words, swapping out the ones that make it sound like poor Emily is extremely stuck up her own arse, and fix the spelling and grammar errors. How is it that some people still can't use the right their/they're/there? But if I'm going to take my job as an email-writing mentor seriously, I'll choose a different tack. In my mind I think about that fishing philosophy, the one that tells you it is better to teach someone how to fish rather than simply handing them the salmon, and decide to give her some vague, but helpful, pointers, tell her to try again and come back.

*

It takes Emily and me an hour and a half to write the perfect email, another hour to cleanse the feedback itself (removing any language that might result in a fire), plus a further twenty minutes to triple-check the email addresses on the distribution list, but I'm there when she eventually hits send. Being a mentor is so time-consuming and distracting.

So distracting that I almost forgot about Mia's opinion of me and the fact we have stopped really talking to each other. I haven't had a message from her in eight days.

'Well done. It's just an email, but it's an important email. Joan shouldn't have made you do that, but you did it well.'

'Thanks. And really, thank you for the help.'

I shake my head. 'Don't worry about it.'

'No, seriously, thank you. Since I joined, nobody has taken the time to help me or explain things to me. I feel like I've learnt more over the last two hours than in my last two weeks. I really appreciate it.'

I can tell from the look on her face that she's being sincere. For the first time in a long time I'm happy that I came into work.

We then do something really awkward, and we have a hug. I'm not too sure who went in first, and I don't think either of us really meant to go in for a hug, but somehow we both got confused about what our arms were doing, and then weirdly and silently egged each other on until we found ourselves in this position. This sounds like a very poorly conceived sexual harassment defence, but I think we both enjoyed it.

Chapter 16

In need of escape and comfort, I've been home so often over recent weeks (I think this is my third weekend home on the trot) that my mum's dog Hugo and I have now built up a lovely friendship. Up until now, he and I have had a fairly competitive relationship. Mainly because as soon as Hugo entered our lives, it was obvious that my mum loved him more than she loved me or my brother. My mum never remarried after my dad died, and although she seemed perfectly happy by herself, she's much happier with Hugo. Truthfully, a large part of me doesn't blame her for preferring the dog over her own children. He's never in a bad mood, he loves her cooking, and he doesn't bark or bite.

He's also a great therapist. I've never been much of a walker, but the spinning questions in my head spin a little less manically after a dog walk.

Today's route is a safe one. I am not emotionally stable enough to take him somewhere new, somewhere I could potentially lose him, so instead we are doing a loop through the hay field, and will then cut through the playground before heading back home.

Luckily, he seems to have a good time wherever he is,

and we are both getting something out of it. Hugo has been intensely sniffing leaves that only appear to be inconsequential, and I'm giving off the air of being a successful dog owner. If only these stupid flies would leave me alone, I could think without any distraction. I'm trying not to be offended that they're finding my personal scent more appealing than the cow shit in the neighbouring field, but it's hard.

And I really am in need of a think. I can't get Mia's words out of my head.

The thing with Mia is that she and I have always thought very differently, but we tend to end up in the same place. It's just that I usually choose a slightly more scenic, one might say meandering, route. Take the way we became friends. We both studied History, and even had a couple of the same classes, but we lived in different halls, and only became friends once we bonded over our mutual appreciation of the south-west corner of the university library. She liked it because it was quiet and well positioned next to a lot of her required reading. I liked it because you could get a great view of Rupert MacDonald, who had fantastic shoulders. I'm pretty sure she initially found my presence quite aggravating (after all, I wasn't really there to study the books), but soon enough she became used to me, and then one day even began to actively look for me.

Eventually we ended up spending a lot of time together, getting into the types of mischief you can only get away with at uni, the types of mischief your fresh air and natural-light-starved brain thinks is OK. And University Mia was a great Mia. She was a Mia that used to go to children's playgrounds on the way home from a night out and spend hours on the wobbly horse thing, yelling to everybody and nobody that she was a princess and we should bow down to her. She was a Mia that didn't mind being a drunken kleptomaniac, making me help her haul home an actual human-sized martini glass – the ones dancers sit in during the risqué nightclub scene in movies. We couldn't get it through the front door, no matter what angles we tried, so we left it in the middle of a roundabout. But my fondest memories are of the random conversations we would have on the stairs. We would have stopped for a short hello, but two hours would pass without a goodbye. The more awkward the location, the longer the catch-up.

And she is my biggest cheerleader. I guess this is why her words hurt so much. Her support was something I thought I could always count on, but now I'm not so sure.

And it hurts.

The one thing I keep replaying in my head, the one thing I can't get away from, is how she said I never fight for anything.

And I keep having this niggling feeling that she is right.

I'm not too sure when it happened, but if I'm brutally honest with myself (which I'm often not, and instead tend to procrastinate when it comes to self-evaluation, probably out of fear of what I will see there), I find it easier to remove myself from any kind of area of competition rather than take what feels like constant defeat. Defeat in my work life, defeat in my love life, even defeat in my living situation. So instead I've given up.

Mia is right. I don't fight. And I am hiding.

I hide behind a smile, I hide behind a joke, I hide behind my own front door.

But I shouldn't. As mundane as the task was, helping Emily felt good. So maybe I shouldn't feel bad that I'm not the star sales exec this year. Maybe instead I should feel good about the contributions I can and do make, at work and everywhere else. Everyone has a role, I just need to figure out what my role is and start to play it.

Maybe my pathetic outburst on New Year's Eve, my resolution to date, was the right sentiment but the wrong action. I don't need to date. I need to do things that make me happy.

'Hugo, this is it!' His head picks up from the bramble he's sniffing, and he looks back at me with his big wide eyes and pure face, clearly picking up from the tone of my voice that something big is about to happen. 'I'm gonna get off my arse and start doing shit.' I do a mini fist-pump in the air, glad that nobody is around to see.

He comes running towards me, as if he's excited too, even though I know he hasn't understood a word I've said. I cave instantly and give him a biscuit.

'I'm proud of us. You've been such a good boy on this walk and I've . . .' What have I done? Hugo runs off, no longer interested now that the snacks are gone. 'Well, I haven't actually done anything yet, but I'm going to. And that's a step in the right direction.' I start walking again.

'You gotta hold me accountable, OK, bud?' I look at Hugo.

He's gone oddly still.

'Bud, you OK?'

I look around, searching for what he can see, and immediately regret letting my guard down and feeling confident in my dog-handling skills. I bet the little shit knew this was coming. I bet he used the whole walk to lull me into a false sense of security and confidence. Just for this moment. Right when I'm feeling all buoyant and self-assured.

There are three things that make Hugo crazy – his doggy kryptonite – and the sight before us, a girl's teddy bear picnic-themed sixth birthday party, has all of them. In less than two seconds I can see a vast quantity of other dogs, food and large cuddly toys. In this case, by 'toys' I mean many, many teddy bears and a beautiful, white, ride-on unicorn, with the birthday bow still attached. I should not have walked into the playground. Going to the playground on a weekend is a terrible idea.

'Oh shit.' I fumble for the lead, nearly cutting off my airway in the process. I knew it was a mistake to drape the lead around my neck. 'Hugo, *sit*.'

Hugo doesn't sit. I try to get out the bag of special, high-value snacks to be used only in emergency situations when Hugo is required to behave particularly well. A dry biscuit isn't going to cut it this time.

Normally quite self-controlled, one might even say 'a wuss', he usually stays right by your side, so close you often knee him in the face. But not now. Not with the trifecta of doggo excitement.

He's off and, as a result, so am I.

Scarred by my brother telling me I run like a penguin

when I was ten years old, I haven't run much since, and as such I'm pretty sure I now run more like a penguin than before, but even more slowly.

'Hugooooooo! Stay! Hugo! Sit. Hugo! Hugo, no!' The last shout comes out a lot quieter than intended – mainly because I'm struggling to breathe, run and shout at the same time.

And, with a speed and agility that he rarely shows, Hugo has herded the dogs into some kind of dog conga line, which proceeds to zoom straight through the (no longer) beautifully laid-out picnic, destroying any food they don't manage to snaffle, through the pond via a deep quagmire of mud, and back out. Straight for the unicorn.

I try again. 'Hugo! No!'

To an outsider looking in, it probably looks quite bad. Indeed, for an insider looking in, it looks quite bad.

And also, so *quick*. If I wasn't so mortified, I would actually be quite proud of our Hugo. The other dogs put up absolutely no resistance, and were easily persuaded to join in the destruction. Hugo is a leader of dogs! Hugo could go into politics!

Hugo has just torn off the unicorn's horn.

I always thought that dogs were meant to be intuitive to the feelings and emotions of those around them, but as we all scramble to get hold of our respective beasts, I can't help but think that Hugo looks extremely proud of himself, which is totally at odds with the inconsolable wailing of the nearby children and the extremely angry and flustered faces of the parents.

Hugo back on his lead, I look around and take stock of the destruction. There is a lot of it, and, like an Escher drawing, the longer you look, the more you see and the more inter-connected everything is. But unlike an Escher drawing, there is a clear beginning. And it all leads back to Hugo. Most of the teddy bears are in the jaws of their new (furrier) owners, the cake is smashed, and wrapped presents are now ripped open, their insides spilling all over the place like roadkill, many smooshed with mud. Even the balloons have made a run for it, caught up in a nearby tree.

Someone who looks a lot like an angry Birthday Girl parent comes over to me, filling me with more dread than I would care to admit.

And so I decide to lie.

'I am so sorry. You see, Hugo, my dog, is a rescue I recently adopted from the jaws of death in a notorious kill centre somewhere in the . . . Spain. And he must have suffered a terrible accident with his previous owners, because he's been left petrified of teddy bears and birthday parties. We don't know what happened, but it must have been awful.' Looking at him, you can tell he's anything but scared. I don't know if I've ever seen him so happy. Part of me is pleased he's having such a good time. 'I am so sorry,' I say again. 'If I'd known you would be here, I would have been so much more careful. I can sew the unicorn horn back on. Really, I'm quite good at sewing.' I hear a noise and look over at Hugo. Despite still being on his lead, he's managed to sneakily get hold of the unicorn horn, and is now callously ripping it up and spitting out the fluff as he goes. If he doesn't want the fluff, why is he so determined to get it out? 'Or maybe it would be best if I buy your daughter a brand new unicorn?'

'Hugo! My love! How was your walkies? Were you a good boy for Bea?' My mum is at the door the instant we walk into the drive. I can smell roast chicken. Sometimes I don't know why I ever moved out of home. I detach his lead before he dislocates my shoulder. From the speed of his tail, you would think he hadn't seen my mum in months. 'Of course you were.' She bends down and lets him lick her face.

I don't want to ruin the perfect image she has of Hugo, but I'm going to need her help.

'Erm, Mum . . . I don't suppose you know where I could get a ride-on unicorn from, do you?'

She looks at me as if I have finally lost my mind.

'Oh, it's not for me.'

Chapter 17

Are you coming today?

Peter's message pings in. I read it from my seat on the sofa, and then put the phone face down on the table without replying. I've been sitting here for so long that my bum is uncomfortably warm, but I have no desire to move.

It feels like it's only been a couple of weeks since the last Games Night, but I'm shocked when I realize a couple of months have passed.

It's hard keeping track of time when you have made absolutely no progress in life. Having sourced the mythical unicorn with Mum's help, I now have the time to start doing the shit that makes me happy, but I keep having false starts. There is too much stuff I could do, but I don't really know what I should do. A typical case of analysis paralysis.

But it's not my lack of life progress that has stopped me from going today. As soon as the date was put in, I knew I wouldn't attend, although part of me would have loved to see how the May Pole theme manifested. Hosts get bonus points (that carry no value and are purely nominal) for coming up with the most bizarre celebrations and tenuously themed snacks. I wonder if all the food will be served on sticks.

I hope my lack of a reply is reply enough.

Unlike Mum, who escapes to a different country on this day every year, I never do anything on the anniversary of my dad's death. I can't be around people in case they smile in the wrong way. So I always take myself off and spend the day alone. Or at least I try to.

Today I plan to do a jigsaw puzzle. Dad loved a jigsaw puzzle.

I can hear him teaching me how to prepare the pieces and follow his instructions. Flip them, face up. Separate the edges. Cherish the corners. Sort by colour. Pick out any special pieces. And begin. As soon as you start, the picture instantly becomes clearer. It's a kind of magic.

I open the box, tip the pieces on the coffee table and begin flipping.

An unquantifiable amount of time later, there is a knock at the door. I ignore it. I'm not expecting anyone. I have no music playing and they won't be able to see my shadow under the door. As long as I don't move.

So I don't move. I even try not to breathe.

The knock comes again.

'Bea?' It's Peter. He found me on this day at the end of second year. I had planned to spend the day with Fred, but I missed the train. He saw me crying on the platform and cancelled his plans. Since then he normally always checks in, by phone if not in person. I'd thought Games Night would stop him from coming this year.

'Bea, I know you're there. At least I hope you're there, otherwise this is very odd.' I hear a shuffle. I imagine him with his ear against the door, listening for signs of life. 'You don't have to open the door, but I wanted you to know that I'll be here for ten minutes, and if you want to let me in at any point during this time, you can. And if you do, I'll share my spring rolls with you.' I can hear the shuffle of a plastic bag so I know he's telling the truth.

But I hate sharing spring rolls. They always come in uneven numbers, making it so awkward.

'OK, I lie. I actually bought two lots of spring rolls so we can each have our own.'

Seven minutes have passed and I open up to let him in. Peter is sitting with his back to the door, making this tricky. He smiles up at me and then crawls across the floor before eventually unfolding to a standing position.

'Hi.'

'Hi.'

He looks across my shoulder. 'What jigsaw are we doing?'

He puts the food on the side as he heads to the table. I rip the bag and start opening up the flimsy plastic take-away boxes before putting the spring rolls on plates, choosing to use the posh guest china that my mum insisted I buy. By the time I reach him, he already has his puzzle face in place. A face that looks both intense and also at peace.

'Did I miss much today?'

'At Games Night?'

I nod.

'No.' He bites into a spring roll. Evidently it's still hot; he pulls a face and breathes as if he's giving birth. 'Actually yes. Sophie's pregnant.' The spring rolls are clairvoyant.

Sophie lived down the corridor from Mia at uni. She has very fine features and married a very handsome man. I imagine their babies are going to be very attractive.

'Mia was asking after you.'

I try to act casual.

'She was?'

He nods. 'She was. She seemed, er, tetchy today.' He takes another bite. 'Unusually on edge. I almost felt a bit sorry for Mark. Poor guy couldn't do anything right.'

I don't know what to say, so I remain silent.

'So –' he draws the word out – 'what did she say to you? Do I need to go beat her up? Because I would do that for you.'

I smile. Peter would definitely come off worse. Eventually I say the only thing I can – the truth. 'Nothing I didn't need to hear.'

There is silence for a while.

'Well,' he says, licking his fingers, 'I'm sure Mark would appreciate it if you called her.'

'I will.' But not quite yet. When I go back to her I want to have made some progress, or at least come up with a plan.

It occurs to me that finger food and jigsaws don't really mix, so I get up, head over to the sink and tear off some kitchen towel. I wander back and pass a piece to Peter, who nods a silent thank-you.

'So how are things with you and Alice?'

He keeps nodding. I'm not sure what that means, but apparently it's the only answer I'm going to get.

'And how are things on the dating scene for you?'

His eyes can be so intense sometimes, I have to look away. I'm not great at deep and meaningful conversations, particularly sober at 5 p.m., but for Peter I try. Peter, who came all the way here with spring rolls to make sure I'm OK. I think Dad would have liked him.

One of the greatest things about puzzles is that they give your hands something to do and provide a perfect cover for avoiding eye contact. 'Well, I've realized that it wasn't really dating that I needed. Or wanted.' I pop in a puzzle piece. 'What I need to do is work on the things that actually make me happy. The things I want to succeed in.'

I am not entirely convinced these words all go together. Especially because Peter is staring at me, kind of vacantly.

'So you've stopped dating?'

It's a little bit more complicated than that, but essentially: 'Yes.'

He goes back to the puzzle and tries to force a piece in.

'I don't think that goes there.' I look again. 'Actually, maybe it does, but flip it the other way around.'

He does exactly that and it fits perfectly. He looks extremely proud of himself.

'Thanks for coming over, Peter.'

Today is not my favourite day, but him being here has made it slightly less shit.

Chapter 18

Now that I have a vague direction, I really want to get on with my life, but other people still keep getting in the way.

Other people like Joan. Why is she always such a cretin?

Work never gets me angry, but she's managed the impossible.

She's also angry back at me. And she's here, standing over my desk.

Turns out Cathy was so impressed with Emily and the feedback that she wrote an email to our boss suggesting Emily be promoted.

Now, obviously Emily is not going to be promoted, as she still has no idea what she's doing and has been with us for less than three months, but my boss was so taken aback by the fact Cathy had anything positive to say that she brought it up in the planning meeting, the planning meeting we have just come out of. The planning meeting where Emily publicly thanked me for the help I'd given her.

And Joan, Emily's 'manager', was irrationally pissed. Pissed because apparently I'd interfered with Emily's training. Personally, I think she's pissed because the praise and spotlight weren't on her for once.

'You have no idea what you're doing. Emily is my assistant, not yours. I gave her that task so she would purposefully mess up. She's an assistant; she needs to know what it's like to fuck up.'

My heart starts pounding and I can feel my face flush with indignation.

'She doesn't need to get tricked into messing up by her manager, who is meant to be teaching her. Instead of being so upset your game didn't work, you might do well to focus on the fact that Emily used her initiative and did a really good job.'

I am standing – when did I stand up from my desk?

'She's my assistant, not yours. Back off.' Her sneer becomes even more pronounced. 'Need I also remind you that I rank above you here. I could get you fired.'

'Then get me fired.' At least that way I would have time to get on with my life.

Joan stomps off round the corner and leaves me, but I'm not alone for long.

Penny's happy, endearing face appears from over the partition. I assume she wants the gossip, so I turn and face her, clearing some perching space for her on my desk.

'Ugh. I hate Joan.'

But what appears on my desk is not Penny's bum, but cake. And prosecco.

I look up. I have no idea how, but I think Penny might have missed the whole fight between me and Joan, and has instead chosen this very moment to rally the troops, who are now appearing behind her, singing me Happy Birthday. A day that I had been even more keen than usual to ignore this year, with no Mia to help me grudgingly celebrate.

I don't know whether it was my outburst or the two glasses of prosecco that I drank, but I am feeling oddly empowered. And pissed off. And energized. And like I really need to get myself out of this situation. I need to start taking control.

The issue is, I keep putting it off. I keep getting distracted by the small irritating things in front of me, and forget the bigger picture that sits behind. I flash back to my epiphany at the end of Hugo's walk. The epiphany that came shortly before the de-horning ceremony.

I need to be held accountable.

And so I decide to message Peter to ask, on the off-chance he has any time, for his business advice.

Of course – Saturday?

As in this Saturday?

I kinda hope he says no – this seems very soon.

Yes.

I exhale, and shrug a shoulder.

Perfect. Thanks, Pete. x

'Well, honey, I want you to have fun this evening. So go out, have some dinner. Why don't you see if Mia can go, and let it be on me. Just tell me how much I owe you. And go somewhere nice.'

I'm walking home from the tube having left work bang on 5 p.m.

'Thanks, Mum.'

I don't tell her that I have no plans this evening. And I still haven't told her that Mia and I aren't currently talking.

'I'm almost home, so I'll let you go now.' I lose signal as soon as I enter my building, so I always hang up before I reach the turn in the road. I don't like the idea of talking right outside and giving my neighbours such easy access to my conversations.

'Can't wait to see you this weekend. You're still coming to Olivia's party?'

'Yes.' Olivia is my niece. Her birthday isn't for another week, but she's still at the age where you want to celebrate your birthday, so our joint 'celebration' is now dominated by a four-year-old.

'Great, I'll give you your card and present then. I love you.'

'Love you too, Mum.'

And with that I hang up, pop my phone in my bag and get out my keys.

And immediately walk into a wall. Well, not an actual wall, but a human wall.

'Sorry!'

I look up. And into a face I recognize. His jawline is burned into my memory for all time. It's Colin, the hot boiler man. I am vaguely aware of the group of friends surrounding him, but his face has me transfixed. A noise escapes my mouth. Part shock. Part awe. Part, a large part, awkward. Eventually I remember to speak.

'Colin!' It comes out a few decibels higher than normal and a lot louder. 'Bea.' I place my hand on my chest. 'You fixed my boiler a while ago.' I make the shape of a boiler with my hands.

Luckily his friends have moved on. I force my hands down and hope the urge to mime has stopped.

'I remember.' A man of few words.

'Right. Yes. Well.' Accidentally bumping into people you vaguely know isn't something that happens frequently. And when it does happen, most of the time you should pretend that you don't recognize them, so both parties can move away without any awkwardness. 'Thank you for that, by the way. My showers are now the perfect temperature.' I giggle. This conversation is an uncomfortable one to be part of, even for me, an expert in awkwardness.

'No worries. If you ever need anything else, let me know.' He then smiles and holds it there for a long time.

One of his friends shouts at him. 'Come on, you bell end!'

'I should go. We're off to the pub round the corner.'

I raise my eyebrows and nod. I have never and will never go there. I'm not a neat freak, but it looks extraordinarily unclean.

'Will I see you there later?'

'Oh, no, I can't.'

'Busy?'

Shamefully free, actually, but I don't want Colin to know that. I draw attention to my bag. It looks big enough to house a laptop. It doesn't. But it does currently house some lovely 280-GSM linen-effect card in aquamarine.

'Work.'

'Well, if you change your mind or, like I said, need anything else, let me know. You've got my number.'

An hour later and I'm frozen to the spot, staring at my phone.

It is my birthday. I should treat myself.

I look down at the takeaway menu from the Chinese round the corner. The number of dishes I'm thinking of ordering is a tad excessive.

But then an errant thought pops into my head, and once it's there I can't get it out.

I reach for my phone.

Hey. Are you still at the pub?

I hit send. And off it goes. To Colin.

Oh God, he might not have *my* number. So I send another.

It's Bea, by the way. With the boiler round the corner.

To save me from watching my phone and getting increasingly anxious, I leave it on the side while I go to the loo.

As I walk back, it pings, and I cringe inwardly as I think what he could have replied with.

But I'm taking control today, I can do this. Like ripping off a plaster, I open the message.

You done with your work? ;)

A winky face. Surely this is flirting.

My game playing isn't that strong – it never has been and it never will be – so I might as well be my uncool self right from the start.

> I have actually. And I wondered if you might want to go
> for a drink one night?

I'm proud of myself for hitting send. Even if he doesn't reply, I think the mere act of sending the message and putting myself out there takes some balls. Or the female version of balls.

Boobs?

Have I finally grown some boobs?

But I needn't have worried. His reply is instant.

> Tonight?

I am brave, but not quite that brave.

> I know you're with your friends, and I thought this might
> be more of a 1–1 situation. So not tonight but soon?

> Most defiantly. Let me know when you're free and I'll be
> their.

I can't help but judge him for the spelling mistakes but I can hear my vagina singing already. Perhaps she isn't really dead, but hibernating. Colin and his jawline could be the thing to wake her up.

About half an hour later, still undecided about how much Chinese food to order, another message lands.

> Fancy a visitor? x

Absolutely not. I don't want him to come over. I want to have the evening to myself. I want to eat my wontons in peace.

But I also worry that if I say no, that will be it. A drink will never happen. My vagina will have to crawl back into hibernation. She would have been fine staying hibernated, but the possibility of freedom has made her restless.

Are you serious?

Deadly.

And then another ping.

I'll be there in 2 minutes. x

My vagina is singing a little louder again, but she's totally at odds with my brain, which is listing all the issues with an impromptu visit.

My heartbeat ratchets up, and I look around. My mind is as frazzled as my apartment.

I haven't prepped myself for visitors. I've prepped myself for Chinese food and a movie.

I look down. I'm wearing my favourite crazy-lady silk (OK, probably satin) pyjamas. The ones with prawns on them.

There is too much debris to deal with in two minutes, but I can definitely do something about the prawns.

I run to my bedroom and make a snap decision to wear my only piece of semi-sexy nightwear (a black nightgown given to me by Mia for Christmas aeons ago). I extricate it from the bottom of my miscellaneous items drawer, where it has lived for many years. It's a bit wrinkled, but it's better than shellfish. I strip off, and also decide to upgrade my underwear.

Fuck. I wish I had kept up a waxing regime.

The last time I got waxed I was seen by a trainee, and although the physical scars are gone, the mental scars remain. I haven't been back since and that was three months ago.

OK, I lie, it was six months ago.

A knock on the door. How did he get upstairs? I blame the shitty front door that doesn't close properly.

'Coming! One sec!' On my way to the door I quickly dive into the bathroom and stash some of my more embarrassing self-care items – including facial wax strips and hemorrhoid cream (I've heard it's good on spots) – at the back of the cupboard.

If possible my heart is beating even faster.

Fuck it. No more hiding, Bea. You can do this.

I keep telling my heart that there is no reason to be quite so jumpy, but it's beating so fast and no calming thoughts are making it slow down. A jumpy heart is a good sign, isn't it?

With no other choice open to me, I grow some boobs and open the door.

His face is still extremely beautiful.

'Hi again.'

He remains standing.

'So, you wanna come in?'

'Yeah.'

No guesses as to what happens next . . .

Chapter 19

What happens next is . . .

He walks through the door and I close it behind him.

'The flat is messier since the last time you saw it. Sorry.'

'Don't apologize.' He gives a hint of a cheeky smile. His eyes travel over me. I hope he likes what he sees. I turn my back on him. I know my butt looks great at least.

'I feel underdressed. I would have worn my new shirt if I'd known I'd be seeing you this evening.'

'Oh yeah, sorry. I would have changed, but you were too quick.' I turn back and see that he has a plastic bag with him. It smells like fried chicken.

'Is that a bag of fried chicken?'

'Er, yeah. I didn't want to come empty-handed.'

How unconventional.

Despite him being a guest, I use the old plates I've had since university. The ones that weren't quite white to begin with.

'So you really do have friends who live right around the corner?' I hope this is the kind of question people normally ask in this situation. Not having been in this situation for a long time, I just don't know.

'Yeah, but around the dodgy corner. You won't know them. You're quite posh.'

'Am I?' In my mind Peter is posh, but I guess everything is relative.

'I don't mean it in a bad way, but yeah, you are. You keep your microwave in the cupboard and you have great teeth.'

And there I was wondering if I had picked up a bit of a posher accent, but no. It's my dentistry and storage space that he's using as a marker. I don't think I've ever been complimented on my teeth before. It's not exactly the most romantic of compliments, but it will do.

Unsure what to say, I reply with a noncommittal 'Ha, thanks.' I smile, but immediately feel quite conscious of my smile being too toothy, so pare it back as much as I can whilst still trying to look natural and half shrug. I'm hoping the shrug says, *Yeah. I have nice teeth. And nice . . . other assets (?)* 'Shall we eat the chicken before it gets cold?'

'Sounds good to me. I'm starving.'

We sit down to eat. Because of the multi-purpose room I don't have that many seating options, and I certainly don't have a dining table, so we do a terrible impersonation of the Romans: we lounge. It's pretty weird, so I concentrate on the food.

'Oh my God. Chicken is so good. How and why is chicken *so* good?'

'Why do girls love chicken nuggets so much? What is it?'

'Maybe because if we're really careful we can pretend they're healthy? And also, they taste bloody delicious.'

I realize I'm eating as if I have never been fed before. Cutlery has been left abandoned on the coffee table, ketchup is smeared all over my plate (and probably my face) and my fingers are covered with grease. I possibly should have prioritized a light snack instead of tidying my bathroom cupboard.

'Thank you so much for the chicken. I didn't realize how hungry I was.' It's not a wonton, but it does taste delicious.

I look up and see Colin staring at me.

'I hope I don't sound creepy when I say this, but you look fuckin' hot eating that.'

I look behind me to make sure. He's definitely talking about me.

Oh lord.

I swallow the chunk of chicken I have bitten off before it's really ready to be swallowed.

A mini cough escapes and I say, 'Thanks. You must be mad. Or drunk.'

'I'm not sober, but I'm not that drunk.'

Which is something only drunk people say. Christ, he's hot.

'I got a lot of shit from the boys for texting you in the pub. They kept bugging me, wanting to know who I was messaging. I told them it was none of their business.'

'Well, I'm glad you messaged me back.' I think. I think I'm glad he's here. I think I'm glad I'm doing this.

My thoughts are interrupted by him taking away my plate. 'My mum always taught me to clear up.'

Watching him tidy up feels uncomfortably domesticated, and I don't know what to do. Luckily it's only two plates and one fork (not used by me), and as soon as he's done I wish there was more. I know what to do even less now than I did before.

He's staring at me.

Is this meant to be alluring? Am I meant to find this sexy?

He's taking off his top. I'm glued to the spot, more out of awkwardness than anything else. I don't find this sexy. Part of me finds it creepy, and the larger part wants to burst out laughing. I hope he doesn't expect *me* to undress here.

He's now standing unnaturally straight with only his boxers on, and I reckon it's my turn to make the next move.

I want to touch him, but I'm anxious that I won't remember what to do and where to put all of my limbs. It's been a while. I'm in uncharted territory and I'm unsure what to do.

I move towards him and place my hands on his upper chest.

He inhales sharply. 'Your hands are bloody freezing.'

'Oh, sorry,' I say, and make to move them away. Someone more practised would have thought about this.

'No matter. I can help warm them up.'

I laugh internally (and a little externally). Whether he meant to or not, he just made a boiler-man joke.

For the most part, there is a lack of awkwardness. Sure, there is the occasional tooth-bump, general clumsiness getting on to the bed, inevitable confusion over where exactly all our limbs should go, and hair getting pulled out of my scalp whenever we change position, but it's nothing I can't handle, or artlessly ignore. That is, until he decided to growl like an actual lion and slap my arse. At this juncture I froze.

But all in all, a solid seven out of ten. OK, maybe a five, but still encouraging for a first go.

And now he's snoring next to me in bed. I move a bit to test how fast asleep he is; he doesn't stir at all so I get up and put my nightgown on before clambering back into bed.

For a while I simply stare at his face. I don't know how I'll feel tomorrow morning, but right now I am kinda proud of myself. The memory of the slap and growl is making me blush, but it doesn't detract from the fact that I had sex with the hot boiler guy with great cheekbones. And I think he had a good time.

But it is odd having another human here. It feels like a faux-friendly invasion. I know I won't sleep well. I'm not used to sharing my bed. I sigh and turn away from him and all of his cheekbones; at least this way if he wakes up he'll see the back of my head, not my drooling face. His snoring has become uncomfortably loud, but I don't prod him or poke him. Instead I pull the cover over my ears in an effort to drown out the sound, close my eyes and try to sleep.

Chapter 20

Thankfully Colin left early, and there was only a limited amount of weirdness in the morning – totally due to the fact I pretended to still be (beautifully) half asleep when he left. In truth I had been awake for at least an hour.

Finally feeling like I can face myself in the mirror, I get out of bed and assess the situation. I am happy to report that there is limited damage. There is a slight aroma of fried food, and some grease marks from the chicken on the coffee table/footstool/craft bench, but apart from that, my apartment appears to have got off pretty lightly.

Different story for when I actually face the mirror though. In addition to the old, smudged make-up look, I have a hickey. At least, I think it's a hickey. It appears to be more like a tiger stripe running down the left side of my neck. When on earth did that happen? How on earth did that happen?

Looking at my phone, I see that I also got a text from Peter at about ten thirty last night. I feel a bit uncomfortable reading it; Colin and Peter shouldn't mix.

> Looking forward to Saturday! We will need Post-its – do you have some?

Do I have Post-its? Ha.

> Sorry for the tardy reply. But yes – of course I have
> Post-its.

Actually, I don't, but the stationery cupboard at work does. I restocked them just the other day.

> I did send it quite late, and I know how you love to be in
> bed by 9 (granny). Shall we say 10? At yours?

If only he knew what I had actually been up to last night.
I feel even more uncomfortable. The thought of Peter knowing what I was up to last night fills me with a feeling similar to, but not exactly like, shame. I can't help but think that if he knew, he would be disappointed in me. And I don't want him to be disappointed in me.

So he must not know. It's my business anyway, right?

> Perfect. x

I am unreasonably warm in a turtle-neck. I had to dig it out from the back of the drawer, but it does at least hide the hickey.

I've got my head down in some soul-destroying admin, when Emily once again appears at my desk.

'Bea.'

She's whispering, so I whisper too. 'Yes?'

Her eyes are super eager, and as I look at her, I can see other eager eyes trying not to look in our direction. It's a little unnerving.

'A few of us were wondering if you would help us. There

are a couple of areas we're still confused about, about how things work and what we should, well, actually be doing, and seeing as how you were such a help to me, I thought you might be happy to help the others too. Simple things like how to run a search on the database, what all the different teams do and how they feed into each other, key timings, who the big dogs are so we can try to look professional in front of them, all that kind of information.'

I drum my fingers on my desk. The admin I'm doing is extremely boring, and I'm at risk of falling asleep. I can't believe they don't even know how to run a search. But as much as I would love to help, this sounds suspiciously like more work; work outside of my job description.

I stop drumming. It dawns on me, rather depressingly, that the work inside my job description regularly makes me seek refuge in the stationery cupboard, whereas I actually quite liked helping Emily.

'So? Will you help us?'

Joan was pissed off, and she might actually be able to get me fired for 'interfering'.

'Please?'

I realize that I don't really care if Joan is pissed off. Part of me wants her to be pissed off.

'Sure. But we'll have to do it a bit clandestinely.' Because I do care about being fired. I have bills to pay. Card supplies to buy. Plants to water. 'We can do it over lunch-time. There's a cafe round the corner that never has anyone in it. I'm sure we could take over a table for an hour.'

'Great! Can we start today?'

*

Turns out we took over three tables. There were a lot of people behind the eager eyes, and a lot of questions.

My favourite was definitely the question 'Who are the big dogs?' Turns out one of the newbies had unknowingly emailed a member of the advisory board asking him to come fix the printer. Unsurprisingly she didn't get a response.

But the illicit session went well. The keen beans took so many notes and nodded so enthusiastically that I couldn't help but feel like some sort of weird oracle.

The only issue was, we didn't have enough time. The hour sped past faster than any other hour in the day, and there were still many questions left unanswered.

I look at the clock on the wall. It's analogue, so takes me a shamefully long time to tell that we need to be getting back. By the time we all return to our desks we will have been away for over an hour and a half. Someone is bound to notice.

'OK, guys – I know you have more questions, but we need to go. I promise I'll find a regular time for us to meet up. I'm also very aware that the conversation was really meandering today, so maybe next time we will focus on a specific area. If you guys want to email me over some things you're unclear about, I can come up with a plan, or a list of topics, and we can go through them one by one. Sound good?'

The nodding heads make me smile. I came up with a plan and people liked it.

Something catches my eye and my smile goes stale, turning into more of a grimace.

My boss is at the counter. I'm very surprised to see her here. This isn't the type of establishment I would think she frequents, which is partly why I chose it. I have also never seen her look more like a meerkat. Her head is tilted slightly to the side and her eyes are watching me very carefully. My mouth immediately goes dry. I wonder how long she's been watching us for.

Despite the total lack of saliva, I go over after everyone has filed out. There is no way I can hide from this, so I might as well confront it.

'Hi, Mansi.' I cough and swallow at the same time in an uncomfortable effort to find my voice. 'I hope you don't mind, but we were just going over some questions and issues they're having. We're not about to do anything like start a revolution.' Oh God, mentioning a revolution makes me look even more guilty.

The sound she makes in response is fairly non-committal.

'We only took an hour over lunch.' This is a lie, but it came out before I could stop it.

She nods. She usually has many opinions and her silence is making me very uncomfortable.

'Right. Well, I'll see you back at the office.'

I turn on my heel, panicking as I reach for my throat to check the turtle-neck hasn't slipped.

Chapter 21

Luckily Peter arrived five minutes late at my flat on Saturday morning, five minutes that were well spent trying on all of my scarves to find the one that would hide the tiger stripe most effectively. If anything, it has become even more visible since yesterday – the colour has deepened and it has spread out even further – and I haven't had the chance to wash and dry my handy turtle-neck.

I open the door to see him wearing a huge grin.

'Hey! I brought cookies.' By the look of things, he also has his laptop and a load of print-outs.

I don't know what vibes I'm giving off that say, 'If you come to my abode, make sure you bring food,' but I'm pretty happy about it.

We hug and I get out a guest plate for the cookies. My favourite triple-chocolate cookies. The ones I usually freeze so I don't eat them all in one go. He knows me well.

Remembering why we are here, I feel a bit awkward in my own home once again. My flat normally feels like a sanctuary, but recently I feel as though it's being opened up and left exposed. The exchange with Mia. Thursday night with Colin. And now with Peter. My business is my business; as dirty and badly set up as it is, it's still mine, and I'm very protective of it.

I bite my nails. What if he thinks everything I've done is wrong?

But Peter has done what Peter does best, and has already made himself at home, which instantly puts me at ease. He's sitting cross-legged on the floor, a pose that makes him seem both very young and too old, long limbs unable to position themselves quite right. I look at his kind face and big eyes, a face that has been my friend for many years, a face I know better than my own, and I realize something – not once has he ever made me doubt myself. I feel very, very slightly less anxious.

'Thanks in advance for your help.' I decide to jump. Just a little. 'OK. So I thought I would give you a general overview, and then what I would really love to do is talk about my three main worries – production, marketing budget and what to do with it, and stock control.'

He looks happy enough, so I plough on.

It's been a great morning. Peter has been his usual patient self, helping me to understand a whole load of things I'm pretty sure are quite simple, including a bunch of overly lengthy and unnecessarily convoluted terms.

The wall is covered with Post-its and we have eaten all the cookies. I put the lid on the pen and half throw it on the table.

'My brain is tired. I need to take a break.'

Peter shuts his computer so abruptly it makes me jump, even through the mind fog I currently have.

'Oh, thank God. Can we go get lunch? I'm starving. I only had a lasagne for breakfast.'

'Who has lasagne for breakfast?'

'It's a perfectly balanced meal.'

My brain really is tired, so I let it go.

'I think the market is open. We could go there.'

Peter jumps up from the couch and tugs down on the front of his shirt. 'Perfect.'

Peter earns a lot more money than I do and therefore can afford to live in a much nicer part of town. Not wanting him to judge me for my comparatively dodgy surround- ings, I carefully plan a walk that avoids the worst parts of the local area. I wonder if any of the streets I avoid are where Colin's friends live. Oh God. What if Colin is hanging around? Panic sets in. I should have thought about this before we left the apartment.

I haven't messaged him since we had sex. The only thing I could think to say was 'thank you' and that seemed somewhat insensitive, so I've stayed silent.

Palms sweating, I take us on quite a meandering route. Hopefully Peter won't ask for the reason behind the wiggling.

'I like your scarf.'

I snort. 'Thanks.'

'Why is that funny?'

Oops. 'No reason.' I avoid eye contact. 'So . . . how are things with you and Alice? Last time I saw you, you didn't really give me an answer.'

'Ah yes, the lovely Alice. Well, to be honest they aren't

going very far. She's a great girl, but she's not the one for me. And I am definitely not the one for her.'

'Interesting. Tell me.'

He shoves his hands into his pockets. 'There's nothing to tell really. She's lovely. She's attractive. She's very kind. But she isn't the person I want to be with.'

'Well, who do you want to be with? What kind of things do you want in a relationship?'

I can see him in my peripheral vision, but I purposefully keep my eyes away, trying to give him the safety of perceived anonymity.

'That's a good question to ask. It's either a really long list, or a really short one.'

In an effort to lighten the mood, I grab his elbow and make space to loop my arm with his. I didn't mean for my question to bring him down, but I can feel emotions coming off him in waves.

'Well, you deserve to be happy. And whoever she ends up being, she's a lucky girl.'

We walk on for a while, but he's clearly still distracted. The silence is not quite comfortable.

I decide to distract him with thoughts of food. 'So, what do you fancy for lunch? A hotdog? A burrito?'

'Nope, I can't eat them.'

'What? You love a burrito! Are you still annoyed at me for refusing to go get one with you at two in the morning?' This is one of his favourite university stories. He always loves to tell it, so I always let him. 'Why did that annoy you so much?'

'It annoyed me so much because in the span of three

years you must have asked me to accompany you to the late-night burrito van at least fifty times, and I *always* went with you, despite the fact I know that place didn't have a food hygiene rating.' He gets more animated as the story telling goes on. 'I asked you *once* and not only did you say no, you also threw a book at me. I think I bled a little.'

'Yes, but when I asked, you were always awake. When you asked, I was already in bed.'

'Hmm, I suppose. I've always found it hard to say no to you.' He pauses briefly and then looks away. 'But that wasn't actually what I was talking about. I meant the time we went on a date and then you ghosted me, even though I bought you a delicious and overpriced gourmet hotdog.'

I stop in my tracks.

'When on earth did we go on a date?'

'Second term, first year. I finally plucked up the courage to ask you out, remember? We went to watch the rugby together, I bought you a hotdog with onions and extra gherkins. A real Casanova moment. We had a nice time, at least I thought so. But then you never seemed interested in giving me a second chance. It was such a scarring experience I haven't touched a hotdog since.'

I remember this well; it was a very good hotdog. But my version of events is quite different.

'That was absolutely not a date! There were fifteen people going together! All of whom *you* had invited! That is categorically not a date. You don't invite other people on a date.'

'Yes, but I invited you first, and I only invited the

others because I didn't want you to get overwhelmed or scared or something. You had a tendency to run away. You still do.'

'You are totally nuts. Nuts.' The idea that the two of us would go on a date is preposterous. But he's right – had he asked me out on an actual date, I definitely would have run away.

We walk along a bit further in silence as I absorb this new information.

I'm quite glad I didn't know he meant that to be a date. Could you imagine? It would have ruined our friendship. I don't know what I would have done if I hadn't had him by my side at uni. If we weren't friends now.

It doesn't bear thinking about.

'Thank you for helping me today, by the way – it means a lot.' I'm half fired up and eager to work, and half overwhelmed at my lack of knowledge and the amount I need to do. But it was nice to talk things over. And I was right to trust him; he wasn't at all negative about any of my extremely meandering thoughts and plans. 'Most of the time I have all of these thoughts and ideas, but then when I go to act on them I worry that what I once thought was brilliant is actually useless.'

'You realize that all I did was organize your thoughts into a more logical plan?'

'No! You did so much more!'

He shakes his head.

'Nope, I promise you I did not. This is the glory of my job. I very, very rarely have to come up with any original ideas, all I have to do is organize them. Seriously, when we go back, have a look at your wall. All of those ideas are yours.'

I shake off the praise. 'Well, either way, I enjoyed this morning. It was fun.'

'I'm happy that you asked for help.'

We round the corner and finally reach the food market.

Our arms still looped together, I give him a quick squeeze, look at him and raise an eyebrow.

'How about a hotdog?'

He smiles and shakes his head slightly, kinda like he's waking up. 'Fine. But this time you're buying.'

Chapter 22

The rush of progress in love and at work is stopped in its tracks by a Sunday visit to my brother's house, to play cool aunty for my niece's fourth birthday party. I arrive when the party is in full swing and note that Olivia already has more friends than I do. I also note, with a hint of irony, the large ride-on unicorn that my mum appears to have given her. Hugo seems totally uninterested in it, lying peacefully nearby like butter wouldn't melt. He's a traitor.

My brother, Fred, has always been my mum's favourite. She has more photos of him up in the house than she does of me and his 'artwork' will always have pride of place in the guest loo. Mine hangs in the coat cupboard above the wellies.

And she should be proud of him. I'm proud of him.

He has a pretty perfect set-up. He and his wife Anna make a great team. You can tell they're a good match just by looking at them. The only tiny thing I'd find to criticize, if I really had to, is the way Anna views me as a project. Areas she focuses on include: my job, my side hustle, my clothes, my diet, my exercise regime and my love life. Coming from quite a direct family, her straightforward approach is very different from that taken by my mum and brother, who are instead totally happy to go along with the superficial details I provide.

I plan on avoiding Anna all day.

So here I am tangled up in rope, leading a charge of children through a supposedly age-appropriate assault course whilst wearing a tutu. It was a bit of a tight squeeze. I'm relieved there's nobody here to impress.

On reflection, one foot stuck in a hole intended for a child's foot, I'm not convinced this physical assault is better than Anna's emotional assault would have been. It takes one more kick to persuade me I've had enough of the physical for today.

Finally free, I find a group of adults. 'Goodness. That assault course is intense. Soft play isn't that soft.' They stare at me without laughing, and I know I am not quite adult enough for this particular group. I don't disagree.

Luckily, Fred beckons me over and tugs me under his arm when I'm within reach. 'Come here. Have some birthday cake. It's half yours too. Kinda.'

Never one to turn down baked goods, and feeling like I might have exercised enough to have earned it this time, I pick a larger piece than is probably polite.

Almost as though she can sense I've been up to no good, Anna pops up.

'So, Bea, how's the love life? How's the card making going? How's life at work? How was Mia's wedding?' Straight to the point as ever. 'Fill me in. Let me live vicariously through you.' I take this as a subtle way of her saying, 'You should be doing more with your life.' I don't 100 per cent disagree with her.

I have just enough time to take a rather large mouthful of cake, knowing the chew time will give me some precious moments to fortify myself.

I nod and flap my free hand about, pretending to be chewing faster, and eventually swallow. 'All ticking along quite nicely. I don't want to say too much and jinx it –' a phrase I hope means she'll back off – 'but card-wise I've actually been building out more of a solid business plan with my friend Peter. Work-wise, I've been given some more responsibility mentoring newly hired employees –' sure, this is a bit of a stretch, but it's fine – 'and love life-wise, nothing of note to report.' At this last point I give her what I hope is a subtle look that says, 'Something is going on, but I'm not going to share it in front of Fred.'

Of course I have absolutely no intention of sharing my antics with her, but she doesn't need to know that. I need to make sure I stay close enough to the protective embrace of my big brother at all times, thereby making the subject off-limits.

'Peter?' Fred asks. Right in the middle of a sexy mini flashback to Colin, Peter's name is an unwelcome surprise. Not noticing my discomfort, Fred keeps talking. Mainly to himself. 'I like Peter.' Peter came over a couple of times during our summer holidays at university, saying he needed a break from his lovely but occasionally overbearing mother. The first time he stayed I was uncomfortable; I knew his house had to be impressive, and I worried what he would think of my vastly more humble abode. I have a sneaking suspicion that Peter is the only one of my friends my brother actually remembers.

'Well, that's all wonderful!' Anna's chirpier voice brings me back to the present; I can tell she has limited interest in the anecdote from Fred. 'And what about Mia's wedding?'

My first thought is of that total knob at the wedding who said I *could* have been his next girlfriend. I try to bat down the hatred.

But the hatred melts quickly into worry. Mia and I normally text each other at least once a day, but even her awkward 'trying to be nice' messages have stopped, and so I haven't actually spoken to her since her birthday drinks. That was five weeks ago now.

'Oh dear. Not good then?' I wish my face was less readable.

I'm not OK with admitting that we had a fight, especially as I know Anna will keep prying and will eventually lead the conversation towards a deep dive into my life. I decide to deflect.

'Oh no, but I haven't seen her that much since she got married. She's very focused on her career, which gives her only a small amount of time for anything else. But I think she's good. The last time I saw her it was her birthday. We went to a really trendy bar for a couple of drinks. You would have loved it. Lots of cocktails.'

'Gosh, the days of going to bars seem so long ago.'

It wasn't *that* long ago. Anna invited me to a work do a couple of years back. I was trying to save money so I wasn't drinking, but Anna was totally – and I use this term affectionately – off her tits.

By the time 10 p.m. rolled around, nobody was left standing.

I remember turning around from my conversation with a couple of Anna's co-workers to see one of her non-work friends making out with the barman, another eating nachos directly off the floor, and Anna stroking the walls.

'Hey, Anna. Whatcha doing there?'

'I'm testing for the filth.'

All I could do was raise my eyebrows and nod.

Anna went on, slurring slightly, swaying. 'Yes. I am a good friend, and my good friend –' she pauses and looks down at me through her eyelashes like she can't remember her good friend's name – 'her, over there! –' she points to the person eating the nachos – 'I want to make sure that it's safe for her to eat her nachos from wherever she chooses to eat them.'

'You are a very good friend, but I don't think she's going to need to eat any more after she's done with those.' Anna keeps testing the wall. Her face is getting increasingly close, and I worry that she might lick it. 'Can I get you a drink? Maybe some water?'

That made her stop.

'*Water?!* Water is for the weak! I want another cocktail.'

I looked over at the bar. The barman was still, ahem, occupied with the other friend. But it didn't matter. By the time I looked back at Anna she was merrily sing-shouting a montage of Disney songs to an unfortunate table of people nearby.

I snap back to the present when a rainbow of children run directly across my eyeline.

'Hello, sweetie! Have you said hello to Aunty Bea?'

Why does Anna have to use that high-pitched voice when she talks to Olivia?

I realize that as her aunt I shouldn't say this, but Olivia is a highly intelligent yet weirdly morbid child with the weight of the world on her shoulders. Ask her a simple question and she'll answer it with a shocking amount of thought, always tinged with a depressing edge. Looking at her parents, who are now both singing Disney songs (thank goodness they found each other), I have no idea where she gets it from.

She comes trotting over to me.

'Hey, bug. You having a nice birthday party?'

She thinks before she answers. 'Yes.' It sounds more like a question. 'But I worry that one day I won't have as much fun at my birthday parties. By the time we are old, like Mummy and Daddy, we will have lots of worries and the worries will spoil the fun. Do you still have fun at your birthday parties?'

Where does she come up with this stuff? But then when I try to remember the last birthday party I had fun at, I come up blank.

I can't lie to her. 'I know lots of people who still have lots of fun at their birthday parties. But I do think that the amount of fun you have is in exact relation to the amount of cake you eat. So I think you need more cake.' And with that we wander off on a hunt for sponge.

Later, safe in the quiet of the kitchen, Mum comes in, Hugo closely following behind.

'Bea, you shouldn't be cleaning up.' She says this while adding a load of dirty plates to the pile.

'I'll wash if you dry.'

She nods and grabs a tea towel.

'I've put your card and present by your bag. I hope you like them. You can change them if not. The gift receipt is in there.'

'Thanks, Mum.' I bet she's given me yoga pants. Luckily it's now acceptable to wear them to many different occasions. I hope they're the type with pockets.

'I think this year is going to be a good one for you, Bea. You seem happier today than you've seemed recently. Your eyes look less tired.'

I know she means this as a compliment. At least, this is what I tell myself.

'Thanks, Mum.' I don't say anything more, but I do pass her a plate to dry, whilst quietly hoping her premonition comes true.

Chapter 23

Peter! Guess what!

Today I got accepted into an independent art fair, and at a discounted rate because someone had to pull out at the last minute.

It's only a small step, but it's a small step in the right direction and it feels pretty good.

I text Peter to share the good news. After all, it was his help that got me here. I also type out a message to Mia, as her pushing got me here too, but then I delete it. It doesn't seem like the right time.

Peter's reply comes less than five minutes later.

Want help?

Yes, yes I do.

Part of the new business plan was to get my cards out there. So I emailed a whole load of potential stockists, sent sample cards to trendy cafes, and applied to sell my wares at craft shows. I even dropped some cards on the underground, hoping it might cause a stir. It didn't (at least not yet).

My efforts didn't amount to much. I got a lot of

rejections. More rejections than I knew what to do with. Craft and art fairs were already full or far too expensive. Cafes thought the cards were cute, but said they didn't currently sell anything other than coffee (but if that changed they'd let me know). Shops didn't have any more space, but would get back in touch again come their January stock review. I thought the rejections would make me feel worse than they have, but they've actually been quite kind as rejections go; most people have even said how much they like the cards.

Until now. Today's email is not a rejection. And it takes about three minutes for the joy to turn to mild panic. The show is in four days and I have no table, no set-up, no nothing. I don't even think I have enough cards. I am entirely unprepared.

I would like Peter's help with everything but instead I ask:

> Could you come help me on the day? Maybe you could keep me company around lunch-time?

> That all?

> That's all. And maybe you could bring coffee. xx

> If you're sure that's all you need I'm happy to oblige, but I'm here if you need more.

The next few days are filled with doing things I really should have done months ago. I cancel all my plans, including a yoga date with Tilly, and refuse any additional meet-ups, including another rendezvous with Colin.

Instead, I get insurance for my stand. I come up with a pricing strategy (by which I mean I put actual prices on all of my cards). I beg/borrow (and also steal, in the case of a small succulent – sorry, pub) things to brighten up my display table. I make a sign. I also try to think of funny things for new cards. I fail miserably at this, and decide to recycle some of last year's bestsellers instead. A perk of being unknown is that they aren't recycled in many people's eyes. Every cloud.

And sooner than I would have liked, Sunday, aka Independent Art Fair Day, rolls around, and I've managed to squeeze all my card paraphernalia into the taxi. The driver isn't happy about how long it has taken to load all my boxes, but finally everything is in and I can shut the door. One issue: I can only shut the door with me on the outside.

'You're never gonna get it all in with you inside, love.'

I think for a while, imagining I am playing a game of Tetris instead.

'Hold on, I have an idea.' I open the front passenger door. 'Can I . . .?' I don't wait for his OK before I move the seat back. I rearrange the boxes and shut the door. 'Perfect! That will be fine there.' I hope. I then grab the box that's sitting on the back seat and sit down, with the box on my lap. 'OK! I'm ready.'

We are leaving about thirty minutes later than I had planned.

Clinging on to the box as we round corners unnecessarily fast, I'm a ball of apprehension. Despite all my preparations, I still feel woefully unprepared. I don't remember the brownie stall organization being this stressful. But there wasn't so much riding on that, whereas I want my cards to succeed. Today I take a step towards that goal. Today feels important. Today I will see people's reactions to my cards first hand. I can't help but think that by judging the cards, they're also judging me.

If anyone had seen me this morning, they would already be judging me badly, but luckily only I was witness to my panicked last-minute preparations and changes in plan. The annoying thing is, I'd been worried about the logistics for days, particularly the taxi, but had been so paralysed by fear that I couldn't face it until the morning itself. A terrible idea.

We arrive at the hall where the fair is taking place.

The taxi driver grumbles in my vague direction. 'Where should I pull in?'

I have no idea. I look out of the window, hoping for inspiration.

'It looks like there's a pull-in right up there?' I try to motion with my hand, but the box on my lap is quite precariously balanced.

He pulls in, hitting the kerb.

'Here you go.'

'Thank you so much.' I try to manoeuvre myself into a better position to be able to reach the door handle. I'm an independent woman, but I feel that it's in both our interests for him to help me.

He doesn't.

Finally I manage to open the door. 'Is it OK if I pop in with this one box to find where my table is and then unload?'

Again, he makes no noise, but I take it as a yes and head inside.

'That little shit.'

Having found my space, I'm back outside to unload. I've been three minutes, max, and yet all of my boxes are piled, abandoned, on the side of the road. Apparently he can help when it suits him. It has also started to rain.

Someone with frizzy hair half smiles at me. 'You were in the taxi?'

'Yes.'

She nods knowingly. 'They really don't like waiting. Next time think about using a courier. It's a tad more expensive, but they also have to help take the stuff in.'

'Thank you.' At least I know for next time. Hoping that there is a next time.

One good thing about the massive rush I put myself in was that I was too stressed to look around during set-up, because if I had, I probably would have packed straight back up and gone home.

Everyone else's stands were amazing, whilst mine looked like something you would see at a sad school holiday fair.

There were sparkle stations and nail art salons, jewellers selling beautiful stacked rings, temporary tattoo parlours, and even a cookie art stall.

The only stall that I thought was worse than mine was one that sold teeny tiny boats, like the ones in *Pocahontas*, for £15 a pop. He must be having a laugh. Who would buy those? For £15? They're half the size of my little finger.

The fair opened an hour and a half ago, and I am yet to make a sale.

As I pace slowly in front of my table, I wish I hadn't asked Peter to come. I feel akin to how I did at speed dating: mortified that Peter is here to witness my downfall but glad to have him here for moral support.

I still have an hour before he's due to arrive, and so in that time I set myself a challenge. I will talk to at least five other exhibitors. I can make cards, this I know, but that isn't enough. What I really need is to get the inside scoop. These people have been selling their crafts for years. How do they do it? How can I do it?

My first couple of tries aren't very successful, mainly because when actually faced with a human to talk to, I can't think of anything to say, so instead I have to style out my half-open mouth with an awkward smile. At this rate, I will definitely fail.

Looking around whilst continuing my slow pacing and arm-swinging, I spot my next prey. She's displaying homemade scented candles diagonally opposite me, has a friendly-looking face and is on crutches, so it's unlikely that she'll be able to run away from my advances.

When I finally gather enough courage to head over, I decide to start simply.

'Hello! Hi! Konnichiwa!' Where did the Japanese come from? 'How are you? I thought I'd pop over and introduce myself. I'm Bea –' I reach out to shake her hand, hoping this is something people still do – 'and that over there –' I point to my stall – 'is my stall.'

She smiles at me, which I think is a good sign. Her face is even more friendly up close.

'Hi, Bea. I'm Francesca. It's lovely to meet you. I was watching you set up.' Oh dear. 'I love your succulent. I keep trying to find one like it but I can never seem to see the purply ones for sale.' Tell me about it. 'You're selling cards, right? I love a good card.'

'Me too! Which is lucky, I guess. It would be hard to sell something you don't like. Like cats. I could never sell cats.'

We talk for a while longer, but then more people start to appear, so I meander back over to my stall, trying not to look too eager whenever someone comes near.

Luckily, when Peter makes his appearance (coffee in hand), there are real-life people talking to me and laughing at some of my cards.

He waits for them to leave before coming over. 'How's it going? It looks like it's going well.' He gives me a hug and hands over the java juice.

'Yeah, it's going good. It was a bit rocky to start with, quite quiet, but I think it's getting busier. Although I haven't actually sold any cards yet.'

'Well, it's still quite early. And even if you don't sell a single card, you gotta try these things, right?'

'I guess.' I'm proud of myself for coming. It would have been very easy to cancel, or not even try to come in the first place. Two very Bea moves.

'You must be hungry. By the lack of food stains down your top I would guess that you haven't eaten—'

'I don't *always* spill food down myself.' Although we both know my track record isn't great.

'Go get food. I'll man the fort.' At this he does some kind of soldier-like salute and I can't help but laugh. I don't think he meant it to be funny but I find it endearing.

I waddle off, swinging by my new friend's stall, offering to pick something up for her.

'Oh, no – thank you though. I brought sandwiches.' She points towards what looks like a brick covered in tinfoil. They must be huge sandwiches. 'I've recently quit my job, so I'm trying to save the pennies where I can.'

Interesting. 'Oh, so you haven't been doing this for long?'

'Well, I set up my company a couple of years ago. I worked part-time for a while, but I only went full-time on the candles last month. The regular part-time salary was great, especially in the early years, and I should be fine, but just in case I like to keep the buffer of money I've saved for necessities.'

I start to ask another question, but a group of people approach her stall so I shut up, nod and give a small wave before retreating.

For lunch I opt for a halloumi wrap. Delicious, comfortingly warm, and a lack of spillage potential.

I walk slowly back to my stall, eating my wrap whilst I take in the sights around me. I could imagine myself here – there is a real sense of camaraderie. I like it.

I also note, with a hint of relief, that my cards are as good as the other cards here. I don't think I've embarrassed myself at all.

I weave my way up and down the stalls, and once again find myself looking at the tiny boats. I don't go too close but I also can't look away – he has a customer. He needs to make this sale. If he can sell a finger-sized boat for £15, I can sell a card for £3.50.

Against all odds and common sense, he does it. I'm so happy I nearly drop my wrap.

Having watched the successful sale of the boat, I make my way back to my own cards with a little more optimism.

I took a route that means I've walked up behind Peter. He's talking, really animatedly, to a couple of customers. I can just about hear what he's saying.

'They're great – I mean, feel them.' He picks up a card and passes it round. It will be unsellable after this, but I let it pass. 'That's a card that says you really care.' He reaches for another. 'This one is my favourite from her current collection.'

He passes it to one of the women. She chuckles. 'You're right. I'd never thought about it before, but this card does actually feel really nice.'

'And they're all screen-printed by hand using the highest-quality paints.'

'Are they vegan?'

'The paints?'

She nods.

He nods back. 'Oh, yes. And eco-friendly.'

Of course the paint is vegan (I think), although the eco-friendly thing is probably a stretch. I make a mental note to confirm both tomorrow.

'Great, I'll take this and also the one with the avocado on it.'

The man next to her adds another card to the pile. 'This too.'

Peter does the maths quickly in his head. I'm not there yet. 'We'll call it a clean ten pounds, saving you a whole fifty pence.'

They wander off, holding hands, and I get closer to Peter.

'You're a really good salesman. I should leave you here by yourself for the rest of the afternoon. How's it gone?'

'Great! You have sold –' he counts them off on his fingers – 'ten cards. And someone took your details for their cousin's shop.'

My grin is genuine. Even if I don't sell any more cards, this day already feels like a win.

The afternoon goes more quickly than the morning, and when it's over Peter helps me pack up, an activity that everyone else seems to do extremely quickly, and yet it seems to be taking Peter and me a lot longer by comparison. Maybe because he keeps doing impressions of the customers.

'I think it was a good day.'

'Me too.' And I mean it, despite all the frantic last-minute preparations and my fears that my cards would fail. 'Thanks for keeping me company, I really appreciate it.' And I do. All the worries I felt this morning have gone. And Peter seems to have genuinely had a good time.

'No problem. If I wasn't doing this I would have been sitting in my lounge pants on my laptop.'

I stop packing. 'Lounge pants? Peter, what the hell are lounge pants?'

He makes a hand gesture that suggests this is a common term and I'm the odd one for not knowing. 'Comfortable pants that you wear when lounging. Surely everyone has a pair of lounge pants?'

He continues packing, and so do I. I carefully place the filched succulent into a safe corner of a box. I received so many compliments on it today. It was a good acquisition.

And it really has been a good day: I learnt some interesting things, I sold some cards, I ate a delicious halloumi wrap and I did some great people watching. One girl even sniffed all my cards and then bought the one she said smelt like the intended recipient.

Almost done with packing up, I look over at Peter, who has apparently wandered off and is now talking to another man. He is standing in that casual man stance with feet slightly apart, hips forward, arms crossed, surveying the room. He looks tall. Quite attractive actually.

Oh God. Is it OK that I think Peter looks quite attractive?

I'm frozen on the spot, staring. No, no, I don't think that's OK. Unable to shake the thought, I turn away – perhaps if I concentrate really hard on packing this last box . . .

But as though I have a devil on one shoulder, I can't help but glance at him again. He is looking good. He's still on the gangly side, but he's grown into his features. He really does look quite handsome.

OK. This is a bit awkward.

Is this a bit awkward?

I find lots of my friends attractive. For example, Mia and Tilly are very beautiful, so, rationally, it should also be OK for me to appreciate the fact that Peter has become quite attractive. He's not so odd any more. Or maybe he is, and I don't care. It doesn't mean anything.

I nod and hope I look like a crazy woman listening to my own music, instead of a crazy woman trying to dislodge the unwanted thought that is now stuck in my head.

I can't help but think that Peter's to blame for this errant thought – he was the one who claimed he'd asked me on a date, which has probably put some rogue ideas in my mind. But if he had actually wanted to go out with me back then, he would have made it more obvious, wouldn't he? He would have told me, wouldn't he? It's not exactly like he's been pining for me. He's dated plenty of people in the timespan that I've known him, and he's never asked me out again.

Shit, he's seen me staring. I wave in the hope this camouflages my recent train of thought. He waves back.

I finish off the last bits of packing, tidying up the remaining cards and collecting the final crumbs of rubbish. Money-wise I've made about half the amount it cost me to come here today, but I'm OK with that. Like Peter said, you have to try these things out.

'Are you ready to go? I can order a taxi and help you load up. We could get a six-person car, and if there's room I'll come back to yours and help you carry it up. It'll take half the time.'

This feels weird. I don't think I should be near him at

the moment. I worry he'll be able to sense the inconvenient thoughts I've been having.

'No, that's really kind, but I'm good. It's out of your way and I'm fine. Honestly, it's an easy job to do and it won't take me long.' It will probably take me two hours. Not exactly easy, but I don't want to rely on him for more than I already have – I can't. If I do, one day he won't be there, and then where will I be? I managed just fine this morning (eventually). I can do this now.

'Honestly, I don't mind.'

'No, it's a boring task and I'm good.' I don't want his lasting memory of the day to be schlepping up to my apartment.

He almost looks a little hurt, and I feel bad.

'OK then. Today's been fun. Thanks for letting me come.'

'Thanks for *letting you come*? Peter, if it wasn't for you I would have sold about five cards.'

'Nah. Your cards sell themselves. They're great and so are you. Come here.'

He reaches for me and I give him a hug. He's always been a good hugger, and despite the height difference I fit well against him. He scratches my back in a relaxing way, and I close my eyes, just for a moment . . . He smells so good. Has he always smelt this good?

'Pete, I've changed my mind. If there is room in the taxi, would you mind helping me?'

Chapter 24

Peter was right. Despite the fact his legs did look comically long folded into the front seat of the taxi that was pulled far, far forward, letting him help meant the whole unloading process went much more quickly, and with many more laughs, than it would have if I'd been by myself. Peter's charm even worked on the taxi driver, who was not only fine with the time it took us to load and then unload, but she even helped.

Once all the boxes were sitting by the front door of my apartment block, we took it in turns to ferry them upstairs. This last load we take together, and by the time we reach my door I know I have sweat on my forehead (and fear I also have some on my upper lip).

I'm breathing more heavily than I'd hoped, but stairs have always been my nemesis. The additional weight from the boxes is making them even worse.

We both put our boxes down wherever we can find space, and I do what I hope is a subtle sweat-wipe. I can hear Peter panting too, which makes me feel better.

He looks at me and makes a face as if he's in pain.

'Drink?' I gasp.

'Yes, please.'

I run through the options in my head. 'Water?' I wish I had something more exciting to give him. Water seems like a measly offering, especially after all the help he's given me. 'I might have some squash.'

He shakes his head. 'Water would be great. Thank you.'

I run the tap so it gets cold, reach for two glasses, fill one and pass it to him. He downs it, so I refill it. Again, it's gone before I've even managed to start on mine.

God, he even drinks well. How can someone drink well?

It's his hands. He has really good hands.

'Bea?'

I jolt back into reality. 'Huh?'

'You OK?'

'Yes. Sorry, I'm just so tired.' And confused. Very confused.

'I'll go.'

'Oh no, you don't have to.' Even as I say it, I think he does need to go.

He puts the glass down. 'Do you want to grab a quick dinner?'

Faced with the potential of him actually staying, all of a sudden I feel the need to get him out of my apartment as quickly as possible. I put down my glass and stand up straight.

'On second thoughts, I am actually really tired. You've been great, but all I can handle right now is my pyjamas. I don't have the energy to go back outside into the world.'

'You sure?'

No. 'Yes. Please, I can't be around people for any more of the day.'

He smiles but it doesn't reach his eyes. 'I'm not "people".'

Shit.

'Peter, I—'

'Bea, it's OK.' He looks down at the floor. 'You've had a really long day and I get it.' Then he looks back up at me. 'But I'm not just people, I'm one of your best friends. I'm always here for you, and I'm not going to stop being here, even if you get grumpy or snap at me because you've had enough of me for the day.'

'No, that's not it, I could never have enough of you.' Shit. What was that? 'I mean . . .' Yes, Bea, what do you mean? 'I mean . . . thank you. Not many people would have come to help today, and not only did you help, but you were also really great at it. I don't know if I'll ever be able to pay you back.'

'Bea, you don't need to pay me back. I was happy to help.' His smile eventually reaches his eyes. 'So let me know whenever you need another pair of hands.'

He turns to go, and suddenly, although I told him to leave, I wish he was staying.

'Peter, I really do owe you one. If you ever want to cash it in.'

Chapter 25

Penny once told me that she admired how I always brought my whole self to work. If I'm in a bad mood, I show it. If I can't be bothered to wear office clothes, I don't. If I want to buy at least one oat-milk latte a day, I will.

And so it feels totally OK to put in a maximum of 20 per cent effort the day after the independent art fair. I have other more important things on my mind, like new ideas for cards, finding and eating all the food I can to replenish my energy reserves, and dissecting the dream I had last night.

As dreams go, it started innocently enough, but then it ramped up quite quickly. It's been a long time since I've had a sex dream, and I'm not too sure how I feel about it, but as with every dream, some details were kinda hazy and some were not. On the hazy side were things like the location – I'm not too confident where my dream was taking place. Part of me thinks it was in a beach hut because I remember seeing a large umbrella and possibly a walking dolphin, but I could be wrong about that. But on the decidedly not hazy side were things like the person. My co-star was Peter. I remember being just as shocked about this revelation in my dream as I am in real life.

And what was even more shocking was that he was good. As in, eyebrows-up *good*.

There was one particular moment when he came up behind me and—

Nope. I need to stop thinking about Dream Peter. I can't risk confusing him with Real Peter. Imagine if I jump his bones next time I see him.

My thoughts are interrupted by a squawk.

Penny walks towards me and I ask her, simply with a raise of the brow, what is going on.

'Someone has Joan's mug.'

I double-check my mug – I am safe. My mug is one of the mass-produced, off-white versions.

As my reverie has already been disturbed, I head for the loo. Not meaning to be dramatic, but I have become approximately 95 per cent snot overnight. And because I'm a keen advocate of office etiquette, snot-snorting is only acceptable in the closed confines of the loo.

It's cruel, I know, but there's a part of me that's excited to see what Joan is going to do to the person who has her mug. There's not much by way of entertainment here for me, though I'm sure it'll traumatize the assistants. Come to think of it, I'd better add it to the agenda for our next session – what if one of them gets PTSD on my watch?

Joan's waiting for me at my desk. If she asks me to send an all-company email regarding her mug, I might lose it.

Instead she smiles.

'Can I get you a fresh glass of water?'

Kind Joan looks odd, somewhat manic. It does not suit her.

'Oh, no, but thank you.'

'I ask –' she really spits out the 'k' – 'because you are using my mug as your water glass.'

I look down at my water glass.

'This . . . glass is your mug?'

'It is a specially designed mug with two layers of glass for a superior taste and hot-beverage drinking experience. I spent a lot of time researching the perfect mug.'

It's definitely a glass.

'I'm so sorry. It looks like a glass to me, but of course, have it back.' I gesture to the glass, and as I do, I drop my tissue.

Her whole face flushes red.

'Are you ill? You are ill! Why would you use someone else's mug, their special mug, when you're ill?'

I'm in for it now, and the awkwardness of the situation and the bright office lights are making me need to sneeze.

Please don't sneeze. I shake my head from side to side, trying to knock back the urge. 'Oh no, I feel fine, but I've been talking all weekend, which makes me sound like I have a cold.'

My eyes start to water. Please don't sneeze.

'Hmm.'

She stomps away with her 'mug', as I sneeze as quietly as is humanly possible into my sleeve. But fair play to Joan; a minute later she stomps back with a fresh glass of water.

She plonks it down and gives me another insincere smile. I can think of nothing that would make me sip from that glass. She definitely spat in it.

A few hours later I'm staring mindlessly at my nails. Some days fly by, and some days crawl at a glacial pace. Today is definitely the latter.

Which really isn't helping distract me from Dream Peter. Maybe I should try to arrange to see Colin again? Our messaging has dried up since I cancelled on him last week in favour of fair prep.

Mia would love the mug incident. And now I do actually have some positive life updates for her.

Are you available for lunch?

I get there a bit early, and start fiddling with my bag, and my jacket, and my top, suddenly unsure of myself.

But then I see her walking towards me and I'm just happy to see her, and doubly happy that she's smiling back at me. As soon as she comes within touching distance I hug her. Hard.

'I've missed you.' And then I don't stop talking. 'So much has happened and I've wanted to tell you everything but I felt weird and, wait . . . I'm so sorry.' I don't care that I am apologizing first. 'I'm so sorry about not talking to you and kicking you out of my house. I'm sorry for being moody and not replying to your messages. I love you. You're my best friend, and I hate it when things are even a little bit off between us. I don't feel like myself.'

Mia's hug back is equally firm.

'Bea, oh my goodness. You're not the one that needs to apologize. I'm the one who needs to apologize.' She holds up a hand to stop me interrupting. 'I should never have said those things about your cards, or about you. I love your cards, you know I love them. And I love you. You're my best friend too. I should be the one saying sorry.'

We breathe in sync for a while but eventually let go of each other. I think there are mini tears in both of our eyes.

She's back, I've got her back. 'Shall we get some food?'

As regular patrons of this particular salad bar, it takes us minimal time to help ourselves to each of our carefully curated salad choices. The only variance today is that I've gone for an extra helping of broccoli, in the hope it will make me healthy.

'So, tell me – what's been happening?' I get the first question in so I can eat. I tuck in as soon as the question is out, aiming for the broccoli first. I should have put it closer to the top.

'I'm pregnant.'

Not what I was expecting her to say.

I stop paying close attention to the broccoli and pull it out from the pile of salad much more quickly than I planned, spraying bits of quinoa everywhere in a glorious halo.

Speared broccoli still in hand, I can't not talk. 'Oh my God. This is amazing! You're going to be such a good mum! I can't wait till it's old enough so I can give it margaritas. I wonder what the ickle bug is going to look like. I didn't even realize you were trying to get pregnant. Are you happy? I can't believe we're going to have a baby. When are you due? Tell me everything. How are you doing?'

Perhaps I should have filtered those thoughts a touch.

She inhales and, in a calmer tone than I used, talks me through some of her feelings. 'Well, to be honest it is a bit of a shock. We weren't trying. Obviously I'm happy, I am . . .' She slows down as she continues, 'But it isn't coming at the time I would choose to have a baby. I guess you can't really control these things all the time, but I had thought we would be better at planning it in.'

'So if you weren't trying, what happened?'

'I blame Mark. His cooking gave me such bad food poisoning that I couldn't keep any food down for three days. It was so unpleasant. And it turns out when they say your protection against pregnancy may be affected if you miss a couple of pills, they're not lying. We had sex *once* that month. Once! And from memory it wasn't even that good.' She eats a bite of her lunch, angrily chewing on some spinach leaves. She softens, just a touch. 'I feel bad saying that. The sex was fine, but I'm angry and he's pissing me off. Part of me wonders if he did it on purpose.'

'He wouldn't!'

'No, rationally I know he wouldn't. But – and this is horrible, so please don't tell anyone – when I found out I was pregnant I *was* happy, but I was also pretty sad, and I still am.' She has put down her fork and is gesturing slightly manically with her hands. She's not typically a gesturer. 'I want kids, I've always wanted kids, but kids weren't in my plan for at least five years. We've had to cancel the honeymoon, I'm having horrible morning sickness, I feel fat, and I can't return those ugly amphibious shoes I bought. I tried, but they'll only give me store credit because I can't find the receipt.'

'So take the store credit?'

'They only bloody sell amphibious shoes. And I'm not going to be going to the rainforest any time soon now, am I?'

'Oh, Mia, that sucks. I'm not gonna lie to you. This is huge. A baby is huge. But it isn't any more than you can handle. It might be more than your vagina can handle, but you are going to be a great mum. And Mark is going to be a great dad.'

Her shoulders slump. 'What if my baby knows that not all of me wanted them at first? Do you think they can tell?'

For a moment, in the midst of Mia's huge emotional crisis, I'm so glad to have her back. So glad that somehow the last few months feel like no time at all.

'I don't think they can tell.' I give her my biggest thank-you-for-coming-back-to-me smile. 'Besides, the fact you're worrying about this tells me that you're already on your way to becoming a good mum. From what I understand, the first thing on the job description is to worry.'

At this she smiles a small smile, enough for me to know that she is OK.

'Ugh, I just wanted some time for me. And I know that's selfish, but I feel like I've spent the last five years either working ridiculously long hours or planning a wedding, and neither of those things were really for me – both were for my family. And finally I feel like I have time for myself, the wedding is over and I'm in a good place at work, I have proved myself and am doing things I find interesting at last . . . and I don't want to have a baby and mess that all up.'

'Well, I don't work in your company, so I don't know what it will be like for you, and obviously everyone and everywhere is different, but I don't think having a baby is as impactful on your career projection these days – I think companies have to be a lot more careful. At my company, people leave for maternity, but when they return they go straight back into the role they were doing before, if they want to. I think people are a lot more aware. Having a baby doesn't make you a less important or less capable employee. If anything, it makes you more focused. And besides, everyone has shit going on outside work. And if they don't, they should. Nobody wants to work with someone who only works.' I genuinely hope what I'm saying proves to be true for Mia. But today is not necessarily about truth – it's more about reassurance.

She makes a face. 'When the other girl on my team told our partner in the firm that she was pregnant, his response was, and I quote, "Oh fuck."'

Eek. 'I think he needs to go on some kind of training.'

'I don't think it will help. What's worse is that he's seen to be one of the good ones – he's even been nominated as an advocate for women returning to work. He says he knows what it's like because he has two children of his own. He has no idea. He works away from home during the week and then plays golf half the weekend.'

'Well then, make sure you bring in the baby and hand it over to him when he/she/it is about to drop a load.

Feed it spicy beans in the run-up.' I give her arm what I hope is a loving squeeze. 'Is Mark excited?'

She smiles a very genuine smile. She always has been easy to console.

'That is the one great thing. Mark is over the moon. He would have had babies years ago if it was up to him. But I don't know what it is – like I said, at the moment he's really pissing me off. He's trying not to, but that pisses me off even more. It's probably the hormones, but honestly, everything he does is annoying me.

'For example, last night he was cooking me dinner – a fancy fish-finger wrap with thick-cut chips.' She gets her love of a fish-finger wrap from me; I used to make these for her when we lived together. 'And as I was watching him, I couldn't help but look at him and think, "No. I love you, but right now I find you so unattractive I don't know why I ever let you touch me, let alone knock me up." And he's got this bloody obsession with bowls at the moment, those big bowls that they serve ramen in. And let me tell you, bowls are really hard to store. They take up a lot of room in our kitchen cupboards. I swear, every time he leaves the house he comes back with another bloody bowl. And he only ever buys one at a time. He says he's testing them out, but it just means we're now the owners of a really large collection of mismatching bowls. If he brings another one home I might whack him over the head with it.'

'Do you hate him a bit? Have you told him?'

'I've tried, but every time I start, I burst out crying. Anything will set me off. It doesn't have to be a sad emotion. It can be *any* emotion. Too happy? I cry. Too funny?

I cry. Too gassy? I cry. I haven't cried for years and now I can't stop.'

I didn't know 'gassy' was an emotion, but I let it slide.

'Well then, maybe try to remember that you won't always hate him and this is merely a phase.'

'Good God, I hope it is a phase, because right now I can't even stand the smell of him. I had to sleep on the sofa last night because the scent of him was making me too nauseous to sleep.'

I can't help but feel slightly sorry for Mark. He loves Mia so much but now, because of the shock and uncontrollable hormones, he's public enemy number one.

'Anyway, distract me. How are you?'

'Which do you want first, the funny work updates or the life updates?'

'Let's go funny first and then life.'

As I had suspected, Mia was the perfect audience for the Joan mug story, laughing at all the right moments. She was also the perfect audience for the life updates. We're well past the allotted hour for lunch, but she didn't want me to stop.

'I'm so proud of you.'

I've only just finished telling her about Colin's growling. I haven't even reached the card progress yet.

'Proud? I slept with the emergency boiler man.'

She nods and makes a face that says, 'Yeah you did. And it was good.'

This next thing I need to say is going to be tricky. I go slow so I don't mess it up.

'There is something that I think you will be genuinely proud of though. I've been putting more work into my cards.' I avoid her gaze. 'The argument we had, or whatever we want to call it, well . . . I didn't like it, but you were right. I haven't been fighting for anything, I haven't been trying hard to succeed . . . I have been hiding a bit.'

'Oh, Bea, I didn't—'

Now I look at her. 'No, you were right. I'm sorry that I put you into a position where you had to kick my arse. But you did, and my arse is now a little more in gear.'

'It is?'

I smile. 'Yes. It is. Peter's actually been helping me. So I now have a plan, and things to concentrate on, and last weekend me and my cards actually went to a real-life fair.'

'Bea! That's great! Why didn't you tell me? I would have come!'

'Well, I didn't know what to expect – it might have been a total flop.'

'And was it?'

I think. 'No, it wasn't. I didn't make much money, but I did learn some things. And actually, one thing I did learn was that my cards are pretty OK in comparison to the other cards out there.'

'Eek! This is great! Can I come to the next one?'

'Sure.'

I then go quiet. There's one thing I still haven't told her about.

'You look shifty. There's something else. Spill it.'

She knows me too well. I do want to talk to her about Dream Peter. I want her to comfort me and tell me it will pass. But part of me wants to ignore it. What if she thinks I *like* him like him? She'd never give it up.

But I can't keep it from her. 'IhadasexdreamaboutPeter.'

'More slowly for those of us with human hearing?'

I force myself to say it again.

'I had . . .'

A few words at a time.

'A sex dream . . .'

Looking anywhere but Mia's face.

'About Peter.'

I sneak a peek. Mia's eyes aren't blinking and she's gone really still.

'Please go on.'

'Do I have to?'

She breaks into a smile. 'Yes.'

I hide my face.

'It was good.'

'Good, or –' she raises her eyebrows – '*good*?'

I raise my eyebrows to mirror hers.

'Wow, didn't see that coming.' Once again, it's like Mia doesn't know what to do with her hands. 'OK, and what do you think this means?'

'It doesn't mean anything.'

Her eyes burn into me.

'OK, so Peter and I have been friends for so long. You know this. I was probably friends with him before I was friends with you.' I say 'probably' because I genuinely can't remember – it was that long ago. 'And he really is one of my best friends. I can't help what my dream brain thinks about.'

'Is that all?'

'I think so.'

'Do you think that maybe, just maybe, there is more going on between you and Peter?'

'No. My dream brain is my dream brain, and my actual brain knows that me fancying Peter is a bad idea.'

'You realize you just said that you fancy Peter.'

'I don't fancy Peter.'

'You just said you did. Are you sure you don't fancy him?'

Am I sure?

'I'm sure.' I nod and say it again with a touch more conviction. 'I *am* sure.' His face pops into my head. 'Ugh. I think it's because he said something the other day about how he once asked me on a date.' Mia makes a face at this, but I plough on. 'And I've seen him a lot lately and the Colin thing has put sex thoughts into my head. And I know that my brain has taken two very separate lines of thought and mushed them together.'

'You can't deny that Peter is looking quite good these days.'

I can deny this.

'I can see that all of my friends, be they male or female, are very beautiful. I can appreciate the new clothes and his more mature look, but just because I might be a bit lonely doesn't mean he's anything more than a friend.'

'Do the right thing and admit that a part of you fancies him. You realize that a boyfriend is basically just a friend that you have sex with, right?'

I get a flashback to the dream, to him kissing my neck, my ear, my mouth, and me wanting him to kiss my neck, my ear, my mouth. I flashback to him breaking off the kiss, and looking at me hungrily, knowing that my own dream eyes would be looking back at him in exactly the same way.

Back in the room, I worry that Mia can tell where my mind went.

'OK. A small part of me might fancy him.' Mia starts to speak but I cut her off. 'But quite frankly none of this matters anyway, because he doesn't fancy me back and this is only a weird phase that I am going through. Besides, we're not compatible. His family, his job, his earning potential, his intelligence. His hair! They're all far superior to mine. It's too much for me to go up against, and I don't want to be the girl who gets judged for boxing well above her weight.' Mia shakes her head. 'And don't shake your head at me – it's a thing. It's a thing that happens.' Monologue over. 'So that's it. These are my thoughts. So, tell me. What do you think?'

'I think you just spouted a whole load of horseshit.'

'I've never heard you swear before.'

'Well, your stupidity deserves it.'

Pregnant Mia is even more forthright than un-pregnant Mia.

There's not much I can say to that.

'Listen to me. That boy has loved you for the last ten years, and if you don't know that, then I honestly don't know what to say. I never brought it up because I assumed you knew. It's so obvious. It's so obvious that even Mark has noticed. And for the record, you two are unbeliev-ably compatible. You round each other out. And don't tell me that you would be punching; he's the one that would be punching. Your dream brain isn't getting confused, your dream brain is trying to wake you up and tell you that you like Peter as a friend *and* as something else.'

I'm still sat here with my mouth wide open.

'And don't give me any of this friends-can't-be-boyfriends nonsense. I don't know where you get that from.'

I think on this for a moment.

But no.

She doesn't get it.

It's pathetic to admit that I'm still affected by the memories made by a seventeen-year-old Bea. A seventeen-year-old Bea who had her heart crushed by Sam, her one-time best friend and first boyfriend.

It's pathetic to admit that I had thought we were going to get married. Nobody gets married to the boy they started dating at fifteen.

It's pathetic to admit that his parting words to me – 'I wish we had just stayed friends' – still haunt me to this day.

It's pathetic to admit that I tried to console myself by remembering how his dirty sports clothes could stink out the whole house, but I still felt really alone.

It's pathetic to admit that I cried for him even though my dad had just died.

She doesn't get it. She's looking at me expectantly. I should explain it to her, but I don't want to.

'We've been friends for so long. It would be too odd to be anything else now. I wouldn't know where to start. I can't fancy Peter, and Peter doesn't fancy me.'

Chapter 26

The most productive thing I did on Monday following my impromptu lunch with Mia was find a good deal on a spa weekend. Our friendship back on track, we decided to pamper ourselves and get facials that we – well, I – can't afford, and wear extremely large, towely bathrobes all day long. I am so happy to have her back. Even my mum can tell that my mood has improved. Her morning messages have finally eased off.

Thanks to my productivity, a few weeks later I'm precisely as I hoped I would be. In a bathrobe that is perfectly towely and far too large, sipping a summery Aperol Spritz – very fitting for July – and sitting on a lounger next to a miraculously unoccupied pool with Mia by my side. I am very content. It was a great idea to escape the city.

'So, tell me. Why haven't you met up with Colin the hot boiler guy again? What's been stopping you? Your love for Peter?'

I roll my eyes. Subtle. 'No. And stop it. That was quite a while ago now, and we fell out of touch. I've been very busy. I haven't been able to schedule in any admin time, let alone time to actually see him.'

'Admin? You need to file papers to have sex?'

'No – admin. My bikini line. Admin.' It was bad enough when we had sex before. Now it's taken on a resemblance to Hagrid.

'Ooooo, *admin*. I don't have time for that.'

Mia isn't very hairy, so it probably doesn't make a huge difference if she relaxes on her hedge trimming.

'But back to Peter.' She reaches into her bag and pulls out a stack of paper at least an inch thick. 'I had some down time at work this week, and thought I would do some research. At lunch the other day you mentioned that you wouldn't even know where to start with making Peter something more than a friend. From what I read, your situation seems to be quite a common one. You've put him in your "Friend Zone".' She thumps the stack of paper on the table, dangerously close to my drink. 'This research should help you get him out of there.'

I look at it.

'I made some notes and highlighted the sections I found most interesting. I've also written up the key findings on the top couple of sheets, but it's well worth reading the whole thing.'

I flip the edges. 'Mia, there must be two hundred pages here.'

'Two hundred and ninety-three actually, but some of them are double-spaced.'

I stare at the pages for a while, too stunned to be able to read any of the words.

'Thanks, I guess.'

My phone beeps.

'Bea! You aren't meant to have your phone on you! We're meant to be relaxing.'

'I know, I know, but I'm conditioned to be more stressed if I don't have my phone on me. It's like a new kind of Stockholm Syndrome.' I'm also very grateful to have a reason to put her research down and ignore it.

The text definitely distracts me. I am entirely unprepared for what it says.

'Holy shit.'

'What?'

'No way.'

'What?'

'I can't believe it.'

'Tell me, or I'll take the phone off you and look myself.'

'Tilly's engaged.'

I feel so guilty that I haven't seen her or spoken to her since before the fair. We don't have the type of friendship that needs constant feeding, but I feel completely out of the loop and it's all my own doing.

'Hold on, hasn't she been going out with that guy for like, a second? How much do we know about him? Are her parents OK with this? Do we need to stage an intervention? Or are we happy for her?' It's really easy to forget that Mia and Tilly have never met.

'Well, she spoke to me about wanting to marry him, but I didn't get the impression that it was imminent, so I didn't think a huge amount about it. But I guess I should have.'

'It seems very quick.'

Not even trying to hide the illicit phone any more, I'm

texting madly to find out more details. My messages are littered with spelling mistakes, but in times of peak excitement, a couple of spelling errors are acceptable. 'Holy shit.'

'What?'

'That can't be right.'

It's Mia's turn to roll her eyes. 'Not this again. Tell me.'

'They want to get married on New Year's Eve. *This* New Year's Eve.' Thinking back, she did lap up every detail of Mia's wedding, and was bizarrely concerned with some of the more boring logistics – lead times for suppliers, increased prices for New Year's Eve, issues with travel. Maybe she was doing preliminary research.

'Are you serious? That's five months away! Does she know that everywhere gets booked up for New Year's Eve years in advance?'

'I guess she doesn't care. Or maybe she has a plan. Maybe she already has it all sorted.'

'Don't offer to help.'

I grimace and look sideways at Mia.

'Too late.' I'm hoping my offer to help will go some way to make up for being an absent friend in recent months.

She simply sighs and puts her head back on the lounger. 'Don't say I didn't warn you.'

I spend another couple of minutes excitedly texting, and then decide to hide my phone when the chat dies down. I paid a lot of money to be here. I want to be here.

And I'm due to be called through for my first treatment – the outsourcing of my admin.

I look at Mia. Her eyes are still closed, but she must be able to sense that I'm free from my captor.

'We still need to come up with a plan for you to confess your undying love to Peter.'

'OK, let's calm down. I do not love Peter. I said that a *small* part of me *might* fancy Peter. But I'm not going to do anything, now or indeed ever. Peter and I are just friends.' The reality is that I'm much better friends with Peter than I ever was with Sam; should anything ever happen between us I imagine the hurt would be that much worse. He's often the one who helps put me back together when I need it, but if he's also the one to break me, what happens? Who would I go to? 'I'm not going to flush our friendship down the drain because a small part of me might fancy him.'

'Well, I don't see how you can stay where you are either, so you might as well try.'

She has a point there. It's possible that even the thought of potentially fancying Peter has changed my ability to remain his friend.

Bollocks.

All of a sudden, I wish I'd opted for a massage instead of a wax.

But Mia has to be wrong. There's a reason Peter and I have never been anything more than friends, and that reason is because we shouldn't. My plan is clear: I will stop fancying him.

'There are some good tips in there,' she says, pointing to the stack of paper.

My phone pings again.

'You really should turn that thing off.'

'I'll quickly read what it says and then I promise I'll turn it off.'

> I've been thinking about that favour you owe me.

The text is from Peter. I feel my face redden.

> I'd like to cash it in. I have a work function coming up that I really don't want to go to but can't get out of. Come with me and save me from my colleagues? There will be free food and all the prosecco you could want.

Mia was right. I really should have turned my phone off.

Chapter 27

'You haven't replied to my text.' Peter doesn't even bother with a hello before getting straight to the point.

It is Summer Games Night and someone has already taken the emergency strawberries out of my hands before I have even been able to cross the threshold. Apparently, someone mistakenly put all the non-emergency straw-berries into the Pimm's, leaving none over for the Eton Mess. What a disaster. Luckily I was late and could pick some up on the way.

'Oh, sorry. Mia and I were on a spa day and I didn't get any messages until later, and then by the time I looked at my phone I was all dazed. I didn't mean to not reply.' Of course this is exactly what I meant to do. I ignored the message in the hope he would forget that I hadn't replied and would then find someone else to take to his work event. Before I can stop myself, I keep going. 'I would love to come though.'

At this he gives me a hug, and I don't know how to feel.

I break the hug off a little abruptly.

I try to hide my discomfort by digging into my bag. 'Your birthday card.' It isn't his birthday until next week but I know he's away with work then, and he's not the type to think about having a party. I pass the card to Peter, along with my traditional present – highly over-priced American sweets, the small red fish that contain all the E-numbers but taste absolutely delicious. I give them to him every year, and every year he opens them up straight away and gives me the first one.

This year is no different.

I take the sweet quickly before he shields them from everyone else.

I can barely hear his thank-you over people nagging him.

'Come on, Oddly! Just one. I only want one.'

'Thanks, Bea. This is my favourite present every year.' I smile back at him, until I see Mia looking at me from across the room, dice in hand, ready to roll. Her eyes are saying a lot.

I avoid her gaze and instead look around the room. We always optimistically hope to play outdoor games for our summer meet-up, but obviously everyone is busy for most of the summer, so we've missed the month of sunshine and now it's raining again so we've been forced back inside. I don't know what game I want to play, but I gravitate towards the card table, abandoning Peter whilst he continues to defend his fish. It looks like they're playing Racing Demon. It's quite a fast-paced, aggressive card game. Often we only get through a couple of rounds before the shouting starts and we have to split up.

I sit down and start shuffling the pack of cards in front

of me. Everyone else can shuffle like a professional card dealer in Vegas, whereas I just smear the cards around.

'So, Bea, are you going?'

Rahul, sitting to my right, disturbs my card-smearing reverie. He's the best cook out of all of us, and although he isn't hosting today, he often brings delicious snacks. A part of me decided to sit next to him in the hope of preferential treatment.

'Sorry, I wasn't listening. Am I going to what?'

'Our ten-year History reunion.'

'Oh God, no.'

I continue to 'shuffle'.

'Yes, you are. You bought a ticket.' This is Mia, who is shouting from the sofa, collecting someone else's money. I'm not close enough to count, but I can see wads of fake cash on her side of the board and assume she's winning, and winning comfortably.

'What? No I didn't.'

'Yes, you did. We bought the tickets together.' It must have been way back at the start of the year. Too long ago for me to remember.

I go back into my memory box and search it for anything that resembles me buying a ticket to a night of unnecessary emotional torture.

'Nope, I don't remember this.'

'Check your emails. The ticket is in there.'

Ah yes, the email inbox. A better, more reliable memory box. I put aside the badly shuffled cards, only for someone to immediately pick them up and shuffle them much more proficiently, and get my phone out from my pocket.

Bollocks. As soon as I see the email, I remember the terrible (yet part of me is jealous that I didn't come up with it myself) reUNIon logo pun.

'Ugh. Why did I say I would go?'

'From memory, you were hoping Rupert MacWhats-hisface would be there.'

At this I blush.

'Rupert MacDonald. And you remember his name – stop trying to pretend that you didn't notice him when he stretched and his T-shirt would ride up a little.'

A couple of the girls nod in agreement and my eyes immediately go to Peter. I hope he doesn't think that just because I would ogle Rupert MacWhatshisface I only find muscly physiques attractive. Because I don't. I mean, I do but . . . argh.

'OK, fine. He did have a good body. And you are coming.'

But I barely hear her answer, because somehow, in between thinking about Rupert and worrying about Peter, I'm now wondering what it would look like if Peter's shirt rode up a little when he stretched.

Having accidentally won a game, I retire to the kitchen and refresh my glass.

'So?'

Mia barges in behind me.

'Hey.'

'What's this about you and Peter going out?'

I busy myself at the sink. 'We're not going out. He has a work thing and doesn't want to go by himself.' I look around the kitchen. It appears we are alone but I have no idea how sound travels in this apartment, so I make a shushing motion and hope that Mia gets the point.

'I think it's a date and you haven't admitted it to your-self yet. What are you going to wear?'

'Nothing.'

'Well, that will cause a stir.'

'I don't actually mean "nothing", Mia. I haven't thought about it because it's not a date.'

'Have you read the research I gave you?'

'No.' It's currently gathering dust on my windowsill. I keep ripping more and more strips off the top sheet as makeshift gum wrappers.

'Well, you should. But honestly, I think it could be as simple as getting drunk and shagging him.'

I look through to the lounge. Peter has taken my spot next to Rahul. In an unusual turn of events, it looks like they're preparing for a second game of Racing Demon.

'I hate to tell you this, but you're really going to have to get over your obsession with me and Peter. Even if I did fancy him, he doesn't fancy me.'

'Oh, for goodness' sake.'

I shush her and motion to all the other people in the next room.

She continues in an angry whisper. 'Let's look at his recent behaviour. He spent the whole of my wedding staring at you. He built a business plan for you in his free time, despite the fact he gets paid to do that during the week. At my birthday drinks, he brought someone else with him, but nevertheless proceeded to spend more time talking to *you* and looking out for *you* than for her. *And* he's just asked you out on a date.'

'You're seeing what you want to see.'

'Yeah, well, right now I see an idiot.'

I'm still not used to pregnant Mia. I'm not sure what to say.

'Oh God. Sorry.' She dabs at her eyes. I don't know how we arrived at tears so quickly after insults, but we did.

'Don't be.' Her comment did sting, but I'm going to choose to ignore it. The tears are more shocking. 'Pregnancy makes you really straight-talking. I kinda like it. I kinda fancy you right now.'

Chapter 28

Once again, Mia was right. I should have thought about what to wear. But I didn't, which is why I now find myself in a dress that I panic-purchased earlier in the day, despite the fact it's far too expensive for my budget. I feel extra guilty as I rang my mum in the shop, forcing her to share my anxiety about the cost.

She's already put the money in my account.

And it is a beautiful dress, even though it isn't quite *me*.

It turns out the 'work function' is actually a really weird, super niche awards ceremony hosted by a comedian who used to appear on televised panel shows. According to Peter, the company he works for bought a whole table but only his team were obliged to go, and funnily enough they were finding it hard to fill the other seats, meaning everyone in his team – including the intense speed dater, Al – has been obliged to bring a plus one.

I'm so intrigued about Al's plus one that I almost forget how extremely awkward I feel about the whole thing. Almost. But now is not the time to let Dream Peter back into my head, especially not as I can now see Real Peter.

He looks a little nervous this evening. Handsome, too, in a dark-grey suit.

I reach out to him. 'Hey.' I give him a quick hug. 'You OK?'

'Yes, I'm good. Are you good?'

'Yes, I'm really good.' I try to use a calming voice because he really does look nervous. It's an odd role reversal. I hope he is OK. We haven't quite let go of each other yet.

'Bea, you are beautiful.'

I turn pink and finally let go of him. I squirm a bit.

I'm particularly bad at receiving compliments in normal life, let alone at a fancy do where I feel like a total imposter in my new dress, my new shoes and my favourite underwear.

'You too. You couldn't scrub up well even if you tried.' That came out wrong. He's frowning at me now. 'I mean, you don't need to scrub up because you always look good.'

I hope I recovered that well enough. He really does look good.

This is not helping me keep Dream Peter at bay.

'Well, thank you for coming. Having you here will make the whole evening much more fun.'

'Of course. I told you I owed you one.'

'Quite, but I actually had fun at the fair. I worry that tonight will be full of highly awkward conversations. You've met Al –' I nod – 'so you know how odd he is. But he's actually one of the more normal ones amongst us.'

He holds out his arm for me to link with and we walk into the room.

'I'm excited to meet your work friends.'

'Really?'

'Yes!' We walk on a little further. 'But I'm more excited about the free food.' I feel Peter relax a bit beside me.

Much to my dismay, when we reached the table we realized that we weren't sitting next to each other. Instead, my name had been placed next to Peter's boss on one side and Al's date, a surprisingly normal girl called Beth who works for a charity, on the other. And thanks to the seating arrangements, with Peter's seat being directly opposite me, all night long I've been forced to look at another person's plus one fawn over him. She made him laugh once, and I had to suppress a pang of jealousy.

Batting away the urge to punch her as she begins to pull him to his feet, I realize that she's trying to get him up and dancing. Unlike me, she doesn't know about Peter's lack of dance skills. She's about to be in a world of pain and I almost feel sorry for her feet. Having wanted to look at anything else all night long, now I can't tear my eyes away.

But he doesn't go off with her. Instead, he moves away from her and towards me.

'Dance with me.'

'You can't dance. And I'm far too sober. I'll feel every accidental injury.'

'I know, but that woman doesn't care that I can't dance. And I can't be on the dance floor with her. She'll eat me alive. It was bad enough at the very well-lit table. I dread to think what she would be like on the dance floor under the cover of semi-darkness. Save me. Please.'

I look at her. There is a lot of determination in her eyes. She has an air of confidence that only continental Europeans have about them.

Then I look at Peter.

I can't help the laugh that escapes. 'You actually do look a bit scared.'

'I'm more than a bit scared. I'm petrified.'

He grabs my hand and we go to the dance floor.

I have been close to Peter before, but as he pulls me to him, I don't quite know where to put my hands. Everywhere suddenly feels too intimate.

The awkwardness is replaced by pain when Peter steps on my foot.

'Sorry.'

I can't help the sharp inhale but: 'It's fine, you've done worse.' He definitely has. 'Do you remember the time you gave me a black eye?'

'Yes, yes I do remember that. But ceilidhs are notoriously violent.'

'Violent? They're choreographed dances.'

'Yes, violent choreographed dances.'

'Maybe with you around.'

It's only when the song has finished that I realize we danced the rest of the time in silence, my hands somehow finding their way up, pulling myself closer to Peter, my head relaxing against him.

The lull in the music helps me to clear my head. I step away and say the only safe thing I can think to say.

'I'm going to go get a drink.'

*

Once at the bar I'm able to breathe again.

'He's quite the catch, that one, huh? Are you guys going to try the long-distance thing?'

'Sorry?' I turn towards the voice and find myself looking at Al, who has cornered me at the edge of the bar.

'The long-distance thing? I assume you'll be doing the long-distance thing when Peter moves to Australia in January?'

Peter is moving to Australia? In January? This coming January? Oblivious to my turmoil, Al keeps going.

'I was quite annoyed when they offered him the placement over me. It's a great opportunity to go and set up the new digital arm.' He takes another sip of his drink. 'Or I suppose you could move with him. I can't remember from our five minutes what you do for a living. Will you be able to move with him?'

I feel dizzy.

'Oh, no, I . . . I'm not . . . We're not—'

'Of course, it's only for a couple of years. They could fly by. Between you and me, I think the London office doesn't really want to let him go.'

A barman comes over to take our order, but all I can do is stand there like a guppy, because, fuck . . .

I don't want him to go either.

Chapter 29

I fucking fancy my fucking friend and now that fucking friend is moving to fucking Australia.

After Al let the news slip, I made up a very pathetic excuse about drinking too much prosecco and escaped home. I haven't messaged Peter since, and he hasn't messaged me with his news either. I wonder if that was why he looked so uncomfortable at the start of the evening. Meanwhile my thoughts remain very confused. This is precisely why dating friends is a bad idea. I'm sad enough that he's moving away; imagine if anything had actually happened between us.

Luckily, helping with Tilly's wedding is proving to be quite a nice distraction. Apparently six bridesmaids weren't enough to pull this thing off in time. We're currently at a lunch-time cake-tasting appointment. I eat when I'm anxious. The samples have had to be replenished twice already.

'Do you think the vanilla sponge is boring? Are people bored of vanilla? Or is it a classic for a reason?'

I shovel another bite into my mouth to refresh my memory. Unable to answer, I shake my head.

'No –' I try to get out some words anyway – 'it's delicious. So light and fluffy.'

She takes a tiny bite.

The smiley baker sits down opposite us. 'Have you decided?' Being a cake baker must be the best occupation in the world. Imagine always being within easy reach of sponge. No wonder she's so smiley.

I look over to Tills.

'Yes. Vanilla for the big tier, lemon for the middle tier and gluten-free carrot cake for the top tier.'

The cake lady claps. 'Perfect! A wonderful combination.' She stands up again. 'Let me go get my diary to write down all the details.'

'Thanks for coming today.' Tills faces me.

'Are you kidding? Eating is the only sport I've ever excelled at.' As if to prove a point, I take a bite of the chocolate cake. Part of me thinks she made a mistake with the vanilla, even though it is really fluffy. 'Are you OK though? You do look quite tired.'

'It's just all this wedmin. I should have listened to you when you told me I was nuts to try and organize the whole thing in five months. I've had to cash in all the favours people owe me, and I think it's all on track, but there are some things I don't think I'm going to be able to do. I didn't appreciate how many things there were to arrange. We're only able to get this cake because another customer dropped out.'

'Ooo! Interesting. Did you get the gossip? Is the wedding no longer happening?'

'Bea, that is terrible!' She takes another bite. 'But no. Apparently the bride's father is now making the cake.'

'Well, more fool them. This is delicious.'

I take yet another bite, despite the fact I now feel quite ill.

Tilly frowns and gestures towards my fork. 'I've only ever seen you eat like this when you're anxious. What's up? Are you stressed about my wedding too?'

I swallow my mouthful. 'No, no, no.'

'If it's not the wedding, then what is it?'

Tilly doesn't know Peter, so she would be a good person to talk to, but she's currently so in love with being in love that I worry her advice won't be subjective.

'Honestly, nothing. There is nothing making me anxious.'

'I don't believe you.'

'Really.' I cross my heart with the fork and fling crumbs everywhere. 'I swear.'

Tilly takes a sharp inhale of breath and I know she isn't done with her interrogation.

Luckily the cake lady comes back with her diary and a pen. 'OK, where were we?'

My phone alarm goes off and I jump, even though I was the one to set it.

'Sorry.' I turn it off and look sheepish. I have another session with the assistants that I don't want to be late for. 'I need to go.' And not a moment too soon. Tilly still does not look appeased by my answers. 'I don't suppose you have a box for the rest of this cake . . .?' I gesture at the leftovers and see Tilly look at me with slight disbelief.

Chapter 30

By the time reUNIon day rolls around, I am fully practised in the art of distraction. My flat has never been so clean. My wardrobe has been reorganized so it's now colour coordinated. I can do a fishtail braid in my hair. I've made so many cards that I've almost completed my store Christmas orders already, and it's only just October. I've also been actively not fancying Peter. Actively not fancying Peter has made me very productive.

If I stop fancying Peter, I'll stop feeling so confused, and I'll feel better about him moving to Australia – I'll only be sad as a friend.

Unfortunately, my brain didn't quite get the memo and chose Wednesday as the night to have another Peter dream. It was one of those dreams that seemed very real – no walking dolphins in sight. We were an item, and it all felt natural and familiar; it was even more disturbing than the sex dream.

Even my phone is mocking me. He's always in my 'frequent contacts', no matter how many other people I message, and even though Tilly has knocked him down a spot due to all of the wedding-related messages. Today's drama was about the florist. I had to spend about an hour in the stationery cupboard talking to someone about the availability of dahlias.

Almost as though he knows I'm watching my phone, a message from him pings through.

Hey – hope you have fun at the reunion this evening. x

I don't message him back. It's not as if there was a question in there anyway. Or any life-changing, Australia-related news either. Why hasn't he told me? I can't believe I've gone from avoiding Mia to avoiding Peter.

I put my phone away, head up the steps and through the imposing wooden doors.

I'm early for an event I don't particularly want to go to.

But I arrived early to help control the nerves. I don't know exactly why I'm nervous, but I don't need to make myself more nervous by being late and sweaty. I also need to find somewhere quiet, out of the way and a walkable distance from the venue to change my shoes.

I wait for Mia in the loo downstairs. She says she's ten minutes away. An uncomfortably long time to wait in the loo if anyone has seen you go in. But I'm here now, and so here I will remain.

When she does eventually text me to say she's on her way to the loo, I venture out of my cubicle and pretend I've been touching up my make-up.

Hellos over and hands washed, Mia is keen to get going. 'Come on, let's head up before the queue for drinks gets too long.'

My entrance is not exactly as I'd hoped (walking upstairs in these heels and this fitted skirt isn't easy) but we make it. However, my relief is soon over when we walk into the function room. If I named the top fifteen people I never wanted to see again in my life, at least twelve would be in this room.

The only saving grace is that I think I can see the shoulders of Rupert MacDonald in the corner. I realize with shock that I don't know if I would recognize him face-on, having positioned myself on the table behind him for three years straight, so when he turns around I'm none the wiser.

We get our drinks – cheap wine for me, elderflower cordial for Mia – and then peruse the room. One skill I have proudly developed during my time on this planet is an instinctive understanding of where to stand for superior canapé access. Tonight is no exception.

The only issue is that Harriet is already standing in the perfect spot. Harriet, my arch-nemesis.

My dislike of her was instant. I think it was her voice that first alerted me to her existence; she sounded (and still sounds) alarmingly like some kind of bird. Disturbingly, she also always wore matching cardigans and tops. I don't know how she did it. I also don't know why she did it. I assume they came as a set, but goodness only knows where she found so many to buy. If memory serves, she was particularly fond of a pastel yellow. But most frustratingly she was also very intelligent, and would always show me up in our tutorials. She would be the first to take out the required reading from the library, she could remember even the smallest of details, and her vocabulary was second to none.

Let's not fool ourselves. I didn't dislike her. I hated her.

But everyone else seemed to love her, which of course made me hate her even more.

I've remembered one more thing. She would write on paper from her 'Daddy's office', insisting it was the best.

Mia beams when she sees her. I shrivel and prepare my ears for an onslaught.

'Mia, oh my goodness, you haven't changed a bit! It's so good to see you!'

They do three ceremonious air kisses before Harriet turns her attention to me. 'I'm sorry, I don't think we've ever met. I'm Harriet.'

Obviously, we have met before. She recognizes me – she just wants to be a bitch. Fine. I can deal with that.

'We took about six modules together over three years and were in the same tutorials for most of them. But don't worry. It was a while ago. My name is Bea.'

'Oh, Bea, of course. Sorry – you've changed so much.'

She means I've put on weight. She's not wrong, but she is rude.

'You too.' Ha! 'But I guess that's only natural . . . it has been a long time since the Cold War. Learning about it, obviously.'

'Obviously.' She not-so-subtly angles away from me. 'So, Mia, what have you been up to?'

I keep my face as open and approachable-looking as possible, but inside I shut down. After tonight I will never have to see these people again. I will never be hood-winked into coming to another one of these things.

At least at school reunions you get to wander around

previously forbidden places like the staff room, but here I am scared to walk away in case I look like a crab and give Harriet even more ammunition.

It's such a random collection of people too. I doubt the majority of these people ever spoke to each other at university, so why do they think they'll have anything in common now?

I'm reaching the maximum amount of time I'm able to listen to Harriet's voice and start to look for an escape route. I resort to an oldie but a goodie – I finish my drink and head away for a top-up. As soon as I move, mini burgers come out, and yep, they head straight to where I was standing. Still, missing a mini burger is a small price to pay for the safety of your future hearing and sanity.

It's like a minefield of foes in here, and I can't see a safe way to the drinks table. I opt for the route that has the most backs facing my path.

Safely at the drinks station (a table covered with a whitish cloth), I ask the person behind the table for another glass of red wine, and I'm left exposed as she hunts around for a new bottle. Apparently someone underestimated the popularity of the red.

'Hi.' I turn to face the voice. 'You probably don't remember me but, well, this is embarrassing, we kinda used to study together. I'd always sit in front of you in the library.'

Holy shit! It's the man I potentially identified as Rupert MacDonald. I was right.

His voice is different from how I imagined it to be. It's quite, well, feminine.

'Hi. And actually yes, I do remember. I spent a lot of

time staring at your back.' Oops. 'Because we were in the library, I mean. I spent most of my time staring at anything that wasn't actually a book.' Awkward.

'Yeah, I get what you mean. Honestly, I always sat there because I felt I would be letting everyone down if I didn't show up.' He has no idea. 'Like we were all studying together and if one of us failed, we all would. That's what I told myself anyway. It's the only way I got good enough grades to pass.'

'Hey, you gotta do whatever works for you.' Like ogling a stranger's back for three years. 'So what do you do now? Except go to awkward social gatherings.'

'I'm a curtain manager.'

'Oh! Cool!' A what?

'Yeah, it's slightly unusual I guess, as careers go. I get to see a lot of shows. Although I've been on the same show for the last year, so it's probably time to move on. It's pretty fun though.'

'Yeah, I can imagine.' I'm getting there. Curtains at the theatre. Can't be as simple as it sounds. 'So what does it entail? I'm so intrigued.'

'Well, I basically open the curtain at the beginning of the show, close it for the interval, and repeat for the second half.'

Huh. It is as simple as it sounds. It's not the life I'd thought Rupert would have. I'd assumed he would work for a bank and be a part-time model. I find it quite inspiring. He's following his dream.

Thankfully the person who went to hunt down the red wine has returned, and not a moment too soon. I don't really know where else to take this conversation. 'Here's your drink. Sorry about the delay.'

'Oh, no worries. Thank you.' I turn back to Rupert. 'It was really nice to talk to you. I hope you have much success with . . . finding new curtains to open.'

Oh God. Did that sound like a euphemism?

I smile, hopefully in a kind, not a creepy, manner, and turn away.

Something adjacent to a laugh cuts through the noise of the room. It's Harriet. I wonder if my strength has replenished enough to re-join the circle that has formed around her. I wander closer to the group.

'. . . and then when we realized it was tap water we all got up and left. Who would serve tap water to people you should be trying to impress?'

Nope. I can't help it; I shake my head. She's not someone I need to make more effort with.

I sail straight past, suddenly finding a painting in the corner of the room very interesting.

I think the painting is really very bad, but I do the head-tilt thing anyway.

'I think I would demand to get my money back if I'd commissioned a painting of myself and it came out like that.'

I turn towards the face behind the voice; I don't recognize either.

'Hi, I'm Bea.' I hold out my hand. I still don't know if people still shake hands any more, but it's too late to back out now.

'Michelle.'

'I don't think we met at uni.'

'I don't think we did either.' She meanders closer to the painting. 'Good lord, I don't know why I came here this evening.' She looks so confident. Her dress isn't one I would choose, but it makes me want to go out and buy more clothes with colours. 'Well, no, that's a lie – I know why I came. My husband made me come, but now I'm here and I wish I wasn't, so I've been trying to find somewhere, or someone, safe to hang out with. That woman's voice –' with a nod towards Harriet – 'is driving me *nuts*.'

I can't help but let out a laugh. 'Oh, thank God. I'm so glad it's not just me.'

'It isn't. I think my husband took one module with her in first year, learnt from his mistake, and chose all his other modules based on whether or not she was also in the class.'

'Who's your husband?'

'That man over there with a handful of snacks.'

'I like him already.'

'Me too. Although I would like him more if some of those snacks were for me.'

'So why did he want to come?'

'Apart from the food? I think he genuinely wants to know what people are up to. I think he's actually interested. I lean towards the idea that I keep up with everyone I want to keep up with anyway.'

'I'm in that camp too.' I take a sip of the horrible wine.

'So, seeing as I know nothing about you except for the fact we went to the same university but never met, tell me about yourself.'

Tell her what about myself? 'What would you like to know?'

'Anything you're willing to share.'

I exhale and shift my weight from one foot to the other. What do I want her to know? I remember my prepared answers, but my run-in with Rupert has left me feeling like it's OK to just go with the truth. So I do.

'I am *so* frustrated with how I've been living my life. For years I've been working at a job that I don't particularly like, I avoid any kind of real intimacy, and I'm uncomfortable about the idea of putting myself out there because I'm so afraid of failure. And I do all this because I think that doing these things, or not doing these things, will make me happy, or at least keep me from being unhappy, but they don't. I've been burying my head in the sand.' I keep my eyes on the painting. 'I think I'm coming out of it, and I think I know what it is I want to do, but I still don't quite know how I'm going to do it, and I'm still really afraid that I'm going to fail. And the irony is, the further I go down this path and the more I try not to fail, the worse failure is going to feel.'

I'm on a roll now and I can't stop, so I keep going. My hands are flapping everywhere, and I'm at risk of spilling the wine.

'But I can't keep going through life like a zombie. I want to work for myself. I want to cut myself out a little piece of the world, a unique identity that is totally mine. I want to work at something that actually feels like *me*, something more creative, more challenging.'

I breathe slightly more deeply. Michelle is looking at

me. She's either processing all the words I just threw up or she's working out an escape route.

'Oh, and I've also just realized that I fancy my best friend.'

I feel lighter than I have in months. My jaw has even stopped clenching.

'Sorry. I think I might have taken that a bit too far.' I look down at my glass. How strong is this wine?

'No, you didn't. I get it. I come from a family of lawyers. I studied law at university. I even got a first. And then I decided what I really wanted to do was own a shop, where everything was an item I had picked out and curated.'

'How did that go down?'

'At first, not well. But now they see I'm happy.' She smiles. 'I think they needed some time to come to terms with the idea that their version of happy wasn't necessarily mine.'

She's right. Someone else's version of happy isn't necessarily my version of happy.

I am going to stop going to yoga.

'So, what is it that you actually want to do?'

Maybe kickboxing?

Despite wanting to be more confident, I can't help the slight insecure grimace that I make. 'It sounds ridiculous, but I make cards – as in greeting cards. Mainly funny ones, plays on words. They're for the sophisticated pun maker.' I try to pull a sophisticated face.

I expect her to nod in general understanding, but instead she asks, 'Do you have any on you?'

'Yes, actually I do. These are some I've been working

on during my down-time at work.' I rustle around for them in my bag and hand them over. 'They're mock-ups, but you can get a feel for them. High-quality paper, high-quality puns.' I do a goofy grin and a shoulder shrug. Both came much more naturally than a sophisticated face.

She spends some time inspecting them, both the puns and the paper. She also sniffs them. Maybe I was too harsh on the lady at the fair. Maybe lots of people sniff cards.

'These are actually pretty good. And funny. I was worried I was going to have to pretend to laugh.'

'There are a lot of jokes that get culled for that very reason.'

'Can I keep these?'

'Sure. If you sell them, feel free to give me a fair share of the money.'

She just laughs. 'Sure thing.' She puts the cards into her bag. She looks like she's about to leave.

'Here.' I rummage around in my bag and find a business card. I'm so glad I made some for the fair. And that I had most of them left over. 'This is my business card. I don't know what you sell in your shop, but if you're ever after a card supplier, let me know. I promise I'm not normally so . . . talkative.'

She nods and takes the card. 'I'll bear all of that in mind.' She magics up one of her own with far less fanfare than I needed and passes it to me. 'Here are my details.' She motions behind her. 'Now I'm going to go collect my husband and see if I can encourage him to take me to dinner. It was nice to meet you, Bea.'

'You too.' I smile and do a mini wave as she retreats.

From the looks of things he doesn't need much encouraging.

Now that Michelle has escaped, both me and the reunion, I get my phone out so nobody else talks to me, and message my mum about Harriet. She also disliked her intensely, solely based on my reviews, and I know she will relish the fact that Harriet is still wearing matching layered outfits.

Chapter 31

Whilst I'm still in wedding mode (and not fancying Peter mode) and currently in the midst of a neon-driven online shop (essential prep for Tilly's eighties-themed hen party), Joan's face pops up in front of my desk. Unfortunately I was too distracted to notice her until it was too late to run away.

'Hey, how are you?'

She sounds far too chirpy and nice. She must want something. I double-check my glass, just in case it's accidentally her mug.

'I'm good thanks, you?' Sometimes I hate pleasantries, but sometimes pleasantries are all you have.

'Yes, very well, despite the awful weather.' Ah, weather talk, aka the bridge between pleasantries and requests. 'I wanted to say thank you for the help you're giving Emily and the others. I don't know quite what you've been telling them in those little sessions of yours, but their work is going through a lot more smoothly. Less confusion and reworking.'

This is interesting. This almost sounds like an apology. I like it. Although I do not appreciate the term 'little sessions'. These 'little sessions' have been going on for months, and are now accompanied by a helpful digital guide I created.

'We are so alike, you and I.' I stop myself from scoffing in the nick of time. I most certainly hope not. 'We just want to make sure we get the very best results.' She takes a long inhale and I wait, not in the slightest bit eagerly, to hear what she's going to ask for. 'So anyway –' finally we get to the request – 'I was wondering if I could suggest a couple of topics for you to cover. I'm having issues getting through to Emily on some development points, and, well, you seem to be able to talk her language, and so I was hoping you would be able to speak to her about them?'

She has some nerve. She condescendingly calls them 'little sessions', but then requests more topics to be added.

I churn on an idea and come up with something I think I might enjoy.

'Fine. Sure. Send me over the topics you think need covering. But you'll have to give me your reasoning behind the development areas. And you'll have to remember that people don't improve exponentially overnight.' And then I add the cherry on top. 'And you'll also have to be willing to take some feedback from me too.' Emily has told me a lot about Joan's managerial skills, which I think mainly amount to Joan shouting at Emily through doors. I like Emily and she doesn't deserve to be shouted at.

Joan chews her cheek at the mention of me giving her feedback.

'Fine. Deal. I'll send a list through this afternoon.'

With today's wedmin all done and Joan's list not yet hitting my inbox, my afternoon is oddly free, punctuated by a quick trip to the new coffee shop around the corner. The coffee is fine, but I am delighted to find that the food samples are generous in size, taste and variety, covering both the savoury and sweet palate.

Perhaps it's the bewitching combination of sugary baked goods and caffeine (especially as the former was free), or possibly the fact I have escaped the office, but I feel liberated and decide to do something I haven't done in a while.

I sit down to drink my coffee in the actual coffee shop.

As I watch all the people, I realize that everyone here is working. It would be gloriously dangerous for me to work here – they would have to reassess their taster policy – but it would also be just plain glorious. I have never been productive in an office. I need change. I need snacks. I need good coffee.

And then I realize. I have space and time now. So I put down the coffee and get out my phone.

I scout out more potential new stockists.

I email Michelle with a mini follow-up.

I make my personalized Christmas cards – a 'Boast in the Post' – available on my online shop. I hoped they might help phase out those awful family update letters aunts seem so keen to send at this time of year.

I write a backlog of social media posts.

I imagine what my studio might look like when I'm rich and famous.

I start doodling new card designs.

It feels good.

*

When the end of the work day eventually rolls around, I feel very satisfied with myself.

Normally I love escaping, alone, to the sanctuary of my apartment on a Friday evening, but tonight I'm not in the mood.

I could just accept my fate and go home but I don't want to. I could go to the pub with work 'friends'. I could text Mia to see if she's free. I can*not* text Peter.

I text Mia. She's not free.

I ask who's going to the pub after work. Joan is the only definite. Penny is busy, and Emily has a date.

Still not ready to accept my fate and still determined not to text Peter, I meander through my phone and my recent messages, using it to jog my memory and remember what friends I actually have.

I don't think I could handle more Tilly right now.

My mum and my brother are too far away.

Colin.

I *could* text Colin.

It's been quite a while since he branded my neck, but since the spa day I've been following the beautician's advice and have been keeping up my admin, meaning my vagina is prepared for visitors.

Why does Peter's face loom in my mind every time I think of my vagina?

We've all heard the phrase, 'If you want to get over him, you've got to get under someone else'.

I can do this.

He might even bring chicken.

Chapter 32

Colin's knock comes sooner than I hoped it would, as I am currently in a downward swing of confidence, unsure if I've done the right thing inviting him over.

Knowing I can't leave him outside (no matter how many excuses I come up with in my mind), I open the door.

'Hi.'

'I brought chicken.'

'I thought I knew that smell.' I'm impressed with my fake confidence.

He comes in, gives me a kiss that has more tongue in it than I would have chosen, and puts the chicken in the kitchen.

It isn't a nice kitchen, and I only rent the apartment, but I really want to put the sweaty, greasy bag on a plate and preserve the nasty countertop that I am now apparently overprotective of.

But there's no time; he turns around and heads towards me, his intent clear in his eyes. And because I'm pretending to be a confident sex-tress instead of someone who feels uncomfortable about where he put the chicken, I try to get my eyes to give him a sexy look.

He stops and leans down. I use his shoulders to steady me, and edge up on my toes. It's quite awkward. Nothing like the dream with Peter.

Not the time, Bea. I really need to get him out of my head. Colin. Colin is here. Colin wants to have sex with me. I might want to have sex with Colin.

We kiss.

The angles are all a bit off. It isn't giving me the tingles. It's not that it's bad, but it isn't setting my world on fire.

Am I asking too much for my world to be set on fire?

It's probably me; I am probably the reason my world isn't currently on fire. I need to stop worrying and thinking, and instead allow my world to be set on fire. By Colin, the chicken man.

He breaks away quickly. 'Let's take this to the bedroom.'

I look towards the counter.

'But the chicken will get cold.'

Apparently that isn't a good enough reason. He smiles and guides me, a touch more aggressively than I am comfortable with, to the bedroom. He does have a nice smile, and he is a good kisser. And he did bring chicken. And I have nothing else to do. Let's do this. Get under someone. I wonder if he will growl again.

He starts undressing. Why is he always so keen to get naked?

Personally, I hate this part, but not necessarily because I don't want him to see me naked. Something I'm grateful for is the growing acceptance I have of my body and all its lumps and bumps. I know I could do with more gym time and less chicken, but my body is my body, and it has housed my soul well for the last thirty-something years.

But what I don't like are witnesses to me undressing.

I'm very aware that I undress like a toddler. I bend in the wrong places. I take things off in the wrong sequence. My feet get stuck. Nothing about the way I undress is sexy, which is unfortunate as the undressing happens at a peak moment in the run-up to sex.

By the look of things, my awkward undressing hasn't dampened his desire. That's good, I guess.

We resume the kissing and his hands start wandering as we lie down on the bed. Mine won't move from his shoulders.

Then he starts moving his head lower. I might be plucked and primed and aesthetically ready for him, but I don't want his face going there.

So instead, I grab his penis.

He can't go further down if he can't move his penis. He moans and stops moving down, thank God. Bribery and distraction work so well – maybe I'm good at this. Maybe I could actually enjoy this.

'Sit on my face.'

Wait, what?

'What did you say?'

'Sit on my face.'

My vagina is in risk of retreat.

'Ummm, no thanks, not right now.'

He grabs my neck, and I am definitely not OK with it.

'Sit on my face.'

All of a sudden I panic. Shit balls. I don't know anything about Colin. Why have I done this? It all feels very wrong. My vagina has fully retreated.

I shake my head. 'Please stop.'

He lets me go. Thank God.

'I'm really sorry, but you need to leave.'

He looks at me with a very confused face.

'What? I won't grab you again, if that's what you're worried about. I was just in the moment. I can get kinda kinky sometimes.' He gives me a face that I think is meant to be reassuring. I do not find it reassuring.

'I don't think – I'm sorry – I realize that I was the one who invited you here, but I don't want you here any more. Please go.' He doesn't move, so I make myself clear. 'Now.'

A while after he's gone, I pull on comforting clothes and head out of my bedroom.

Massive plus point – he left the chicken.

I put the chicken on a plate, wipe up the grease left by the bag, and decide to eat it all by myself. I don't think I can handle noise, so I don't turn on the TV, but I do need something to quiet my mind, so I look around my apartment for distraction.

As I sit down, I can see Mia's stack of research. I read her key points. Just out of interest.

Chapter 33

Having initially been very proud of the fact I did nothing towards organizing the hen party, I'm now starting to fear that *nobody* has done anything towards organizing the hen party. Everyone has already spent a fortune without actually doing anything. So far all we've done is wander around outside, getting wetter and colder. We are all looking tired and deflated. Our group chat explodes with a series of suggested locations and maps. I pretend to look, but as everyone else decides where to go, I'm actually answering emails and arranging bumper card deliveries ahead of Christmas. Apparently people love a festive boast.

Finally, we end up in a very poorly lit bar that appears to have cornered the market in memorabilia featuring palm trees and bright pink flamingos with sunglasses. It's perfect, and the slightly sticky floors add to the overall ambience. There is only one downside: two bar staff, and more than twenty people to serve all at once. As I wait at the bar, I'm reminded of Mia's birthday. And Peter saving me from an hour-long wait.

It's as if my brain can't escape him, no matter how hard I try not to fancy him.

It takes about thirty minutes for us all to sit down

with prosecco, but we've finally managed it and have commandeered the seating area at the back. Our gentle and sometimes stilted chatter comes to an abrupt end when one of the bridesmaids, I think her name is Nicole, stands up.

'Hello, ladies! I'm Nicole,' (yes), 'and I'm this *gorgeous* gal's maid of honour!' For some reason, maybe relief at being inside, or possibly because we now have a face to blame for our cold feet, we all whoop at this. 'And tonight, we are going to have some fun! Drink up because we've organized some activities –' you could have fooled me – 'and we need to leave here in about fifteen minutes!'

The mood shifts. Everyone has just got comfortable and now we're going to have to drink our overpriced prosecco too quickly to enjoy it, probably get a bit burpy, and then head back out into the cloud of rain.

Throughout my many years, I have learnt that at moments like this, you have two options. Option one: you accept that you're going to be miserable and hope to slip away early. Option two: you dive right in and hope that your enthusiasm can lift everyone's spirits.

Option one is definitely more Bea. But in an unusual turn of events, I go for option two. I'm already wearing eighties dance gear and Tilly deserves a fun hen party.

In hindsight, the shots I ordered were a good and a bad idea. They really separated the group, but luckily for this version of me who was eager to have a good time, I had more takers than leavers, and when our fifteen minutes were up, I'd made at least three new friends. We marked each other out by putting our compulsory temporary hen party tattoos on our foreheads.

But from Nicole's perspective, I imagine I was quickly becoming her worst nightmare. I was shouty and overly enthusiastic, as apparently that's the way this party gal rolled. But this party gal was also a secret weapon, Nicole just didn't know it yet.

Because although I was getting less sober, I was also getting more shouty and enthusiastic, so when Nicole asked for us to move on, I quickly became the person who was up and chivvying. I even held out people's coats to speed up the process. As if I was somebody who enjoyed organised fun.

And as soon as we arrive at our actual destination, I rather wish I hadn't chivvied.

We're at a gym.

What on earth are we doing at a gym?

'Ladies!' An extremely camp man sashays around the corner. 'We are here today to become Queens! Queen Beys!'

I have no idea what that means. Did he say my name?

'I'm going to guide you through her most iconic work of dance – "Single Ladies".'

On any normal day this might fill me with dread. But the current version of me, the one who does tequila shots at 4 p.m., actually claps and runs to get a space at the front, eager to watch (and try my very hardest to follow) what the dance instructor is doing.

And he is *good*. He makes me want to dance. He makes

me want to become a Queen Bey. But unfortunately his skill only goes so far. Every time I spy myself in the mirror, I'm not positioned how everyone else is. He knows I'm bad and at first he tries to help me, but soon gives up, saying, 'You gotta work with what ya got.'

And I don't got this.

I should have had more tequila, so at least I won't be able to remember the singular pain and humiliation that comes with being particularly bad at enforced group activities. But towards the end of the hour, despite the overall lack of coordination possessed by our dance troupe, he still insists on putting on a show, a show with Tills as the lead Bey.

I make a mental note to delete all footage of this. An act that everyone will thank me for.

And right at the part where we are all supposed to be bending down and stroking our bums, the lights go out. The music stops. There must have been a power cut.

The scene is quiet; a couple of people try to be proactive and take charge, a couple of others squeal.

But then a different song starts playing. Disco lights are going off everywhere. And someone dressed as a delivery man and holding a box comes in.

'I've got a special delivery for Matilda Bertram.'

Nicole's face is a picture of pure joy. Holy shit. She's organized a stripper. Most of me, and apparently everyone else, is shouting 'Yaaaaaaaas'. And just like that, all the wandering around in the cold and damp, the dancing and the rushed prosecco, has been forgiven and forgotten. Even the dance instructor is smiling.

Chapter 34

The hen party continued pretty much as anyone would have expected. Stripper, squealing, shots, dancing, confessions of love and questionable snogs. And the party gal version of me showed little sign of slowing down. Espresso martinis really keep you going.

But as soon as midnight strikes, the lonely hour hits. Some people, who weren't quite as dedicated to the party train as I was, have already left. Some claimed they had to get the last train home. Others said they had an early start the next morning. Some snuck out without so much as a wave.

And Tilly is nowhere to be seen. Even the hen has gone home.

It's clearly time for me to bow out semi-gracefully. I retreat to the safety of the loo.

But the queue for the loo is long and lonely. As I stand, lightly swaying, I can't help but notice how loud everyone is being now that there is no music to drown them out. The girls next to me are talking about their boyfriends, both of whom sound horrible. So I try to block them out. But blocking out the noise means I quietly think about Peter. He wouldn't be a horrible boyfriend.

I think about the way he always used to bring me a cheese and crisp sandwich whenever I was hungover. The way he helped my mum with the crossword by working out the answers and then giving her easier clues. There was one particular night I remember crystal clearly – we were sitting on a random bench, late at night on the way home, not saying a huge amount. But looking back, I wonder if I could have leaned across and kissed him. I didn't, of course. Because we were just friends.

But I don't think of him as just a friend any more.

I break out of the line.

I don't need to pee. I need to tell Peter how I feel. I need to tell him now, before he goes to Australia. I need to tell him now, before I bottle it.

I need two burritos and a taxi.

Chapter 35

I ring his doorbell a couple of times, not 100 per cent confident I'm at the right place.

'Bea? What are you doing here?' He squints a bit in the dark and turns on another light. 'What are you wearing? What the hell is on your forehead?'

I had forgotten about the Lycra. And the tattoo.

'It was Tilly's hen party. Are you going to let me in?' It's cold. My feet are doing a mini march on the spot.

'Come in. I'll make you tea. Are you drunk?' Yes, very.

'I brought burritos.'

'With guac?'

'And two types of beans.'

'Perfect.'

'Not for anyone who comes across you tomorrow.' Gross. Why did I have to go there? Fart jokes are never appropriate, but especially not tonight. I'm meant to be the most attractive version of myself tonight.

'So how was the party? From the look of things, pretty good.'

In my eighties dance gear, I feel very colourful against his grey walls. I should leave, I'm too drunk for this.

'Yeah, it was fun. I'm sorry. You're in your pyjamas. I

woke you up. I'll leave you alone. You can have both of the burritos.' I give him the bag and turn to leave, but he makes a move to try and stop me.

'Whoa, hold up.' A familiar hand on my arm. 'Bea, these are not pyjamas. These are my lounge pants.'

His smile makes me smile and I don't want to leave.

'It's cold, it's late. You're exhausted. It's *well* past your bedtime. Why don't we eat the burritos and then you can sleep here and go home in the morning.'

That does sound very tempting, and suddenly all I want to do is sleep. It's so nice and warm in here; despite now having a boiler that works, I rarely turn it on.

'Are you sure?'

He gets out a couple of plates and forks, and more than a couple of flower-patterned napkins that I'm sure he didn't buy himself. It's nice to think that he still lets his mum buy him the essentials.

He passes me all but one of the napkins. 'You spill.'

He's correct there.

'So, tell me.'

My eyes go wide. 'Tell you what? There's nothing to tell.'

'What happens at a hen party . . . there can't be nothing to tell.'

'Ha.' I'm relieved, but also a little disappointed. 'Nothing salacious happened. Just the usual. Strippers, group bonding through humiliation, whipped cream, shots, questionable dancing. You know.'

'They sound much more friendly than the male version. If I ever coerce someone into marrying me, I don't think I'd like to have a stag do. I don't know if I'm strong enough to survive. I think I would cry.'

The talk of marriage makes me clam up a bit. This conversation feels quite loaded. I manage to throw out a single word. Hopefully a lack of words will also mean a lack of mind-reading.

'Really?'

'Really. I've been on quite a few and they keep getting worse. Every stag do is bigger than the last. And the last one ended with the groom almost getting his manhood taken off by a baby bull. Men are competitive, and ideas are getting riskier with age. I'm not excited to see what happens on the next one.'

'Men?' I scoff in a forced, comedic way, hoping to get my heartbeat back to normal. 'Boys, more like.'

'Hey. I'm a man. I own lounge pants.' He motions to his legs. 'I've mowed a lawn.'

I look through the window. I can only see a wall. 'But you don't have a garden.'

'I didn't say I mowed my own lawn. I'm not a masochist. I would pay someone else to do that. I don't want my lawn to look terrible.'

'Again, you don't have a garden.'

'Details.' He shrugs and shovels a forkful of burrito into his mouth.

We sit in silence for a while. Not long, but long enough for the stare to get too intense. I break first.

'The burritos are probably cold and gross now, sorry.'

'I love burritos in all their forms and temperatures. Thank you for bringing them over.' He sits back against the sofa. 'I feel like you've been avoiding me. That maybe that night with me and all my work colleagues scarred you.' He has no idea. He touches my knee and I look up. I'm normally quite awkward with physical interaction. I never know what to do when someone touches me, but Peter's hand feels comforting. 'You really OK? You almost seem a little sad.'

'I'm good, really. It's nice to see you.' Despite his attempts to make me feel comfortable, I still feel a little exposed and unsure of myself.

'You too. I have to say, you look quite fetching in eighties gear.'

I hide my face in shame.

He pulls my hands away and uncovers my face. He gently tucks my hair behind my ear and smiles his slightly crooked smile. It makes me happy. I realize seeing him smile is one of my favourite things.

I came here to tell him the truth. Oh God, this is the moment I should be telling him I fancy him. But I can't because I don't fancy him.

I love him.

I don't know why it's taken me so long to realize. I love his stupid hair and I love the way he smiles. I love his terrible sense of humour and his too-loud laugh. I even love the way he dances. I love his attempts at cooking, although I feel safer when he orders in. I love how my apartment feels when he's in it. I love how he looks out for me no matter the situation. I love how he can follow my thoughts, and I love how he translates things for me so I can understand them. I love how he makes me feel that I'm OK just as I am.

But I will understand if he doesn't love me back. I don't particularly love me right now. I have to know if there's a chance.

But instead of saying all of that, I kiss him. It seems less scary.

He kisses me back, and for a moment everything is perfect. But then he gently pushes me away.

'Bea.'

I can't read what his eyes are saying, but I can't face rejection. Not tonight. Not from Peter.

'Please, just kiss me.'

And he does.

Chapter 36

Oh. Shit.

I'm in Peter's bed. What the fuck happened last night?

I stay very still, staring at the ceiling until I can be sure that he isn't asleep next to me. Where is he?

Why did I drink tequila?

Oh God. I kissed him. I know I kissed him. I remember that. That was nice. Oh God, that was stupid.

Why am I so stupid?

Oh my God. I was getting naked. I remember getting naked. Oh my God. We had sex. I am in his bed and we had sex in his bed. Shit. Fuck. Tits. I wish I could remember it.

I didn't even tell him how I feel. This was one thing I needed to do well and I did it very badly. I did it so badly I didn't do it at all.

Don't panic. Just think. What do I remember? Be calm. It's important to be calm. Follow the breadcrumbs. I remember bringing burritos. I remember him touching my hair. I remember him telling me I looked good in Lycra.

I remember kissing him.

I remember him leading me into the bedroom.

Oh God, my head hurts.

I remember some limbs. I remember undressing. I remember undressing and, oh God, telling him I wasn't toned.

I am not toned. I meant to get toned, but I like cookies and chicken too much. I'm sorry.

Oh fuck. Why do I insist on shitting everything up? What the fuck is my problem? Why did I put him in this position?

I don't feel well. I feel bad. I need to feel better. I need to rewind time and act like an adult. I also need a sausage sandwich. A sausage sandwich will make me feel better. I wonder what vegans eat when they're hungover? That is not a helpful thought.

I really need a sausage sandwich.

Or maybe I need to be sick.

I definitely need to get out of here before I make it worse.

I turn over. Peter's side of the bed is ruffled, but empty. He's gone. The clock, the same crappy one he's had since I first met him, tells me it's 8.42 a.m. Oh God, why is it still so early? I already want this day to be over.

I sit up. I'm glad he isn't here to see this. I can't imagine I'm looking my best.

Vertical is definitely worse than horizontal, so I stay still for a while in an effort to stop the nausea.

What have I done? Why did I do this?

What if he left because he didn't want to see me either? What if I made such an arse out of myself that he couldn't bear to look at me? Have I finally done enough to make

Peter, who is comfortable around anyone, stop talking to me? I am an awful human being.

I struggle out of bed. I spot a couple of random bruises on my legs, but I can see both of my shoes, which is a win, and all of my clothes. Some kind of grumbling noise escapes from me.

I don't want to put the horrible plasticky Lycra back on. Being that shiny and skin-tight was OK last night, but in the cold light of day it further highlights my shame. Peter's neighbour is probably camping by her window, waiting for his inappropriate guest to reappear in yesterday's clothes.

It really can't get much worse, so I borrow one of Peter's jumpers. It will cover most of what is indecent (at least on the outside), and paired with the cheap Lycra leggings, my outfit could look like a fashion choice instead of a hen party hangover. I tell myself that I'll wash the jumper and send it back.

Once dressed, the idea of leaving the relative safety of the bedroom doesn't fill me with joy. I don't know what's waiting on the other side. The apartment feels empty, but I still spend some time listening at the door before deciding to risk it. I open the door as quietly as I can, which takes more effort than it should, but I can't help the delay in communication between my brain and my limbs.

Peeking around, I can't see any trace of people; there is no movement, there is no noise. I can, however, see the remnants of the burritos, which look even less appetizing now than they did last night. I'll take those with me. I might have messed everything up with Peter, but leaving him that cold, globular mess to clean up is a step too far.

I wander around, making my way slowly to the kitchen, and come across his gallery wall.

I hadn't really looked at it before, but I do now. And right there, slightly up and left from the centre, is a picture of the two of us. It's a picture I know well; I have it Blu-Tacked above the accessories station in my bedroom. It's a nice photo. We look happy. We also look cold. From memory, this was taken at the end of the first term at uni, when all of our essays were written and all of our classes had finished. Of course we were happy then, we didn't have a care in the world. And I hadn't just ballsed up our friendship.

I have to get out before he comes back from wherever he's escaped to. I took advantage of him and his kindness, and the idea of him trying to tell me it's OK when I've made a prize arse out of myself is too much.

I grab a pen and hover over a notepad of his.

> Sorry I fucked everything up. It won't happen again. Bea x

Doesn't quite cover it.

I drop the pen, crumple up the note and run away.

Chapter 37

By the time Monday rears its ugly head, I'm technically sober, but still haven't been able to shake the hangover guilt. And all I can ask myself is whether it's acceptable to ghost one of your best friends who you had drunken sex with until they move away to the other side of the world.

I don't know the answer, so I'm slowly working my way around the office with some very bald tinsel. Everyone around me seems determined to be full of festive cheer, but I know that in reality we are all facing a month of work deadlines, poor diets, and parties every night. All in order to be able to take off that precious week between Christmas and New Year when nobody knows what day it is.

It's all too much. I reach for the inflatable Santa.

'Bea, can you come in here please?'

I didn't think bosses were allowed to shout at assistants any more.

It takes all of my energy to straighten up and walk over to Mansi's office door.

'Can I help?'

She says, 'Shut the door,' and nods to the chair. 'I'm going to have a frank conversation with you. As a warning I'm terribly hungover, and so this might be more frank than even I mean it to be.'

I sit in the chair to await my fate, and start to pick off my nail polish. I wish with all my heart that I had called in sick today.

She takes a sharp inhale of breath as I try to steel myself. 'You have been a pain in the arse since I hired you. But I can't blame you because I'm also a pain in your arse. And I've come to the conclusion that we aren't the ones for each other. I don't need you as my assistant.'

Holy shit, is she firing me? I was expecting something bad, but I wasn't expecting to get fired.

'That said, I can't help but value your . . . unique contribution to the company.' I wonder if she is thinking specifically about the joke wall I created in the kitchen. 'And over the years, you have become as much a part of this company as I am. You have grown on all of us, except possibly Joan. And now you've cut out an interesting niche for yourself.'

Hold on, is she giving me a raise?

'But you're not suited to being an assistant, and I do need an assistant, now more than ever.'

I need a map to help me navigate my way through this conversation.

'I'm trusting you with this information because, well, I have no other choice, and I have never doubted your increasingly begrudgingly given loyalty to me.' She's right. I've never once shared any of her secrets, including her apparent love for making felt animals, despite having to open all of her mail, containing many, many boxes of felt, patterns, googly eyes, glue-gun sticks, twine and, most recently, alpaca wool. 'I'm adopting a child, which is why I've been out of the office more than usual lately.'

Oh God, maybe she's been making the felt animals for the kid she was hoping to have. Now I feel awful.

She goes on. 'But this means that I will need a more involved assistant so I can spend more time at home. I don't believe you want to be a more involved assistant.'

I'm sitting on my hands, making sure I stay deadly still until I know what is going on.

'So, I have a proposal for you, one that I urge you to seriously consider.' She takes a dramatic pause. 'When we first started out and I hired you, I remember you were great at many things, even things that you had no real background in. This is the moment where I apologize to you. I have done you a disservice; I should have found you a more suitable, more challenging role that made the most of your strengths, but instead I kept you as my assistant, a selfish move on my part.

'And so we find ourselves here.' She makes a gesture with her hands that prompts me to look around her office, wondering precisely how literal she is being.

'Now, I've also been keeping track of your card business –' business is still a stretch at this point but I'll take it – 'ever since that unfortunate headline mix-up. I saw your business plan on your desk last week. I shouldn't have snooped, but I did and it made for interesting read-ing. It's ambitious.'

She looks at me pointedly and I think I'm meant to say something.

'Yes, it is.'

'It will take time.'

'Yes, it will.'

'The cards are funny.'

'Thanks.' This comes out more like a question and I frown a little. 'How do you . . .'

'I looked them up online.' She says it as if that was the dumbest question I could have asked.

'I do not need or want you as an assistant, but what this company does need is something that I think you could be quite good at.

'I've been watching you with the assistants ever since I stumbled across your mentoring session in the cafe. I'm impressed, as are they, I believe. And I'm of the opinion that the sessions have made a difference in the work-place. For the better. I also noticed how you handled Joan.' She uncrosses and re-crosses her legs, and makes a face that looks like she smelt cabbage soup being reheated in the communal kitchen. Interesting. 'Our attrition rate is shocking, and it costs us a lot of money and time to hire in and train up new people. Too much money and far too much time. I want to try and stop this. And to stop it, I think what we need is someone to help on board our rotating door of assistants so they feel more confi-dent from the start, and someone to look out for the development opportunities we offer. I hope that with time and more support, the door will rotate a little more slowly, and we will have fewer skills gaps. I want to see if you can be this person. Indeed, I believe you already are.'

'OK.' Again, it comes out more like a question.

'But, and there is a but, this is a role we cannot currently offer full-time. So your salary will be pro-rated for three days a week, with a review after six months to see how things are going, both from your perspective and mine.'

Huh. Interesting.

'Think about it.' She adjusts her power blazer. 'This could work out quite well for you. And me. It will give you more time to dedicate to your . . . puns.'

She stops talking and looks at me.

'Can I take some time to think about it?'

She nods, once.

'When do you need me to decide by?'

'I would like to start looking for an assistant right after Christmas. So if you could tell me by next Thursday that would be appreciated.'

'Well, thank you.' I'm not too sure what to say. I definitely won't say the right thing, and I haven't had any chance to prepare something, so I go with my gut. 'There were a couple of compliments in there somewhere. I really appreciate it. I'll think about your offer and let you know by Thursday.' I go to leave, but before I do I turn around. 'Sorry I'm a terrible assistant.'

She looks at me above her glasses and I wonder whether this is a mannerism you automatically pick up as you gain power, or if there is some secret class you can take.

'Don't be. I was also a terrible assistant. Probably worse than you are. But then I found what it was I wanted to do, and you need to do the same. I'm trying to find a solution that works for both of us.'

'I don't know what to say.'

'You could go get me a ridiculously sugary festive coffee. Unless that falls outside your job description.'

'I'll make an exception this time. Anything else?'

'Yes. I haven't bought a Secret Santa present yet, and the party is next week. Next Thursday in fact. A big day for you.' She gets some money out from her purse. 'When you're out getting coffee, could you also pick up a suitable present?'

I shouldn't have asked.

'Who's it for?'

'Just get something you would like. I'm sure that would work fine.'

'OK.' I nod.

'Good. Now go. Leave me in peace.'

She shoos me out and I narrowly miss the door frame on my way out.

I grab my coat and bag, and, like a bee to honey, or a bored office worker to any potential gossip, Penny appears.

'You heading out?'

'Yeah, I'm doing a coffee run. And buying a secret Santa gift.' I roll my eyes at this.

'Great! Can I come with you? I need fresh air otherwise I might fall asleep.'

Having bought a pine-tree-scented candle and novelty Christmas mug, Penny and I head down the road to the cafe with all the food samples.

'So what did the boss have to say?'

I don't think I should tell Penny anything until I know what I'm going to do myself.

'Could we talk about something else?' I feel bad; it goes against the work wife code.

'No worries.' I can tell from her tone that she is, in fact, a little worried. 'What else is going on with you? You've been quiet today.'

I can't roadblock her out of two conversations, and besides, it might be good to talk about it. I hid in shame all of Sunday and I haven't yet found a way to confess to Mia, so I fill her in on all the details. Or at least the ones I can remember.

Having just reached the cafe, we stand in the middle of the floor blocking the natural path of customers, and only move when the update is over.

'I think it's a good thing you told him how you feel.' Penny tells everyone how she feels all the time.

'But I didn't. I just launched myself at him. And now I can never *actually* tell him how I feel, because I've ruined it by acting like a drunken fool. And now I don't know what to do. He hasn't messaged me, so I guess I'll take his lead.'

'Why? Why not text him? That's what I would do.'

'Yes, but you're beautiful. And beautiful people can get away with that.' And I can be stubborn. Very stubborn.

'I'm not even going to address that comment.' Penny gives me a look. 'So what are you going to do about it?'

'Get a fake tan and do my nails?'

She rolls her eyes at me and I think she also tuts.

I pick up the coffees. Obviously I also ordered one for myself.

Penny is still looking at me.

'So?'

I grab a handful of samples to take back to the office.

'I'm going to pretend it never happened and move on.'

Chapter 38

Next Thursday arrives, and although I've made a decision, I'm still nervous about it. I'm sitting at my desk, unmoving except for my thrumming fingers.

I spent the whole weekend thinking everything through. I kept wanting to call somebody and talk over my reasoning, but of course the one person I wanted to call was Peter. He's always been good at organizing my thoughts, even if right now thinking about him still has me scrambled, not least because he hasn't messaged me at all since that night. Sure, I haven't messaged him either, but he hasn't even bothered to tell me that he is moving to Australia. Doesn't he think I deserve to know?

Because I couldn't call Peter I did the most Peter-like thing I could, and used Post-its to organize myself. They kept falling off my wall, but they were still helpful. And once all my thoughts were up there, it was clear my heart was saying 'jump', and eventually my head couldn't argue any more.

I look back at the photo I took of the Post-its, the evidence I need to remind myself that I've made the right decision.

Mansi looks up from her computer as I knock on her office door. I wonder if she can already tell what I'm going to say. 'Have you come to a decision?'

I remind myself that this is the right decision. I have one life; I might as well make the most of it.

'Yes. I'd like to take you up on your offer, but I have some terms that I want to discuss with you first.'

She smiles and nods. 'Come in. Let's talk.'

I leave her office feeling more confident than I have in a while. She agreed to pretty much everything, even a pay rise; the only hard no was to my (half joking, of course) suggestion of bringing a dog into work. It would help morale. She even agreed to become something of a mentor to me.

Mostly, I feel relieved and proud at making a decision, and taking the route that requires the bigger leap.

I sit back at my desk, only to jump out of my skin when Penny jumps up in front of me.

'Penny, you scared me half to death.' She is smiling semi-crazily. 'Why are you so happy?'

'Why am I so happy? Why are *you* so happy? I don't think I've ever seen you smile so much. Is it Peter?'

And like that, my free and easy happiness bubble has burst. Because no, I was not smiling because of Peter, but I wish I could be.

'No, it's not Peter.'

She changes the subject quickly after my admission, so quickly that I know she's come over with a purpose.

'What is it, Penny? What do you need?'

She shrugs casually. 'Nothing, but I was wondering what you were going as this evening?'

'What am I going as?'

'What are you going as? To the Christmas party?'

In my sea of Post-its I have forgotten about the Christmas party, and I don't want to admit to Penny that my costume-wearing quota for the year has already been reached with my eighties get-up for Tilly's hen – the night I slept with Peter, who I am definitely not thinking about. I pull a face and tell her a white lie.

'I might have forgotten it at home.' This is a white lie because this is what *might* have happened. She doesn't need to know that what *actually* happened was that I decided, many weeks ago, that I wouldn't dress up.

'Oh no! Well, no worries – due to an online ordering error I actually have a spare, so you can dress up in my second costume and we can match!'

This, my friends, is karma. It just normally takes a little longer to bite you on the arse.

'We aren't the same size at all – whatever outfit you have will never fit me.'

'Trust me –' I do not – 'it will.' The glint in her eye fills me with fear.

And rightly so, as a few hours later I'm looking in the mirror and the person looking back at me isn't anyone I recognize.

'Why did I let you put me in this?' I hold my arms out and spin from side to side.

'You look amazing!'

Penny is standing next to me, her reflection a stark contrast to my own. She is wearing exactly the same outfit as I am, but she looks glamorous and chic.

'No, *you* look amazing. *I* look like a child wearing a box. Which is actually pretty close to the truth.' We are both dressed as presents, but somehow the proportions work better on her.

We enter the 'party room', which is the board room, but badly disguised with streamers, a fake Christmas tree and what can only be described as a singing disco ball, which goes particularly crazy when the music is interrupted by ads. On the snack table I think I can also see a bowl of the children's vitamins, the ones which turned the kids different colours.

Why does such a wonderful time of year come with so many terrible parties?

'I need a drink.'

Penny nods. 'I'll come with you.'

On the way to the drinks area, Chris, the office pervert who proudly announced with glee after the last office move that he could see my desk from his new position, appears out of nowhere.

'Bea, you look like you want to be unwrapped.' He winks. Everyone knows I'm a fan of a pun, but not in this situation. I do not want to be unwrapped, and no sentence ever previously uttered has made me want to hit someone more. I am disappointed in myself for not being as confrontational as I could, and possibly should, be. But I say nothing and walk away, though I do make a mental note to send him on a compulsory course about discrimination in the workplace as part of my new role.

After grabbing a drink and some snacks, making sure to hide extras inside my box, I am abandoned by Penny, who is too kind to ignore the boring office people wanting to talk to her.

Pondering the point of a work Christmas party, I can't say I'm enjoying myself, but I have to confess that they're good for one thing – putting everyone on an even footing. Everyone here feels just as out of place as the next cracker, no matter if you're the MD or the newest assistant. Everyone feels odd wearing fancy dress in a room where we normally hold our quarterly reviews. And everyone is hoping that with the new year will come a new range of memories to wipe out any shameful acts and secret confessions shared on nights exactly like this.

Doing a scan of the room, I can tell that nobody feels more out of place than Joan. She's wearing a sad homemade outfit that I think is meant to be a Christmas pudding. On a baby it would probably look endearing. But Joan isn't a baby.

I decide to go speak to her; after all, I believe Christmas is a time for forgiveness.

'Hi.'

She turns and seems genuinely happy to see me. 'Oh, well hello there, Bea.'

I'm glad I came over to say hi, but I don't quite know what to say now that the pleasantries are over. I really want to avoid a boring, predictable conversation about Christmas plans. Mainly because I have none except going home and eating all the mini chocolates and cheese I can find.

But she takes a big inhale of breath, and it sounds as if she's going to take the plunge for me.

'So . . . any plans for Christmas?'

Later in the evening, too many wines in, Penny hunts me down with a determination I rarely see in her, and takes me to the stationery cupboard for a confessional. We barely fit with our costumes on – I have to reverse shuffle in as there's no room to turn around. I've barely managed to shoehorn myself into the closet before Penny starts talking.

'I needed a moment with you to tell you that you are my inspiration.' She pops a vitamin into her mouth and keeps going, chewing frantically. 'Over these last months, you have become such a force in the office. But not like a Joan force; you've become a force for good. A summer breeze. And it has inspired me. Every night for the last two weeks I've been wandering around my apartment totally stark naked, except for my shower cap, trying to figure out what to do with my life. What my thing is. You!' She points at me. 'You've found your thing! You're shining and happy! I want to be shining and happy too! Tell me how to be shining and happy!'

This is news to me, as I always saw Penny as the shinier, happier person out of the two of us.

'Pen, the shine comes from my illuminating foundation.' I joke in an effort to make her smile. I don't want to downplay or ignore her, but it's hard to tell if this is how she really feels, or if this is how she feels when she is fuelled by sugary vitamins and cheap, office-party alcohol. I make another internal note to block out some time to talk to Penny about this more seriously. And more soberly.

After making my mental note, a noise I've never heard before comes out of Penny. I would classify it as a groan made from a mix of exasperation and shame.

'Also, I think I kissed Chris.' I gasp in shock and I know the whites of my eyes are showing. 'On the cheek! I'm not that drunk.' She hangs her arms so they flop down on either side of her. 'But I did also have the most awkward hug with Mansi after I told her I thought she was great and that I really admired her and thought she smelt nice, but she really isn't a hugger. Then I got stuck in my costume.'

'What? How did you get stuck in your costume?'

'Well, I didn't know how to leave the conversation with Mansi, and so I sat down on the floor, thinking it would be a funny way to escape.' As she speaks she tries to recreate her movements. 'My arms were kind of hugging my legs, and my legs were all tucked up inside the box, but then I couldn't get up as I didn't have room to manoeuvre my arms out, and there also wasn't enough room to stand up with my arms in there, so I just scuttled around on the floor until I reached the stairs.'

I pass her some of the snacks I've been hiding in my costume.

'I wish I had seen that.'

'I wish you had too.'

Chapter 39

The fourth and final Games Night of the year is obviously always Christmas themed. My Christmas jumper is freshly washed but I'm struggling to feel in the mood for mince pies. I'm not sure if I can face seeing Peter this evening. He must be moving in a few weeks. I wouldn't know; he still hasn't told me.

For the first time this year, Games Night is actually held in the evening. Although as it starts getting dark from three thirty, it feels a bit like we are in a perpetual night. The overhanging trees are looking particularly evil this evening.

I near Rahul's flat – he's always a favoured host because of his food. However, I've chosen to risk missing out on the most popular food options by purposefully running late. The more people there before me, the more diluted Peter will be.

I approach the door and ring the doorbell. I can hear lots of people inside, and someone shuffling to open it.

'Bea!' Mark smiles at me from the other side, and welcomes me in with a hug.

It looks like everyone who has ever attended a Games Night has shown up this evening. The hallway is packed.

There are far too many people to play games, but it doesn't look like anyone minds.

It's also really warm, a stark contrast to the outside. I start to panic and my neck gets really itchy. There is barely enough room to take off my coat.

Luckily, Mia comes to help. The lack of space and multiple layers mean I've got a little twisted. She looks really pregnant now.

'I know, I'm huge.'

'You're not huge, but it's now very obvious that you're pregnant.' I hope this is the right thing to say.

'Ugh, and I'm so warm all the time. I'm so grateful I got accidentally pregnant when I did. I couldn't imagine being this warm in summer.' She hangs up my coat. 'It's cooler over here, follow me.'

It takes us a while to reach our destination next to the big windows in the lounge, mainly because there are so many people here. People I haven't seen since the last Christmas Games Night. I don't have a huge amount to say to them, so I'm happy to have a reason (Mia's body temperature) to move on, but it's nice to see them anyway.

We reach the window. Mia perches on the sofa arm and I stand opposite. I look around. No Peter in sight. I'm relieved.

I definitely feel relief. I definitely do not feel sad.

I turn my attention to Mia. It's been some time since I've seen her.

'So, have you decided how long you're going to take off for mat leave?'

'The whole year.'

'Good!' She had been thinking of only taking three months.

'Although Mark wants me to give him a couple of months as shared leave.' She shakes her head. 'We haven't decided anything quite yet though. If I'm pushing this thing out, I want to reap all the benefits I can.'

'So, what made you change your mind?'

'Well, I've been doing some research –' obviously – 'and a lot of studies say that going back after twelve weeks is actually quite unhealthy for the baby and the mother.' She leans forward. 'Also, I like the idea of having time to just be a mum. And watching daytime TV.'

Rahul is walking over. He has a plate of food in his hand.

'This is for you. I didn't want you to go hungry. Not when you're eating for two.'

He hands Mia the plate of food and she thanks him with a mini tear in her eye. It's a beautiful plate of food. It's crammed with all the good things. I have my eyes on the fancy sausage roll.

Rahul retreats, probably back into the kitchen.

'The shittiest thing about being pregnant is that you're only actually meant to eat about two hundred extra calories a day.' She picks up what looks like an onion bhaji. 'But if people don't know and feed me extra, I won't correct them.'

She takes a bite and moves the plate closer to me, a gesture that says it's OK for me to take something. I go for the sausage roll and look up to confirm my choice is acceptable to her. She nods yes.

I take a bite. It's delicious. He's put some cranberry in there, and the pastry is so buttery and flaky.

'So what's been happening with the cards?'

I'm sure I look like a hamster when I smile, but I can't help it. I want to smile, but I still have quite a lot of sausage roll in my mouth. Once I swallow the sausage roll, I fill her in on my decision to go down to part-time, all the new orders, the popularity of the personalized boasts in the post and, hot off the press – 'Do you remember that person I met at the reunion drinks? The cool one with the husband who doted on her? Michelle?'

Mia simply shakes her head. She was too busy talking to the Queen of the Cardigans to notice my new girl-crush.

'Well, she's running a Christmas pop-up next weekend featuring a bunch of independent crafters, makers, artists and the like, and she asked if she could sell my cards.'

'That's great!'

I nod. 'It is, and if they do well, she would look to stock them in her stores on a more permanent basis. I thought she only had the one shop, but she has, like, five, so this could be really good for me.'

'That's amazing! I am so proud of you!'

I just nod. I see Mark in the corner.

'So, how's the bowl collection coming?'

Her demeanour changes impressively quickly. She looks down, as if she's slightly ashamed.

'Don't talk to me about the bowls.'

'Why can't I talk to you about the bowls?'

'Because I feel really guilty about the bowls.'

'How on earth can you feel guilty about the bowls?' We've said the word 'bowls' so many times that it's started to sound wrong.

'Because I found out why he's collecting them and it turns out I'm a horrible human.'

I dip my chin and look up at her. I know she's done something bad. 'Go on . . .'

She sighs and lets it out. 'After I threw one at his head, he informed me that, apparently, many years ago I made some offhand, totally unremarkable comment about being pregnant and really looking forward to eating ramen out of a bowl that's resting on my baby bump. And so that's why Mark has been collecting all the bowls. He wants to make sure that when my bump is big enough, I have the perfect bowl to eat ramen out of.'

We are both quiet for a moment. That is really lovely.

'I bet the perfect bloody bowl is the one that I broke after I threw it at his head. I've been offering him guilt blow jobs for days. He hasn't taken me up on the offer yet, so I'm still in purgatory.'

Poor Mark.

'Please can we change the subject? I can't think about the bowls any more.'

I've already filled her in on my biggest news. But I can't possibly tell her the Peter news. I can't bear to let her know how badly I messed it up.

Luckily I don't have to. She gives me something else to talk about.

'How are Tilly's wedding plans going?'

'Well, as it's Tilly, it's actually all going OK. She's had to go with her second-choice band, but apart from that it's all fallen into place quite well.' So well, in fact, that I suspect she already had the venue and caterer booked before getting engaged.

'Of course it has – that girl is charmed.' I feel a bit bad that this is Mia's assessment of Tilly. One thing I've learnt from spending more time with Tilly is that she works really hard to be charmed.

'Actually, she—'

I hear a laugh. Was it Peter's laugh? It sounded like it could be.

'Did you hear that?'

'Hear what?'

I look around. 'I thought I heard Peter.'

She looks around very casually. 'Nope, I don't think you did.' From her face, I know she knows I'm hiding something. 'I don't think he's coming this evening.'

'Oh.' My shoulders fall. 'OK, well, that's good.'

She tilts her head.

'Bea, what happened?'

It takes less time to tell the story than I thought it would, and at the end she doesn't need to keep digging. She knows I've shared everything, warts and all.

But she does still have some questions.

'So, which part of this story brings you the most shame?'

Sometimes I really wish she would beat around the bush a bit more.

'There are a few.' I count them off on my fingers.

'Firstly, the fact we had sex and I don't remember it. Secondly, the fact I threw myself at him and he pushed me away. He *pushed* me away. And last but not least, the fact he hasn't messaged me since.'

'I would hasten to add that you haven't messaged him either. But I'm glad you told him how you feel.'

'Argh, why do people keep saying this! I didn't tell him, I launched myself at him.' I wish there was a way to know what he was thinking without actually having to ask.

'Meh, actions speak louder than words. I'm sure you'll survive this.'

How can she be so casual? 'I don't know if we will. I found out from one of his work colleagues that he is going to Australia for a year, which kinda puts a time crunch on working all of this out.' Although I'm not sure time will help.

'He's going to Australia? He hasn't said anything about that to me.'

'He hasn't told me either, but he is. His friend, Al, told me.'

'Are you sure?'

I nod.

'Well, you guys have been through worse.'

I scoff. 'What have we been through that's worse?'

Her eyes go back and forth, as though she's actually flipping through the memories in her mind.

'OK, maybe not worse, but you couldn't not tell him how you feel. And so we're clear – how do you feel?'

'Right now? Ashamed. And I blame you for the mess

I'm in. It was your stupid advice that made me think it would be OK to go over to his house.'

'Do not blame me for this.'

'You were the one who told me to get drunk and shag him!'

'I would never say anything so crass.'

She is infuriating.

'Ugh. I can't believe he pushed me away and I just kept at it.'

'You're always so plagued with self-doubt. He probably pushed you away because he was trying to be a gentleman.'

'I really wish that the flashbacks would stop. Every now and then I'll be doing something really inane, totally content in my own head, and then WHAM!' I hear myself asking him to kiss me, and I feel his lips on mine.

I rub my head, trying to get rid of the ache that has appeared there.

And now, the thing that's making me most sad is also the thing that's giving me the most hope. Once he's in Australia, I won't have to worry about facing him, but it also means he'll be gone. Mia reaches over and hugs me.

'It was definitely not my finest moment.'

'No, but not your worst either.'

I can't help but smile. 'No, probably not.'

Chapter 40

The headache that formed on Games Night hasn't left me. Peter has kept totally schtum, and as a result my anxiety and worry have skyrocketed.

And to top it off, Michelle's Christmas pop-up is upon me.

I'm weirdly nervous about seeing Michelle again. I'm hopeful (and worried) about how my cards will sell, but more than that I want to make a good impression on her. I'm very aware that trying to make a name for yourself in a completely different industry comes with all the same political issues you find in any office job, possibly more so in the independent crafting business. I have a sneaky suspicion that crafters (who are essentially scissor-wielding folk who have gone slightly stir-crazy from being left at home alone for too long) are particularly sensitive.

I see Michelle, who is wielding a clipboard, and head over with my two boxes. This time I've only had to bring cards and the succulent, for luck. As my cards are part of Michelle's shop, I don't have a whole stall to dress, only a display. The taxi ride went off without a hitch.

'Michelle! Hi.' I hope she recognizes me. 'I come bearing cards.' If she hasn't this should prompt her memory. 'Where would you like them?' I ended up bringing more than she asked for, but it turns out that trying to forget about Peter makes me very productive.

'Bea! Honey, it's so good to see you. We're full steam ahead. You're over there,' she says, pointing to a couple of cleverly converted easel-like contraptions. 'You can see your sign above your area. Are you happy to dress it yourself?'

'Yes, of course, very. I'll go do that now and get out of your hair.' Talking of hair, she looks amazing: she is wearing a well-fitted jumpsuit with a bold print. If I were organizing a pop-up, I would not look so fashionable.

'Thanks, honey. I'll come find you after I've sorted out all the last-minute logistics. Sorry, it's gone totally crazy.'

I scoot away, hoping I didn't add to the last-minute fray, and display my cards alongside the filched succulent. I add a mini red and white striped scarf around the pot to make it look more festive.

As I'm packing up the boxes to use again later, Michelle comes over.

'These look great!'

'Thanks – I brought a few more than you said, I hope that's OK.'

'It's your space, you can do with it what you like. I'm just happy you were able to come.'

This is the time for me to emphasize how very excited I am for the opportunity, to show her how much I could add to her repertoire.

I get ready with my spiel and take a big breath in.

'I—'

'Michelle!' My speech is interrupted by another

clipboard-wielding person. 'Michelle! We have a problem. The guy we hired to play Rudolph isn't coming. His train is stuck.'

'OK, that's OK.' Michelle's face suggests this is not OK. 'We can find someone else. We have the costume. All we need to do is find someone who can fit into it, and is OK with kids.'

'They need to be DBS checked.'

I can't fucking believe it.

This is my moment. I raise my hand.

They both look at me, a hint of annoyance in their eyes. I don't think they want to be interrupted. Especially by someone who apparently thinks they're still in school.

'I, uh, I have a DBS check. I mean, it's a couple of years old, but I don't think they have an official expiry date.'

I can see Michelle's eyes travel up and down my body, taking vague measurements. When they reach my face, they light up.

'I think you've just saved the day.'

When I first put the costume on and looked in the mirror, I really tried to be one with Rudolph. But two hours later, I'm ready to cry.

I thought the present outfit was cumbersome, but this is far worse. I can't breathe very well as the costume has a full-on reindeer head, I keep tripping up over my enlarged feet, my vision is severely restricted, there is no secret hiding place for snacks, and despite the fact the costume is on the large side, I have a massive wedgie that I can't undo because my hands are now hooves.

But, on the flipside, I'm proving my worth to Michelle, even if in a slightly different manner to the one I'd envisaged. Still, the hope of acceptance keeps me going. I've forced my way on to her team, and now I need to keep these kids entertained and not knock any of them over. This task is trickier said than done, as although moving is hard, talking is impossible, and so the only way I can entertain them is through movement. It's quite the conundrum.

I check the clock to see how long I have left in this thing. Thirty minutes. Thirty minutes left and then I'll be free.

The kids currently being distracted by an elf, who can both talk and walk more freely, I take the opportunity to look around and gauge how my cards are doing. Having no peripheral vision means that I keep having to turn my whole body in the direction I want to see. I rotate about ninety degrees and find myself staring straight at Peter. I think an errant antler hits him in the head.

'Gosh, sorry, it's quite busy in here, huh?'

I am momentarily stunned, but then realize he has no idea who's inside the costume. So I nod.

'Well, I'll let you get back to it then.' And he meanders off, totally unaware of all the feelings and questions his presence has caused.

Peter is here. All of a sudden this costume simultaneously feels like a heat prison and a protective cloak.

Why is Peter here?

I rotate back to the horde. The kids are still being entertained by the elf, so I decide to follow Peter.

He takes quite a circuitous route, which due to my size and logistical issues I can't follow, but he does eventually stop at my card station. Because of where I'm positioned, I can't see his face. I want to see his face.

I try to manoeuvre myself subtly around a dangerously overloaded display of festive china – cute stacking mugs that together form a happy snowman – and edge closer.

The girl next to him picks up one of my cards and chuckles. Despite my focus being on Peter, my heart can't help but do a little happy dance at the noise. She likes a card! And she's a random stranger! This is so exciting!

He looks at the girl, and now I can see his profile. He looks tired and stressed, but he still smiles and she smiles back at him. I instantly want to hit her. 'They're funny, right? I know the person who makes them.'

Her smile, if anything, gets even more dazzling.

I'm about ten seconds away from marching over when a group of dawdling fools walk right in front of me, blocking my view and restricting my ability to listen.

Once they've cleared, I try to shuffle closer, but it's really hard to do because I'm about three times larger than my normal body size.

I feel a tug at my arm and turn towards it. It's the elf.

'I need you back.'

'I'll be there in one minute, but I need to watch this first.' After I speak I remember that nobody can hear me through the padding.

I try again with my arms.

'Please, they're tyrants. I can't control them any longer.'

Resigned to my fate, I nod, and look back briefly at Peter, who is now walking out of the shop.

Chapter 41

Finally, after the day of costume-wearing hell and a morning spent journeying on an overly full train that's stuffed with presents, we've reached the Christmas holidays, the eating and drinking challenge that we've all been training for over the last month. And I've been eating even more than usual this year. I haven't told either Mum or Fred about my decision to go down to part-time, and with great anxiety comes great hunger.

Possibly because my mum is alone, it's tradition for both Fred and me to converge on Mum's house every year, with Anna and Olivia alternating between her parents and our mum. This year Mum gets all of us.

I can't tell if she actually likes this situation or not. She says she's excited, but her actions tell us differently. The fridge is stocked with food, none of which we're allowed to eat because it's all allocated to a certain meal and a certain time. I had to bring my own snacks, just to be safe. She gets annoyed at all the extra shoes in her house, she doesn't like the noise, and I'm pretty sure she takes the dog on extra-long walks to escape us.

The first couple of days are always the worst.

'Bea, did you open the wraps?'

Oh shit.

She has her hand on her hip. This isn't good.

I can see Fred looking at me, pretending he isn't looking at me.

'Erm, sorry, yes I did. I had one for lunch.' It was actually a post-lunch snack. 'I thought it would be OK. We don't normally have wraps over Christmas, so I had hoped they'd be safe.' I really don't like confrontation. Had I known the wraps were off-limits, I wouldn't have touched them.

'Well, I bought them as an alternative to bread so we could have turkey wraps on Boxing Day instead of sandwiches, but you've opened them so badly that they're going to be stale by the time we want them.'

A skill of mine is spotting the peel-and-reseal tags too late to actually use them, thereby ensuring the contents of all open packets need to be consumed within two hours or they'll become stale.

I have no defence, so I can only try to placate, a tactic which sometimes works, and sometimes only succeeds in making Mum more irritated.

I stand up and go over to inspect the bag, as if being closer will make my vivid discomfort seem even more sincere. The proximity only makes me feel worse; I really did a number on the packaging.

'I can go out and get more.' If any shops are still open. 'Or we could put them in a bag. Or we could heat them up slightly – I do that with mine when they go a bit stale and it perks them right back up! I promise. What do you think?'

She sighs and shakes her head. 'I knew this would happen. I put a couple of back-up packets in the freezer, so we *should* be fine.'

There are twelve wraps in each packet. I'm bad at maths, but even I can figure this one out.

'So even if we have to throw away the open packet, we still have twenty-four wraps to get through? I don't think we need to buy more.'

Having spent the last six hours trying to avoid the angry puce face, I realize that I've just created the perfect conditions for one to appear. And appear it does. Along with the pulsating vein in her forehead.

'I'm sorry, I'm joking.' I realize I'm not joking. 'But I do think we'll be fine for wraps, and I promise not to eat anything ever again unless I've checked with you first. I love you, Mum. Thank you for looking after us so well.'

And she really does look after us well. Even if it occasionally causes more pain than pleasure.

Fred rearranges the newspaper he's reading, and I take that as a sign that he's relaxing back to normal, seeing that trouble has passed. At least for now.

'Can I help you make the stuffing?'

Fred jumps up from where he's sitting.

'Bea, I need you actually. The stuffing will have to wait.'

He drags me out of the room and I grab my wine on the way out. I have my priorities.

'Don't make me repeat my actions from Christmas five years ago.'

That was a particularly bad year. We never settled into

a routine, so Fred had to text me every time I wanted to make a cup of tea to let me know when the kitchen was safe to enter. I spent a lot of time alone that Christmas. Especially after the texting system failed, leading to a particularly bad mix-up regarding the leftover veg. Fred resorted to locking me into the study and only let me out when Mum wasn't in the house.

'But I didn't know! It's not my fault!'

'Don't eat anything unless she gives it to you.'

'But what if I'm hungry?'

'It's not worth it.'

'So I'm meant to starve?'

'You are not going to starve.'

'Are you calling me fat?'

Once upon a time, when we were a lot younger than we are now, Fred called me fat. It really upset me. I went on a very strict diet for about two months, lost a load of weight (that I put back on quite quickly when I realized I loved food) and cried a lot. Since then, I bring it up every now and then to make him feel bad.

'Come here, you idiot.'

He envelops me in a bear hug. I don't know what it is about a hug from your brother, but they make you feel so safe. I feel bad for anyone who hasn't had the opportunity to experience this.

'Thanks for always looking out for me.' My words are muffled. The hug is lovely, but he's also restricting the amount of air I can get into my lungs.

'You OK, sis?' He releases me a bit, but apart from the fact I can now breathe slightly better, I don't like the distance. I smoosh back in and make him hug me for a while longer.

'I'm fine.' And I am fine. Finally my work is going in a good direction, my cards are working, things are back on track with Mia. It's ungrateful to want more. To want Peter.

I subtly dry my eyes, hoping no tear patch is visible when I do eventually pull away.

I inhale and step back. There's a small wet patch on Fred's top, but I don't think anyone will be able to tell whether it's from tears or a smidge of drool.

Fred is first to talk. He knows I'm not totally fine, but he also knows a hug is the perfect medicine. 'Well, we might as well use this time. Tell me, what have you got Mum for Christmas?'

Every year we say we will compare presents so we don't overlap. Every year we forget. And so every year, we overlap.

'Well, I suppose nobody can ever be too moisturized.'

Chapter 42

Christmas morning comes and goes with the usual bustle of activity. Olivia sneaks into my room to wake me up. Quite how and why children breathe so heavily I will never know, but I dutifully play my part and pretend to be asleep until she jumps on my bed, closely followed by Hugo, who licks every part of skin I've left exposed.

Now that Christmas Day has actually arrived, Mum's mood has visibly shifted. It's as if she can finally relax now that the event is here.

Or she might have taken some kind of herbal remedy. I don't know which it is. Either way, the morning was full of laughter. And now, post-lunch, Olivia is napping in front of a Christmas movie, and the adults (a category I'm frequently surprised to find myself in) are all too full of food and unable to move from the table.

Which means talking.

And talking at Christmas means that people often feel the freedom, or even the requirement, to get extra personal. It's the most stressful conversation I take part in every year, but I'm particularly anxious about it this year – for the first time I have lots of things to share. And lots of things to withhold. And I can't possibly eat any more. My anxiety will have to do whatever it does without me nervous eating.

It starts off light. Anna is finally admitting that she needs to find something else to do other than looking after Olivia. Fred is talking about a possible extension on the house. Mum even admits that she's joining a local murder mystery book group.

'So how are the cards, Bea? Do you want me to look over the plan that you and Peter came up with? I could give it a once-over. I don't know anything about cards, but I'm good with numbers.' Fred offers.

I look at their faces and assess the mood in the room. I can never tell if it's better to ruin a nice moment, or make a bad moment even worse.

Here goes.

'Well, yes. That would be great, thanks.' I take a fortifying sip of wine. As it's liquid I hope it can seep into the spaces between the food. 'And on that note, an . . . interesting development actually. My boss, Mansi, you remember her?' Get to the point, Bea. 'She's put me in charge of staff development at work—'

'Well, that's wonderful, darling, it sounds like a big step up—'

'And she's decreased my hours to three days a week.'

There is a tumbleweed moment.

'But I asked her to. Or, I agreed to it.' They look at each other. The air in the room is very heavy. 'It's a good thing – it means I can spend more time developing my card business, and the job itself is much more interesting.'

I go on, rambling as I get more nervous, filling the void with words.

'I realize this is a big decision, and it isn't one I took lightly.'

There is still silence.

'So, what do you guys think?'

They all look at each other, probably trying to decide who will talk first. It won't be Anna. As vocal as she is, she's still careful in proper family discussions. The real choice is between Mum and Fred.

Fred wins.

'Well, I would like to see the business plan, but I think that if this is what you want to try and do, you're very brave. I wouldn't have the balls to do it.'

My mouth actually drops open.

'Mum? What do you think?'

She actually smiles. 'Honey. All I ever want is for you to be happy. And I don't think you've been happy for a while. If this will make you happy, I'm happy.'

Uncomfortable with any kind of sincerity or positivity, I do what I do best. Distract. 'Anyone for some chocolate?'

I get up, using the table for extra leverage, and squeeze past the chairs. I swear they've moved closer to the wall since I sat down.

'So how is Peter? He's such a good boy to help you with your business plan.' Luckily my face isn't visible to anyone.

I steel myself and turn around with the chocolates in hand, and head back to the table.

'Uh-huh. He was very helpful.'

'I always thought the two of you would end up together.' My mum never usually offers an opinion on my romantic life.

'Me too,' Fred casually adds. He's never offered up any relationship advice either.

'Me three.' Was that Anna?

What is *with* everyone?

'What? When? How? Why?'

'He has a wonderful smile.'

'Why haven't you two ever gone out?'

'You would have very cute babies.'

I have no idea who said what.

'I always thought Peter harboured a bit of a soft spot for you. The first time you brought him here, he followed you everywhere like a little puppy.' Mum looks like butter wouldn't melt.

'Stop! Please.' How did everyone see this but me?

I'm getting very warm.

'I am not going to talk about this with you guys.'

'Why, has something happened, sweetheart?'

'No!' That came out louder and more forceful than I meant it to. I'm probably very red. 'Nothing has happened. Nothing will ever happen. Peter is a great guy. I know this because he's my friend, and yes, he is a boy, but that doesn't automatically mean I want to go out with him.' Even though I do, despite trying really, really hard not to. OK. Maybe medium hard. 'And I don't need to go out with him, or anyone else for that matter, to be happy.' I lose a lot of steam as I say this next sentence. 'I'm happy that Peter and I are just friends.'

Later that night, in bed and alone, and this time also feeling lonely, I look at my phone. He still hasn't messaged me. Even in the quiet years we would text each other a 'Merry Christmas' message.

There are a lot of things to look forward to at Christmas, but when it's all over there are so many emotions, even if it's been a great day. Especially if it's been a great day.

It's too easy to look back at the year. And it has been quite a big year for me.

I feel like I've finally woken up. I've found out that my vagina can still feel things. I have two new and exciting jobs to look forward to. I have forward momentum. It could be argued that I'm actually a pretty OK human. You could even say I'm happy.

But then there's Peter. I keep coming back to Peter.

Maybe Mum is right. Maybe he did like me. Maybe I simply didn't see it.

But whatever he might have felt doesn't make a difference.

What makes a difference is how he feels now. And all I know is that he pushed me away. I might have lost him as a friend for ever because of one stupid evening.

Chapter 43

With only five days between Christmas and Tilly's wedding, my time has been split between various extended family reunions and last-minute wedmin. It's been nice to have a lot to do; it's kept my mind off Peter. At least for the most part. But he's still in the background of everything I do. Even my family have been extra nice to me since the bombardment. It doesn't make me feel better, it makes me miss him more. Mum didn't even say anything when she found out I opened the New Year's Eve nuts two days early.

The situation is hopeless. It's already New Year's Eve. I haven't had any time to see him, not that I would know what to say, and I still don't know how soon he leaves for Australia. I know I should stop being so stubborn and message him, but now I worry that I have left it too long.

My negative mood is making it hard to get in the mood for Tilly's wedding. I said I would go early to make sure the place is looking as it should. I was meant to leave about twenty minutes ago, but I'm currently frozen in front of the mirror. I don't like the jumpsuit I'm wearing; I had bought it hoping to channel my inner Michelle, but it makes my butt look like a pancake. I'm not in the mood to party and be a happy wedding guest.

I sigh, pick up my overnight bag and make my way downstairs. It's only an hour's drive away, but I will never know why an hour in the car always seems so much longer than an hour faffing around at home.

I yell through to my mum and Fred, 'I'm leaving now, guys. I'll be back tomorrow.'

My mum pops her head round the corner. She's already prepping dinner. 'Bye, honey. Drive safe. You look lovely.' She's lying, but I appreciate the gesture.

I pick up the car keys and see myself out.

Even though I left late, I still get to the venue in plenty of time, and it looks amazing. I don't need to do a single thing.

Tilly must have been working all day.

The room where the canapés and drinks (and later dancing) will take place is essentially a greenhouse; a greenhouse that Tilly has filled with twinkling lights. It looks magical.

I message Tilly.

> Tilly – you have done an amazing job. It looks so
> beautiful in here. xx

My phone pings back almost instantly. It's Tills.

> You're here! Can you come up to my room? I'm in the
> bridal suite.

I take my bags and head into the adjoining hotel to find her.

★

When I eventually locate her room, I open the door and a sea of heads turn towards me. I recognize a couple of them from the hen party, including her maid of honour, Nicole. I smile a hello. They're far too busy doing brides-maid things to pay me a huge amount of attention, so I close the door behind me.

I find Tilly at the back of the room with her hair and make-up done, the dress still hanging beautifully to one side.

'Tills, you look stunning.' And she does. Even half dressed, she's a vision.

She looks at me and nods. Unlike everyone else in the room, she doesn't appear to be having a great time.

'Tills? What's wrong?'

She pulls me towards her and I sit next to her on the chaise.

'Bea, thank you so much for everything that you've done for this wedding. I know it seems quick to you.' I start to shake my head. 'It seems quick to me too. And you've done so much. More than any of my actual brides-maids.' She looks at the wider room.

'Tills, I was happy to help. I still have some cake in my freezer.'

'I'm glad.' She swallows. 'You've done so much, and I haven't thanked you properly at all. Today wouldn't be happening if it wasn't for you. I'll make it up to you. I'm not too sure how, but I will.'

'There's nothing to make up.'

'Well, maybe not yet, but I have one more favour to ask.'

'Anything.' The word is out before I really think.

I should have thought.

'Could you do a reading for us? One of Jeroen's sisters was going to do it, but she's having to look after her child who appears to be a small nightmare. I wasn't going to ask you because you've already done so much, but I don't want to ask anyone else.'

Oh God. No. Why me?

I try to come up with an acceptable excuse.

'I haven't practised. Don't I need to practise?'

'I have the reading here, so you can get comfortable with it. I think the key is to go more slowly than you think you should.'

She passes me the reading and I glance at it. It doesn't look particularly long, but I'm too panicked to see any actual words, only a puzzle of letters. I'm only OK to speak in public when I've had a lot of time to practise. The ceremony is in just under two hours. This does not give me enough time.

'But I hate my outfit.' I gesture at myself. 'I'm wearing a really ugly sack that looks weird at the crotch.'

She looks at me. Her eyes definitely linger at the crotch.

'I have an idea.'

Half an hour later, I've successfully squeezed into one of Tilly's dresses and the make-up artist has made my face look like it's glowing in a good, non-sweaty way.

'Bea, that dress looks fabulous on you.'

I look in the mirror and I have to admit, I love the dress. It's exactly the kind of dress I would choose to wear, and it makes me feel both comfortable and confident at the same time. Looking at myself in the mirror, and feeling how I currently feel, it's undeniable that an outfit can give you extra power, kind of like armour.

'Thank you so much for letting me borrow it. I promise to at least *try* not to spill anything on it.' It's quite a light colour – spilling would be bad.

'Bea, it's yours. Keep the dress. Spill on it as much as you like. I've had it for years and never worn it because it doesn't suit me, I kept it because I always wanted it to. But it turns out it was made for you. Take it as a thank-you for today – not the full thank-you, but a mini one.'

Refusing her feels like the natural thing to do. But then I wonder about how I would feel if our roles were reversed. I would want Tilly to take the dress. I would be happy that she loved it.

'Thank you, Tills.'

For once in my life I might be appropriately dressed for the occasion.

The formal part of the ceremony doesn't take very long, and I'm distracted throughout. I want it to go more quickly – so I can get my reading over and done with – but I also want it to go more slowly, so I can have more time to practise.

When it's my turn, I get up and stand at the front where all the other speakers have been standing. I assume this is the right spot. When I finally look up, I lock eyes with Tilly and there's a brief moment where I think I might cry before I've even started.

Then I remember I am wearing The Dress. My

collarbones have been dusted with shimmer powder, and I know I can do this.

Regardless, my eyes start to water as I read.

' "Love", by Roy Croft.'

I swallow and try to slow down my words.

> *'I love you,*
> *Not only for who you are,*
> *But for what I am*
> *When I am with you.'*

I close my eyes, very briefly, and suddenly all I can see is Peter. I open them back up but he's still there.

> *'I love you,*
> *Not only for what*
> *You have made of yourself,*
> *But for what*
> *You are making of me.*
> *I love you*
> *For the part of me*
> *That you bring out.'*

He's sitting cross-legged on my floor, passing me Post-its.

> *'I love you*
> *For putting your hand*
> *Into my heaped-up heart*
> *And passing over*
> *All the foolish, weak things*

> *That you can't help*
> *Dimly seeing there,*
> *And for drawing out*
> *Into the light*
> *All the beautiful belongings*
> *That no one else had looked*
> *Quite far enough to find.'*

He's telling me I am beautiful.

> *'I love you because you*
> *Are helping me to make*
> *Of the lumber of my life*
> *Not a tavern, but a temple.'*

He's walking through my door, bringing me spring rolls.

> *'Out of the works*
> *Of my every day*
> *Not a reproach*
> *But a song.'*

He's dancing with me, only occasionally stepping on my toes.

> *'I love you*
> *Because you have done*
> *More than any creed*
> *Could have done*
> *To make me good,*

> *And more than any fate*
> *Could have done*
> *To make me happy.'*

He's laughing, and I smile back.

> *'You have done it*
> *Without a touch,*
> *Without a word,*
> *Without a sign.*
> *You have done it*
> *By being yourself.'*

As I reach the last lines, I struggle to read them through the tears.

> *'Perhaps that is what*
> *Being a friend means,*
> *After all.'*

When the poem is over, I don't quite know what to do. There is no clapping or anything to signal that I'm done, so I look up. It seems strange to see that nobody else appears to have been quite so affected. Until I spot Tilly. She's crying too.

I hover for a while on the spot before walking back to my seat, accidentally taking the long way round.

How is everyone remaining so still? I can barely stop trembling. I need to move.

I sneak a glance at Tilly. She's looking right back at me.

She's mouthing something to me . . . *Are you OK?*

Yes. I nod back.

But I need to leave.

I sit up straighter. Beyond straight. My butt is poking out behind me and my chest is forward, ready to go.

Tilly is still looking at me. I gesture towards the door, and try to mouth back. *I have to go. I'm sorry.*

She nods and waves me off with her hand and smiles. I know that she knows it must be important.

And it is important.

I leave as quietly as I can, fully aware that this is not very quiet at all.

I have a flashback to Tilly's hen party and breaking free from the line for the loo.

I need to tell Peter how I feel.

But this time I'll find the words.

Chapter 44

Armed with a message from Mia telling me Peter is at his mum's house, I run up to my room, collect my bag and check out as quickly as possible.

I feel guilty leaving, but if there is one person who would understand, it's Tilly.

I stall the car twice before I'm able to pull away. Calm down, Bea.

The drive to Peter's mum's house is two hours long. It doesn't give me enough time to memorize a long speech, but it should give me time to come up with my key points. This is good. Fewer words will have more impact and be easier to remember. I've boiled it down to two. Two key points.

I make the final turn into the unnecessarily long driveway that really deserves a road name of its own. The outside lights turn on as I park. There's no turning back now.

I barely have time to knock before his mum opens the door. This wasn't quite the scenario I imagined, but I don't know why – after all, this is her house, not his. Maybe I haven't thought this through enough.

'Oh, hi!' Does she remember me? If not, I shall remind

her. 'Sorry, I realize this is very random. I'm Bea, Peter's . . . friend from university. Well, one of them. He has many friends. Peter is very friendly.' That sounded dodgy. She's staring at me, expecting more words. I swallow. 'I was actually looking for Peter. Is he here?' I wish I didn't sound so rambling and desperate, apologizing yet again, seemingly for my very existence.

'Bea, hello. Of course I remember you.' She smiles at me, and I'm relieved that she's giving me a friendly face. 'Unfortunately he isn't here – he left about an hour ago. I don't know where he's gone – he left in something of a hurry and I haven't been able to get hold of him. Would you like to come in for a cup of tea? He might come back.'

As kind as her face appears to be, I can't go in. That is a level of intensity I don't think I can currently handle. Plus, my palms are so sweaty I don't think I could hold a cup of tea without dropping and breaking it. And I bet they only have nice cups.

This is all very anti-climactic.

'Oh, that's so kind, but no, no thank you. I shall head back out. I was passing through and wondered if he would be in.'

'Of course.' I know she doesn't believe me. Nobody passes through remote countryside.

'Cool, right, well. It was lovely to see you again, even if very briefly. I'll go now. Happy New Year!' I walk away, and turn back before she shuts the door. 'Maybe don't tell Peter I stopped by – I don't want him to feel guilty that he wasn't in.'

I don't particularly care whether or not she's bought

my pathetic excuse. I feel totally deflated. His lack of presence makes me feel as if fate is preventing us from being together, that there is a reason why we have never been more than friends. Great friends, but still, just friends.

I can't face going back to the wedding, and instead head for home, even though I know it will lead to my family being even nicer to me.

Chapter 45

Midnight comes as I pull into home. It feels fitting to bring in the new year alone and not quite at my destination.

Fireworks start going off in the distance when I open the front door. Hugo greets me, as if he's been waiting for me to return ever since I left.

I hear voices in the kitchen, so I yell through, 'Hey, guys. I'm sorry, I'm back. I left the wedding early to go on a stupid errand and decided to come home instead. I hope that's OK.' I walk towards the kitchen.

I can tell that they've had a nice evening. The dishes aren't yet in the dishwasher, they're part-way through a jigsaw puzzle, and Mum has had at least two glasses of wine. She's going to start giggling soon.

'Hi, honey.' Mum smiles at me. 'Are you OK?'

'Yes, but I would like a glass of wine.' And to drown my sorrows and forget I ever got my hopes up.

'Was the wedding nice?'

'Yes, it was beautiful.' It really was.

'Is that a new dress? I thought you left wearing a different outfit.'

I look down and almost start to cry. I've forgotten about the dress. The perfect dress will now for ever be the dress of broken dreams. I need to take it off. I feel so stupid for letting a poem get to me so much.

'Tilly let me borrow it.' I will definitely be giving it back to her. I don't want to see it again, let alone own it. I put my hands on my hips to emphasize how it's slightly on the small side. 'It's quite constricting actually, I'm going to run upstairs and change.' I head out of the room before they can argue. Not that they would. From the look of things they also feel the need to be comfortable. They're all wearing trousers akin to, well, lounge pants.

Retreating upstairs feels nice. Away from all the eyes.

Once in the safety of my own room, I take the dress off and reach for my favourite set of pyjamas, and, in a moment of peak wallowing, I also decide to put on the jumper I purloined from Peter. It's become something of a security blanket.

As I'm pulling it over my head, Hugo barks downstairs. He never barks, so I hurry up to make sure everyone is OK and stumble on the last step as I take in the scene.

Peter is talking to my mum in the entryway, whilst Hugo stares lovingly up at him.

I know how he feels.

'Peter.' I need to say more words, but I don't know if I know any more words.

'Bea.' He smiles at me, but his smile fades quickly. Is he remembering our kiss? 'How was the wedding?'

'Huh?' I still can't seem to say anything more than vague sounds.

'Tilly's wedding?'

'Ehh.' I nod my head slightly, hoping that the nod will convey what my words would normally help describe.

He looks at me and I remember that I'm wearing his jumper. All I can do is hope he hasn't noticed. I'm painfully aware that the last time we spoke I was begging him to kiss me. I wonder what shade of red my face is.

Out of the corner of my eye, I can see my mum frozen to the spot, eyes darting between the two of us, trying not to look conspicuous, but with a huge grin on her face. She looks like she wants to clap.

'Well, sorry for disturbing you. I thought I would pop over. I realize this is very odd timing, but I had some thoughts on the, er –' he looks at my mum – 'business plan that I wanted to share with you.' He makes to disentangle himself from Hugo, who just gets more in the way. 'I realize it's an odd time,' he says again.

I still can't tell what he's actually thinking. Is this really why he's here – to talk business? When we used to study together he would often get inspiration at the weirdest moments, leaving parties to go home and write an essay. But maybe he feels as bad as I do about how odd things are between us? It makes sense. If he's moving he probably wants to leave with a clean slate.

Mum chimes in, 'Oh no, it's wonderful that you're here. I mean, these thoughts come whenever they come, don't they? Bea told us you'd been helping her, it's very kind of you. You two make a good team.' She winks. I didn't even know she could wink.

Kill me now.

And it only gets worse. Fred comes to say hello, followed by an unashamedly nosy Anna.

Weirdly manly and pretty awkward greetings happen, which prove to be extremely hard to pull off in the tight space provided by the entryway. Fred isn't exactly small, but Peter's limbs really are very long.

It's too much for me to handle and I feel the need for some space.

'Why don't we move into the house and out of the hallway.' Finally I've found some words.

'Great idea. Peter, would you like some tea? Or wine? Either way, let's go to the kitchen.' Mum starts to direct us down the hallway.

'Tea would be great. Thank you.'

Once in the kitchen, I wonder if I made the right choice. The kitchen is bigger and has brighter lights, meaning everyone is suddenly more visible. I imagine my emotions are written all over my still very red and now very visible face. I wish they weren't.

The five minutes it takes to make the tea is the longest year of my life. For once, Peter looks a bit unsure about what to do; he's not meeting anyone's eye. In a weird way, it gives me confidence.

'Well, erm, I don't want to bore everyone with my thoughts. Bea, shall you and I take this into the . . . a different room?'

'Sure.'

We leave and Mum calls after us, 'Let me know if you

need any cookies. I have plenty.' Strange, considering she previously told me they were reserved for tomorrow's afternoon tea.

'Thanks, Mum.' This might be the first time I've ever felt too sick for baked goods.

Chapter 46

We head for the Cave, a tiny cosy room that's mainly used for storage. But it's also the only room that isn't full of my family and isn't a bedroom. The light takes a while to warm up and Peter still isn't meeting my eyes. This might be the longest we've stood in silence for.

I can't remember a time when I've ever felt so nervous. 'Butterflies' is a terrible term for what I'm experiencing. Butterflies conjure up images of sunshine and flowers. What I'm feeling is more like rough seas and battering winds.

I'm not sure I trust myself to deliver the two-point speech. My words will definitely get mixed up if I start talking now. Silence it is.

Finally he looks up, and he does that silly little smile of his.

'Peter, I need to tell you something.'

Fuck. The words came out and I wasn't really wanting them to, but I needed to do something.

And I should keep speaking. Peter is looking at me. Waiting for me.

But now, of course, my words aren't coming.

What is wrong with me? When I want to talk I can't, but when I don't want to talk I do.

I take a deep breath.

'I know you're going to Australia, and I don't want you not to go, but I don't want you to go without me telling you something. I can't leave anything unsaid, and I don't want you to leave with this weird silence between us.'

He makes a noise and I stop him from talking with the universal hand gesture that says 'I'm not done'.

'I have two key points to tell you.' But now I can't remember them. I just know I had them. I've started pacing back and forth like I'm trying to get my daily step count in. 'I went to your house earlier this evening. Well, not *your* house, your parents' house.' Why is the ownership of the house so important? This isn't one of my points. 'In case your mum mentions it.'

'I went to Tilly's wedding.'

I stop and turn to face him.

'You went to Tilly's wedding? Why?'

'To speak to you.' He's so still that I start pacing again. 'Why did you go to my house?'

Yes, Bea, why? Why did you go to his house? Tell him. Just tell him. And for goodness' sake, stop sweating.

I hang my head. 'Ugh, I wish I'd kept the dress on.' The dress would have given me confidence.

'What?'

'Never mind.'

Poor Peter is looking so confused.

'Peter, I'm so sorry. The last time I saw you, well, in truth it wasn't the *last* last time I saw you, but when I came over to your flat after Tilly's hen party, I shouldn't have. I acted like a total fool and guilted you into having sex with me. I'm so sorry. That is not at all how I wanted sex between us to go down. It's not how I wanted anything between us to go down.'

He doesn't look any less confused.

'So, yes,' I breathe, 'I'm sorry about the sex. Well, actually I'm not sorry that we *had* sex, but you pushed me away and I should have left it at that. I'm also sorry that I brought over the burritos.' That was an unnecessary addition to the apology – why did I say that? 'Basically, the first thing I need you to know is that – I am not a perfect person. I can be grumpy and quiet. I can be sad and moody. I don't do the things that I should do. And the things I do, I tend to do quite badly, which is not my intention, it just comes naturally. And I'm sorry if any of my recent actions have hurt you.'

'Are you done?'

'No.' This is going very badly. I look at him. I really do like him. Seeing his face makes me happy. 'Well, point two is . . . I like you, and I wanted you to know. You don't need to say anything.' I really hope he says something. 'So if things have been weird between us, and they have, it's because, well, I like you, and I didn't know how to tell you. So instead I slept with you, and then avoided you, which only made it worse.' I finally stop pacing.

'Are you done now?'

'Yes.' I shake my head and then realize that's the wrong gesture. I nod once.

And then I point my finger into the air.

'Oh actually, no, I have one more thing!' I realize my hand is still up, so I slowly put it down. 'I, erm, I realize that this is a lot. And I've also kind of taken your recent silence and general avoidance of me as a sign that you probably don't know what to say, or don't want to hurt my feelings. And that's totally fine. Like I said, you don't need to say anything. But I wanted you to know how I felt. There is no pressure for you to feel the same. You do you.'

'Right.' His hands are on his hips. Like an off-duty superhero. 'So I think I should clarify some points.' He's using a business-like tone. I wonder what that means. I don't think it can mean anything good.

I wish he'd say nothing and leave, rather than tell me he wants to stay friends.

'Firstly, I'm not going to Australia. I turned it down. Al's going instead.'

Fuck bloody balls. This is going to make hiding a lot harder.

'Secondly, I wasn't avoiding you. Well, I was to start with because I didn't know what to say. And then I was accidentally avoiding you because I had to go to Australia to smooth over the fact I was no longer going to Australia. It was very last-minute and I forgot my phone and it was an extremely busy couple of weeks. For that I apologize, but what I have to say I need to say in person anyway. And then when I got back I tried to get hold of you. I've been going round to your apartment so much that the old lady next door threatened to call the police if I came by again. I came to your work, I even tried to hunt you down at a Christmas fair, but you weren't there either.'

'I was actually.'

'You were?'

'I was dressed up as Rudolph. I think I speared you with an antler.'

'Why didn't you say hello?'

So many reasons.

I shrug. 'I couldn't talk, I could barely even move.'

'I suppose it did look quite cumbersome.' He smiles faintly, but it fades really quickly.

'Bea, we didn't have sex that night at mine.'

What? Thank God. I think?

'I didn't want to sleep with you, I'm not really into taking advantage of inebriated women. You passed out as soon as you lay down in bed, and then you snored all night. It was helpful to know that you were still breathing, but we'll need to talk about the snoring.'

I snored? I blame the tequila. Oh God, he didn't want to sleep with me?

I can't help but interrupt him. 'So, that night . . . I know you pushed me away, but would you ever want to have sex with me?' He is so silent and so still. I really wish I'd made a joke instead.

His face takes on a serious edge. He shifts a bit in his stance, and starts talking really slowly, pronouncing each word very carefully.

'Bea, that night, yes, I pushed you away because I didn't want to have sex with you.'

Oh.

'So you don't want to have sex with me?'

'Bea, please, shut up.' I close my mouth and wait. 'I do want to have sex with you, but I didn't want to have sex with you that night. I have wanted to have sex with you for years. I wasn't going to waste our first time on a drunken fumble. I have plans. I am a man and I have *plans*, Bea.'

This makes me blush.

'I was so happy to wake up next to you that Sunday morning. I was so happy until I came back with breakfast only to see that you'd run away. Bea, you have to stop running away.'

He steps towards me. Part of me really wants to run.

'Bea, you have to know that all I have ever wanted is to be in your life. It's up to you to decide how much. But for the record, I want it all.

'I want to wake up next to you after you've been snoring all night. I want to eat bread that's gone stale because you haven't resealed it properly. I want to buy flat-pack furniture and let you build it. I want to get lost trying to follow your thought processes. I want to have fights with you. I want to have make-up sex with you. I want to make a family with you – dogs or children, or both. Whatever you want. I just want *you*.'

I might be smiling but I'm so numb I really can't tell.

'It's up to you. It always has been. I'll always be here for you because I love you.'

That is a horrible decision on his part.

And I have never been so happy.

I find myself tentatively reaching for him until we're

close enough that I swear I can feel his body against mine, even though I know we're not actually touching.

And just like when my words have a habit of failing me right when I need them most, I freeze when I should really keep moving.

But in the end, it doesn't matter because Peter keeps moving.

He moves one hand to my waist, and one hand to my cheek.

He moves me gently, but firmly, towards him.

And finally, *finally*, he leans down to kiss me.

I am vaguely aware of meeting him halfway, but I'm mainly aware that the kiss is (eyebrows raised) *good*.

I smile at my own stupid internal thoughts and accidentally break the kiss sooner than I would have liked.

'Bea? Everything all right?'

'You know I'm probably going to fuck this up, don't you?'

He nods. 'Yes.'

OK.

Acknowledgements

This book might have my name on the front cover, but a whole bunch of other names deserve to be there. However, that would mess up the beautiful design, so instead I will thank you here . . .

My very first thank-you goes to Rebecca Ritchie (Becky! Holly!) at AM Heath. No words do justice to how grateful I am that you decided to take me on and put up with my emails and animal-print clothing. Thank you so much for believing in me and always being a positive force. And really, really thank you for only making me climb that staircase once.

To the whole team at Transworld – it is an absolute dream come true to work with such a dedicated, passionate and skilled group of people. When this book was a tiny seedling of a thought, I secretly wished you guys would pick it up. And then you did! I am so glad that nobody was around to see that particular happy dance, but thank you for making this very dear wish come true. To Darcy, my original editor and burrata-eating-enabler, who gave me some very key pointers ('Does Bea have to wear onesies quite so much?'); I really hope your leaving had nothing to do with me ☺. To Molly, who valiantly took up the cause after Darcy left (for reasons that had absolutely nothing to do with me, I'm sure), thank you for being such a supporter of Bea and I am so grateful that you like my lists! To Frankie, I knew that one day our paths would cross again – to this day you are still my favourite desk buddy. Thanks also to (deep inhale of breath): Larry, Judith, Josh, Holly, Katie, Hayley, Hannah, Deidre and Jo! I thank you all from the bottom of my heart.

Of course, this book would be nowhere without my friends – you guys rock. I can't list you all, but all of you give me joy and happiness (and in some cases inspiration). A few special mentions . . .

Emily, Anna and Lucy – what an absolute bunch of dudes; let's keep laughing together. A special mention needs to go to Anna who read an early version, told me it wasn't totally terrible and gave me that much needed vote of confidence to keep going. Emilia and Rahul, what great bunnies you are!! Shout-outs also go to: Natalie for my pink hair and the dinner – it's a cooking show too; Hester and Fole; Nikki – thank goodness we reconnected, please thank your mum for me; Marloes for the Dutch name; Emily for the notes on the visual diary; Chris and Saoirse for some of your more awkward soundbites; Jamie for keeping Gill sane and supporting my crafting obsessions; Hannah, Flo, Gill and Rosie for the safe space; Paige for frequently over-sharing and being the inspiration for Penny (everyone needs a Penny) – I so hope that next year is your year. Thanks also to my

American contingent, in particular the Barbarias, the Knotts, the Burleighs and the Franklins. Some wider family members also deserve a shout-out; the Clarkes who all amaze me with their enjoyment of life and never seem to mind when I invite myself along to their family gatherings; and a special mention to Kate McCulloch (who actually married IN to the madness) for being an early reader and title-thinker-upperer, whose only fault is getting too invested in the characters.

Of course, I owe a huge thank-you to my family, who have always been my loudest and most embarrassing supporters. James – thank you for always having my back; Juliet – thank you for showing me that it's OK to have my own voice; DB – thank you for being a great landlord and providing me with protein-rich meals, wine and hugs when I needed them most; Dad – thank you for providing a safety net, without which I wouldn't have had the courage to jump. I am also super lucky because James and Juliet massively married up. Alisa, thank you for being you and for being just as weird as I am (that's meant to be a compliment). Tom, thank you for introducing us to the most violent and competitive card game in existence. And to my amazing nieces and nephews – Lleyton, Caleigh, Rosie and Charlie – your smiling faces make my heart sing. I love you guys a huge amount and am so excited that I get to witness your awesomeness.

But alas, the biggest thank-you of them all has to go to my amazing mum. Gilly, you have given me so much – friendship, laughs, support (emotional, physical and gastronomical), in good times, but more importantly also in the bad. I wouldn't have half as many laugh lines on my face if it wasn't for you. So thanks, I guess?? You are always there for me, and it is because of this that I have been able to fulfil so many of my dreams – thank you so very much. I love you mostly.

And last but definitely not least – the most magical thank-you goes to my readers! (Although, as I write this, the book hasn't actually been published yet, so I guess I might have already thanked 'all' my readers already, i.e. my family and close friends . . . but if there are more of you . . .) I am genuinely chuffed that anyone could possibly be interested in reading anything I have to say – it absolutely boggles my mind and I am so touched that you would take time out of your busy lives to read the words I have strung together! I really hope that in return for your time I have at least given you some laughs.